MURDER ON THE DANCE FLOOR

The first death at the Kismet Klub in Newbury is put down to an Ecstasy mishap, and even when a second drug-related death is connected to the club, it doesn't occur to Superintendent Gregory Summers that there could be a serial killer. He does discover that the deaths are not due to Ecstasy, but to a new, lethal drug – Entium Trilenium. When DC Nicolaides's fiancée holds her hen party in the Kismet Klub, on the same night as an undercover police enquiry, the killer strikes again – terrifyingly close to home. For one member of the CID life will never be the same again.

MURDER ON THE DANCE FLOOR

Murder On The Dance Floor

by

Susan Kelly

Magna Large Print Books
Long Preston, North Yorkshire,
BD23 4ND, England.

British Library Cataloguing in Publication Data.

Kelly, Susan
    Murder on the dance floor.

    A catalogue record of this book is
    available from the British Library

    ISBN   978-0-7505-2749-1

First published in Great Britain in 2007 by Allison & Busby Ltd.

Copyright © 2007 by Susan Kelly

Cover illustration © Brighton Studios.com

The moral right of the author has been asserted

Published in Large Print 2007 by arrangement with
Allison & Busby Ltd.

Magna Large Print is an imprint of Library Magna Books Ltd.

Printed and bound in Great Britain by
T.J. (International) Ltd., Cornwall, PL28 8RW

PROLOGUE

The first murder went almost unnoticed.

Lindsey Brownlow was seventeen, but passed for twenty. She was a tall girl whose full cleavage, tousled blonde hair, subtle make-up and fashionable Bo-ho clothes masked the fact that nature had given her looks no better than average. The bouncers at the Kismet Klub in Newbury never gave her a second glance when nodding her in, unless it was to admire the confident way she sashayed away from them towards the bar, banging her tiny clutch bag rhythmically against her chiffon thigh.

Lindsey was no troubled teenager. She came from a close-knit family, Mum and Dad still together after twenty years, brothers aged fifteen and twelve whom she didn't even hate. On the warm June night when she died, she was nearing the end of her first year in the sixth form and was expected to do well in her A levels: Maths, Physics and Chemistry.

University beckoned.

She wasn't rebelling. She didn't come to the Kismet on Friday nights to get out of her head or to pick up unsuitable boys to make her parents weep. She liked to dance, to flirt; she chatted with her friends and drank a few Bacardi Breezers. Drugs were no big deal. Everyone she knew used them, but nothing heavy, no heroin or cocaine, just E or a few puffs on a communal joint.

This was teenage life in the twenty-first century. All those old people who got hysterical about drugs didn't know what they were talking about, just wanted to stop young people from having a good time.

As Lindsey and her friends liked to say, 'Deal with it'.

The night that she was found convulsing to death on the towpath of the Kennet and Avon canal, a few yards from the club, or klub, her best friend dialled 999 on her mobile and got her an ambulance. The hospital called the police when she was pronounced dead on arrival and her stricken friends explained to the uniformed pair who responded that Ecstasy was Lindsey's drug of choice.

Cheaper than booze, innit?

CID were not called, since the incident was tragic but commonplace. The *Newbury Weekly News* carried an interview with the Brownlow family in which they tearfully begged young people to refrain from illegal drugs. The nationals didn't consider it worth so much as a paragraph on an inside page.

Flowers wrapped in cellophane were left

to rot on the towpath, teddy bears sitting forlorn atop them, their arms wide to the elements.

There was a big turnout at the funeral.

By the autumn, no one but Lindsey's family and friends remembered the loss. The waters had closed over her head and left no trace.

CHAPTER ONE

'Explain it to me again.'

Detective Superintendent Gregory Summers wrinkled his brow in consternation. 'I'm struggling here. Nadia, your fiancée, is marrying someone else, but you've not split up and you still consider yourself engaged.'

'That's it in a nutshell, boss.' DC George 'Nick' Nicolaides sank the rest of his lager in one long draught and sighed with satisfaction. He lived in Newbury and would be walking home from CID's regular Friday night session in the pub, so he needn't worry about the breathalyser.

He patted his stomach thoughtfully, pondering whether to pick up an Indian or fish and chips on the way back. The stomach had been expanding lately but that hardly mattered now that he was spoken for.

'Go on,' Greg said.

'You know I told you that, when Nadge moved in with me, she left her job at the West Middlesex Hospital and signed up with a nursing agency? They found her a post in a big house on the Downs, looking after an old bloke who's dying of pancreatic cancer – geriatric nursing being her specialty.'

'That rings a bell,' Greg agreed, for all the world as if he'd been listening at the time. 'And the word is *speciality*.'

'Whatever. Well, Nadia and Mr Fitzsimmons – that's his name–'

'I guessed that.'

'–got on together like hot cakes.'

'Huh?' Greg said.

'Oh, you know what I mean.'

'House on fire?'

'See. I knew it was something hot. So, after about a month he tells her he wants to remember her in his will and she thinks he means five hundred quid or some token. Only then he tells her he's got no family and wants to make her his sole heir.'

'Is that OK?' Greg asked, after a pause to digest this. 'Won't people think there was undue influence?'

'Maybe if he was disinheriting his kids, or even his nephews and nieces,' Nick conceded, 'but he's all alone in the world. So Nadge says fine by her.'

'OK,' Greg said, thinking, *I bet she did!*

'Well, a couple of weeks go by and he says he's talked to his solicitor about the new will and the brief explained that there'd be something like two million quid in death duties.'

Greg almost choked on his beer. 'Two million? That means he's worth at least five.'

'So – really?' Nick's coarse Mediterranean

11

features screwed up in pain as he struggled with the mental arithmetic. 'That means death duties are forty percent!' he concluded incredulously.

'Iniquitous,' Greg agreed.

'Bloody liberty, more like. So Mr F asks the brief if there's any way round it and the brief asks if Nadia's married and Mr F says no, just engaged to a very nice young policeman.'

Detective Sergeant Barbara Carey snorted. 'I thought she was engaged to *you!*'

'And there are no death duties between husband and wife,' Greg said, finally seeing the light.

'Seems not, so our wedding's on hold and Nadge is getting married to Mr F on Saturday – tomorrow week.'

'What do your and Nadia's parents think about this?' Greg asked. Nick mumbled something. Greg cupped his hand like an ear trumpet. 'Pardon?'

'I said there didn't seem no point in telling them. They're a bit old-fashioned, like.'

'I wouldn't let my wife marry someone else,' DC Andy Whittaker said.

'No, she just ran off with another bloke,' Nick said unkindly. 'That's heaps better.'

'Now, now, children.' Barbara got up and patted the pockets of her black linen-mix trouser suit for money, surfacing with a twenty pound note. 'Same again, everyone?'

'Mineral water for me.' Greg was driving. 'No bubbles.'

Nick handed her his empty glass and went on with his story. 'Anyway, me and Nadge talked it over and we couldn't see no down side. The doctor says Mr F'll be lucky to see in the New Year and then me and Nadge'll be set up for life.'

The whole thing struck Greg as immoral but he couldn't pinpoint why, so he said nothing as Barbara fetched them all another round of drinks. Was he being puritanical? Or did it just seem unfair that a couple like Nick and Nadia should get their hands on that sort of money?

He couldn't see Nick staying in the Job once he was a multi-millionaire, either, which meant losing an experienced detective. On the other hand, Nadia might well decide she saw no reason to share her new-found wealth with him and take off, causing tears before bedtime.

'Will the marriage be consummated?' Barbara asked bluntly as she deposited glasses in front of her colleagues.

'He's old and very sick, Babs. Still, even if it is...'

'It's worth it for five million quid.' Barbara finished the sentence for him.

'Well, yeah.'

She grinned. 'It'd certainly be one of the most expensive shags in history.'

13

'I thought a marriage wasn't legal till it was consummated,' Andy said.

'What do you mean by not legal?' Greg demanded. 'Are you suggesting that a couple are committing a criminal offence between the registry office and the bedroom?'

'Oh, you know what I mean!'

'An unconsummated marriage is potentially voidable,' Greg explained kindly, 'which is not at all the same thing as being void. I don't imagine Mr Fitzgibbon–'

'Fitzsimmons,' Nick supplied.

'–will be seeking an annulment.'

'I wouldn't let another man make love to my wife,' Andy said mournfully, 'not even for five million quid.'

'No, she did it for free,' Nick said.

Andy slammed his glass down on the table and walked out of the pub, the dignity of his exit marred only by the fact that he was forced to stop to deliver an enormous sneeze halfway, making every drinker in the bar turn to see where the explosion had come from.

Greg raised his eyebrows at Nick as Barbara produced a tissue to mop up the beer spillage.

'Well, he shouldn't get on my case,' Nick growled. 'Just bloody jealous.'

He reached across and helped himself to what remained of Andy's pint, placing it next to his own as first reserve.

The more Greg saw of Nadia Polycarpou, the less he liked her. She struck him as hard, even making allowances for the fact that nurses had to cultivate a certain detachment in the face of death. He hoped she wouldn't be tempted to speed Mr Fitzsimmons' passing, but thought she had too strong a sense of self-preservation to risk it.

'That reminds me,' Nick was saying to Barbara. 'Hen night next Friday. Nadge said to invite you. Kismet Klub – that place near the canal. You know?'

'I know it. All right, I'm game.'

'And Angie too, if that's all right, Mr Summers. Nadge don't know many people round here yet.'

'I'll tell her.' Greg glanced at his watch, an automatic and futile gesture since he'd noticed after lunch that it had stopped, presumably in need of a new battery. Hadn't things been easier when you just wound your watch up every morning? 'I'm for home. See you all Monday. Don't forget we have the new DCI starting first thing.'

'And that's bound to cause trouble,' Barbara said.

Newbury CID had been through four chief inspectors in three years – five, if you counted the loaner from Kent who'd been with them briefly the previous autumn during the Gillian Lester inquiry. On the bright side, only one of them had actually died in harness.

15

'What's his name again?' Nick asked.

'Striker Freeman,' Greg said doubtfully.

'You see,' Barbara said, 'that's not even a real name. He'll probably turn out to be Osama Bin Laden.'

'I doubt it,' Greg said. 'He's Jewish.'

'Oh, then I'm thinking weedy and intellectual – Woody Allen type. What do they call them – nebbish?'

'Oh, yes,' Greg said derisively, 'since no one's scared of the Israeli army.'

'You what?' Nick said.

'He served two years in the early Eighties.'

'O-kay,' Barbara said slowly. 'Possibly not a nebbish.'

'He's authorised for firearms too.'

'Blimey! Who do we get next week – Jack Bauer?'

'Isn't he dead?' Nick asked.

'No! He faked his own death at the end of season four. Try to keep up.'

'Oh ... that makes more sense.'

'As I haven't the faintest idea what you two are talking about, it's definitely time I wasn't here.' Greg drained his water and got up.

'You know Dickie Barnes is running a sweepstake on how long he'll last?' Barbara remarked.

'No,' Greg said sourly. 'And have you had a bet?'

'I've got a tenner on six weeks.'

16

'Thanks for your support. With luck, this one won't be scared off so easily – not if he's armed.'

As Greg walked back to his car that Friday night for the short drive to Kintbury, his home of twenty-five years, he could have no idea that the Kismet Klub serial killer was about to claim his second victim. He didn't know that there *was* a Kismet Klub serial killer, otherwise he wouldn't have been whistling a happy tune as he started the engine and looking forward to a peaceful weekend with his girlfriend Angie.

It wasn't yet eight o'clock as he swung out of the police station car park and onto the ring road, heading along the A4 in a westerly direction towards Hungerford. Nineteen-year-old Erin Moss was still getting ready for her evening out at that moment, trying on one outfit after another and letting her mum – who was a youthful thirty-eight, admitting to thirty-three when her grown-up daughter wasn't around to give her the lie – offer advice.

'Not too slutty?' Erin twirled in front of the mirror.

'Maybe a bit slutty,' her mum said with a grin.

'Not for a first date then. Don't want to give the wrong impression. I've got a good feeling about this one.'

She'd got a hot date, or so she hoped – a bloke she'd met over the Internet who turned out to live in Pangbourne, just a few miles along the motorway. She'd never been to the Kismet Klub but Craig was a regular.

'We're meeting inside at ten,' she told her mum.

'Ooh! Last of the big spenders, this "Craig".'

'Nah, 's not as mean as it sounds. They let the girls in free Friday nights. Tenner for the blokes.'

'I'm surprised that ain't illegal,' Mum said. 'European Court of Human Rights, or summat.'

'What about the black top from Primark, the one with the lace at the neck?'

'Try it on, though you'll need to change your skirt then. It don't go. I still wish you'd eat something, love. There's a bit of chicken curry left over – heat up in the microwave in no time.'

'No thanks.' Erin patted her perfectly toned abdomen. 'Don't want to bloat, not–'

'–on a first date,' her mother chanted with her. 'Glass of milk, line your stomach.'

'Go on, then.'

As Mum poured the milk, Greg's car was drawing up in the drive of his 1970s semi, tucked in neatly behind Angie's Renault S. He alighted with a spring in his step, grabbing the bottle of claret he'd picked up on

18

the way.

Erin and Mum went on happily for almost an hour and a half, lovingly bickering, until both were satisfied.

'You look smashing, babe,' Erin's mum said eventually, stepping back for a proper view. 'Right classy. Now you will be careful? I dunno about all this meeting on the Net. You hear such things.'

'I'll be careful.' Erin gave her mum a big hug. She was a sensible girl, with a good job in the office at Camp Hopson, Newbury's quaint department store. It was a step up from her mum's life as an assistant in the staff canteen at Bayer HealthCare and she never came home smelling of grease.

'And you'll get a taxi if it's getting late? Never mind the expense.'

'I expect Craig can drop me off. He's got a car.'

'That's what he *says*,' Mum muttered, but not loud enough for Erin to hear, since she was no killjoy. He said he was twenty-four; he said he worked at Heathrow as an engineer; he said he was called Craig. He was probably forty-eight, unemployed, fat, bald and a Nigel.

'Don't wait up,' Erin called over her shoulder, as she checked her keys and headed for the bus stop.

Oddly enough, Erin found Craig easily at

the Klub and he was everything he'd claimed to be. Even the photo he'd sent her looked like him and was recent. He seemed pleasantly surprised too, telling a tale of a blind date whose photograph turned out to have been taken in 1982 and from whom he had narrowly escaped with his virtue.

He was funny; she liked men who made her laugh. He bought her a drink and they danced and swapped life stories. They had a fun couple of hours before deciding, mutually and without rancour, that they didn't fancy each other enough to persevere with a relationship.

He dropped her home in his Ford Focus at half past one, giving her a chaste kiss on the cheek and waiting till she was safely inside her front door before driving off with a valedictory and entirely illegal toot of his horn.

Erin's mum found her dead in bed the following morning, the brushed cotton sheets still wrapped neatly round her naked body like a shroud.

It broke her heart.

CHAPTER TWO

'I don't understand how this can have happened,' Greg said irritably. 'We have a suspicious death connected to Newbury's most fashionable nightclub and now it turns out she wasn't the first. We're going to look a right bunch of plonkers.'

Dr Aidan Chubb, the pathologist, shrugged his elegant shoulders. It was now Monday morning and he'd been on the go for most of the weekend, following a motorway pile-up on Saturday night, but no one would have been able to tell – his green surgical suit crisp and clean and fresh from the laundry.

'We didn't do a full toxicology on the first girl at the time,' he explained. 'Luckily we'd kept back samples from her organs so I got them done as an emergency last night after I'd got the cause of death for the latest one. At least we're not looking at an exhumation. Well, not yet.'

Greg groaned. 'This was Lindsey Brown? Why didn't we give her the full works?'

'Lindsey *Brownlow*. You know how it is: short of time, short of money. Since the cause of death seemed obvious, the inspector on the night relief didn't reckon it was worth the trouble and expense of a lab report.'

'Which is why all suspicious deaths should be handed over to CID,' Greg grumbled.

'And you'd have ordered the tests?' Dr Chubb asked. 'With constant budget cuts and the lab backed up?'

'...Maybe.'

'And it hardly qualified as suspicious at the time. It seemed like a classic case of death by Ecstasy at a nightclub. Sad, yes, but all too common. Her poor little mates confirmed that she'd been popping Es and she'd drunk way too much water, the way they do. The body was bloated with it. In fact, that speeded up the action of the Entium Trilenium, which is why she collapsed and died outside the nightclub rather than during the night like Erin.'

He spread his hands. 'It was an open and shut case.'

He patted Greg reassuringly on the shoulder. 'CID were working flat out on the Inkpen murder at that time, anyway.'

'Yes, that's going to make a great excuse – we were busy with a woman stabbed in her own garden so we had no room for extra corpses. In future, please form an orderly queue to die in suspicious circumstances in the Newbury area.'

'Want to see the body?' Dr Chubb asked. 'Erin Moss, that is. She's all tidied up.'

'I suppose I must.' Greg followed the pathologist to where the dead girl lay, awaiting transfer back to the morgue drawer, a sheet covering her modesty. Dr Chubb drew it back to display her head.

She looked like a nice kid, Greg thought: not a beauty, just the girl next door, the one you fell for and made a life with. She was wearing quite a bit of make-up but what teenager didn't on a night out at a club? It was smudged now, uneven on her waxy cheeks, her lips pale even with the remains of her tinted lipgloss. She was – what? – five or six years younger than Angie. Her dark hair was cut to her jaw line, with a wispy fringe which made her look younger than nineteen. Most girls that age tried to look older but Erin had clearly not been anxious, in his late mother's phrase, to wish her life away.

'Only child, by all accounts,' Aidan said. 'No father.'

Again, Greg thought, just like Angie.

'Mother's pole-axed,' the doctor added. 'Came in to do the identification yesterday.'

'Hysterical?'

'Not *hysterical*. More like catatonic. I thought I was going to have to call an ambulance for her. Luckily, she had a neighbour with her – sensible woman – to take care of her.'

Greg turned away from the body. 'Well, let's try to salvage what we can. Tell me again what the poison's called.'

'Entium Trilenium, known as Entry, which is ironic as it tends to give people a quick exit.' Dr Chubb pulled the sheet back over Erin's head. 'It's not exactly a poison like, say, cyanide or arsenic. It's a recreational drug, manufactured in a lab: one of the methamphetamines, like Ecstasy.'

Greg groaned. 'I'm not in favour of the death penalty, as you know, but I think I'd make an exception for these chemists who invent new and lethal drugs.'

'It surfaced in the States about a year ago and caused a spate of deaths in the San Francisco area before spreading across the country. Luckily, people got the message and stopped taking it pretty damn quick. Trouble is that the difference between an enjoyable high and a fatal dose is minuscule. In fact, it's incalculable.'

'You mean you could take a couple one night and have a great time...'

'And the next night the same dose will kill you. Right.'

'OK, well I'd better go and talk to the families.'

'And I'm for bed.' Dr Chubb yawned and stretched like a green panther. 'Didn't Babs say something about your new DCI starting today? Only I've put twenty on him lasting three months, so try being nice to him for a bit.'

'Oh, bugger!' Greg said.

As he let himself in at the front door of the police station twenty minutes later, Greg caught Sergeant Dickie Barnes talking to PC Chris Clements, while licking a pencil stub of the sort favoured by old-time bookies.

'I'm offering twelve to one against him being arrested in the next six months and twenty to one against him dying – violence or natural causes. Shall I put you down for–' He suddenly noticed Greg and hurriedly put away the loose-leaf binder he was writing in.

'Sir. Your new–'

'I know!' Greg wasn't forgiving him in a hurry for taking bets on the new DCI's staying power.

He went first to the CID office where he found only Andy and Nick. The atmosphere between them was still strained but he didn't have time to knock their heads together.

Andy spoke. 'Sir, Babs is in your office with–'

'I know!' He explained as quickly as possible the reason for his late arrival. 'Nick, get down to the Kismet Klub and start interviewing the staff about these suspicious deaths. See if they still have any CCTV tapes from the time of the first death in June.'

'Doubt it,' Nick said.

'Well, certainly make sure they don't tape over Friday night's footage. We need to find

25

out who's selling this drug and quickly. Andy, get on the computer and find out all you can about Entium Trilenium, or Entry.'

'How are you spelling that?' Andy reached for his notepad.

'How it sounds,' Greg snapped.

'Yes, sir.'

'What about the dead girls' families?' Nick rose and donned his invariable black leather jacket, even though it was warm for October. He hadn't even the excuse of being born in Greece and feeling the cold since he came from North London.

'Leave them to me,' Greg said, 'or to Mr Freeman.'

His secretary, Susan Habib, was on her feet as he entered her office. She actually seemed to be doing some filing, which was the nearest thing to a miracle Greg had seen that year.

'DS Carey is in your office, Mr Summers,' she said, tight-lipped, 'with the new chief inspector. Since you weren't here when he arrived, I wasn't sure–'

'Yes, thank you, Susan.'

Greg took a deep breath, glued a pleasant smile to his face and thrust open the door of his office. Barbara and the new man were standing with their backs to him, at the window, as she pointed out the landmarks of Newbury, such as they were.

They both turned at his entry.

'Sir!' Barbara said. 'This is DCI Freeman.'

Freeman walked forward with an outstretched hand. He was a little shorter than Greg – maybe five-foot-eight – and had a body which, though stocky, moved with supple ease. Greg knew he was forty-four. He clearly shaved his head and a millimetre of recent growth showed it was because of male pattern baldness – a much better solution than the infamous comb over. What hair there was appeared to be dark brown and his intelligent eyes were of much the same shade.

He was wearing a navy blue suit, but his paler blue shirt was open at the neck. Greg didn't think that his tan running shoes were for show.

'Welcome,' he said, as they exchanged handshakes which were firm but not competitive. 'Sorry I wasn't here when you arrived but we've had a couple of drug-related nightclub deaths all of a sudden.'

'Sergeant Carey's been looking after me,' Freeman said with a smile.

'Babs, can you get down to the Kismet Klub, give Nick a hand interviewing the staff? He'll fill you in.'

'Sure.' Barbara hesitated at the door. 'Isn't that where Nadia's having her hen night this Friday?'

'Is it? I wasn't really listening, to tell you

the truth.'

'Better not close the place down then.' Barbara gave DCI Freeman a big smile and Greg sensed that she already approved of him, which was reassuring since he trusted Babs' judgement. 'See you later, sir.'

Greg gestured the new man to a seat. He sank into his own chair and brought him up to date on the Kismet deaths.

'Sorry to chuck you in at the deep end,' he concluded.

'I like to be busy.' Striker leant forward, his tanned face intense. 'One of the reasons I applied for this job was that I heard that Newbury had more than its fair share of murders – not run-of-the-mill ones either.'

'Yes ... I wonder why that is.'

'So are we treating these deaths as murder?'

Greg sighed. 'I suppose we'd better, although it looks as if they were just fooling around with drugs, so even if we can find the dealer we'll likely end up with a manslaughter charge, at best. I want to start by talking to the mother of the latest victim.'

'Shall I do that?'

'How well do you know the area?'

Striker grinned. 'I have an OS map and a town plan.'

'Let's both go, as it's your first day.'

Striker shrugged. 'You're the boss.'

CHAPTER THREE

The Mosses lived in a housing association flat on the southern borders of Newbury, on the ground floor of a three-storey block, with a patch of unfenced garden at the front, left to easy-care lawn. A punctured red and green ball lay lopsided in the centre of the grass.

The main door to the building had no lock and Greg pushed it open into a concrete stairwell, turning to the right to find the door to flat number two.

A woman of about sixty answered his knock and introduced herself as Gladys Asher, the upstairs neighbour from flat four. She was fat to the point of obesity, in a pair of leggings, their lycra stretched to its limit, and a baggy sweater. Her face was weathered and lined beneath hair dyed an unlikely shade of red. She looked strong, healthy and practical, the sort of person you might want taking charge in a crisis. Greg assumed she was the one who'd accompanied Mrs Moss to the mortuary the previous day, a fact which she swiftly confirmed.

'Julie's got no family,' she explained in a low voice, stepping back to admit them to the hall, 'so I've been sitting with her since the doctor left.'

'The doctor?' Greg queried.

'She was that upset I thought it best to call the GP in, see if he could prescribe something for her. Then I didn't want to leave her alone, in case she tried to top herself.' Greg noticed with approval the lack of euphemism, the 'tried to do something silly' that was so often preferred.

'Erin was all she had.' Her dough face grew sad, the pinched eyes dark with unshed tears. 'Such a nice kid. Why do they do it? A few beers was good enough for us in my day, port and lemon for a special occasion. Too much money about – that's what it is.'

She indicated a door to her left. 'She's in there.' She turned and put a hand to the small of her back. 'Ouch! Slept on the sofa last night. Could of had Erin's bed, I suppose, but you don't fancy it, do you?'

'No,' Greg said. 'You don't.'

'You go in. I'll make some tea.' She vanished through the opposite door. Striker rapped gently on the door of the sitting room and went in without waiting for a reply.

The room was in semi-darkness, the curtains pulled across except for a gap of about six inches in the middle, the lights off. One bar of an electric fire glowed on the far wall although it wasn't cold that morning. Greg remembered from when his son Frederick had died how important physical comforts suddenly became – hot baths, warm fires, a soft blanket, a mug of tea – their simple normality a shield against suffering, anointing the bruises of grief.

Julie Moss sat on the sofa gazing blankly into the glow of the fire. She didn't look up. Striker said, 'Mrs Moss?'

'It's miss. Miss Moss.' She kept her head bowed.

'Miss Moss. I'm Detective Chief Inspector Freeman and this is Superintendent Summers. We're terribly sorry for your loss, but we need to ask you some questions if you feel up to it.'

'We know how hard this is for you,' Greg put in, 'but the sooner we start our investigation, the better our chances–'

She glanced up at last. 'Have you arrested him?'

'Who's that, Miss Moss.' Striker crouched down so his face was level with hers.

'This *Craig*. That's what he called himself. You can bet your bottom dollar it was him gave her the drug, probably slipped it in her drink when she wasn't looking. My Erin would never take drugs off her own bat.'

Greg and Striker exchanged glances. How often had they heard this from a bereaved mother or father? Parents were clueless about how everyday a part of their children's lives drugs had become.

Greg said, 'May I?' He pulled the curtains

back without waiting for permission, letting some daylight in. Turning back, he saw a woman who would normally be pretty, not yet forty – young, these days, to have a grown-up daughter – with a trim figure and the same short dark hair he had seen on the body, now unkempt. She wore a grey velours leisure suit under a blue-checked dressing gown, her feet incongruously cheerful in teddy-bear slippers.

The room was cluttered but cosy, with a cheap but newish three piece suite in cream and brown tweed.

'Tell us about Craig.' Striker sat next to her on the sofa. 'Is that Erin's boyfriend?'

She shook her head. 'Never met him till Friday night. They talked on the Net, you know? What do they call them?'

'Chat rooms?' Greg suggested.

'That's it. Chat room about some pop group they both liked. Some band. She was into House music.'

Greg wasn't at all sure what that was but Striker said, 'Yeah, my girls love that stuff too.'

Julie tried to force a smile. 'You got teenage girls?'

'Two. Not easy, is it?'

'No!' Julie shook her head vehemently. 'Erin was never any trouble. She's the last girl this should have happened to. She was my best mate as well as...' She ground to a halt and took a deep breath. 'I dunno who I'm gonna talk to any more.'

Striker gave her a moment to recover. 'Do you happen to know this Craig's surname, Julie – may I call you Julie?'

'Yeah. No. Didn't know his last name. Not sure Erin did. You know what kids are like today – all casual.'

'I daresay this Internet has its uses–' Gladys, light on her feet for such a large woman, swept into the room with a tray containing four mugs of strong tea, a carton of milk and a packet of sugar. 'But you gotta watch out for the weirdos.'

'Did Erin have her own computer?' Greg asked. 'At home here?'

'Yeah, in her room.'

'Then we should be able to trace this Craig from his email address,' Greg said. 'May we take it away with us?'

'Whatever you need.'

Greg took his mobile out into the hall and put a call through to Andy Whittaker, who was the best of his team when it came to computers. When he returned, Gladys had added milk and sugar to Julie's tea and was practically forcing her to drink. 'I put four spoonfuls in,' she said. 'Hot, sweet tea. My mum swore by it for shock.'

Greg's mum had sworn by it too.

'I'll go and start packing up the computer for Andy,' Greg said. He felt that Julie instinctively trusted the new DCI and it might be helpful to leave them alone together. 'Will you show me around, Mrs Asher?'

'Eh? Oh, all right.' Gladys heaved herself up from the armchair she'd sunk into and followed him into the hall, still nursing her own mug of tea. 'I get you,' she said softly. 'You reckon your boy'll get more out of her if we leave them alone.'

Greg looked at her with respect.

'You may be right,' she added, 'she's not too old to object to a pretty face, even in her state.'

Pretty face, Greg thought in surprise. It wasn't a phrase he associated with a middle-aged man, although Freeman was good-looking enough.

She gave a brief cackle of laughter and led him through a door at the end of the hall. He saw a typical teenager's bedroom, the floor strewn with discarded clothing, the wallpaper almost invisible under posters of singers and film stars. He recognised only Johnny Depp. Even Angie had a soft spot for him – he'd come home a couple of times to find her curled up with a glass of wine, the DVD of *Pirates of the Caribbean* and a big smile.

The room was a narrow oblong and a single bed was pushed against the wall under the window, making the most of the space. It had not been made since Miss Moss had found her daughter's cold body.

The view was of another block of flats some fifteen feet away. There was a bedside table, a built-in wardrobe and a chest of drawers.

The computer stood on a purpose-built stand in an alcove, the sort of metal frame you could pick up at any high-street store for twenty pounds. Greg unplugged it and carefully disconnected the printer and the speakers. He wasn't sure if Andy would need the monitor as well as the hard drive so decided to prepare both, moving them onto the bed with their leads wrapped round them.

'Did Erin have any special friends?' Striker asked, 'on the estate perhaps?'

'Few kids she went to school with,' Julie said, 'but I think her mates were mostly at work these days. She was an office assistant at Camp Hopson.' Seeing his questioning look, she explained. 'The department store in Northbrook Street. You not from round here then?'

'New in town, still getting my bearings.'

She sat up a bit straighter and ran her fingers through her hair. 'Don't suppose you got a fag on you?'

'Sure.' Striker reached in his jacket pocket and pulled out a packet of ten cheap, filter-tipped cigarettes. He shook one loose from the silver foil and held it out to her, clicking a cheap Bic lighter with his other hand.

'Ta.' She sucked on it gratefully. 'You not

having one?'

'I don't.'

'Just keep a packet for the girls, eh?'

'Something like that.' He had found over the years that a cigarette often broke the ice. 'Who would Erin be most likely to talk to about her social life, boyfriends, drugs–?'

'Erin wouldn't have nothing to do with drugs.'

'Julie, I appreciate how difficult–'

'I know! That's what they all say. You think all kids take them, but that's how Erin's father died, see.'

'Oh?' Striker had assumed that Julie Moss was simply separated from Erin's father.

'Before she was born even. Heroin. He was trying to come off it. We'd just met and we were hoping to make a go of it. Talking about getting hitched. He promised me. See?'

'Yes. I do see.'

Striker was familiar with the promises of heroin addicts and the invariable disappointment.

'Dunno what happened – just wanted one last fix, I suppose, and it all went horribly wrong. They said at the inquest that it'd been "cut" with something nasty – kitchen detergent or such like. When I found I was pregnant, I promised myself I wouldn't lie to my baby about what happened to her dad. Erin hates drugs as much as I do. She's got no truck with all that experimenting

36

kids do now.'

Striker nodded sympathetically, although what he was thinking was, *Perhaps it was bred in the bone.*

'If she took a drug last night,' Mrs Asher was telling Greg, 'then chances are this Craig gave it to her.'

'Did you see him? Craig?'

'Nope. Nor did Julie. He arranged to meet Erin at the nightclub. Quite the little gentleman, I don't think.'

The doorbell rang.

'That'll be my constable,' Greg said. He patted the computer monitor. 'With luck, our Craig will have left his details on here somewhere and then we'll see what he has to say for himself.'

Greg had made a private vow to hang on to this DCI, which meant getting to know the man and liking him if it killed him. Accordingly, when Andy had taken Erin's computer away, he invited him to lunch and, when Freeman expressed a preference for Italian food, led the way to the Cucina Romana in a side street near the town centre.

Freeman ordered lasagne so Greg said he would join him.

'You don't keep kosher?' he said, as the waiter left them after wielding pepper pot and parmesan.

He laughed. 'I'd have starved to death on all those millions of hours of surveillance with nothing but ham sandwiches to keep me going. No, I'm not so much Jewish as Jew-ish.'

'So, tell me about the Israeli army.'

'Oh, you know how it is.'

'Ah! That thing where you wake up one morning and find yourself enlisted in a foreign army? Really not.'

'OK, only it was all such a long time ago that I sometimes think it happened in a dream, or to somebody else. I dropped out of university and went to work on a kibbutz, which was great – the camaraderie, not to mention the lovely young girls.'

'Mmm.' Many of Greg's generation had spent time on a kibbutz but he'd never have had the bottle himself and he'd been in the police force full time since he was eighteen.

'Then a couple of my Israeli friends got called up for their national service and I thought it sounded like fun.'

'Fun?' Greg queried.

'What can I say? I was twenty-one, young and stupid. In fact, it *was* fun. Mostly. Admittedly this was a comparatively quiet time, after the six-day and Yom Kippur wars and before the suicide bombings became endemic. I did it for two years and then I came home.'

One of the fundamental splits in humanity, Greg thought, was between those who had killed a man and those who had not. Striker Freeman probably fell into the first category, yet he seemed at ease with himself, comfortable in his skin.

'You married?' Greg asked.

'Sort of. Got hitched shortly after I got back from Israel. Sarah and I separated recently but we're still good friends, spend a lot of time together. You? Married?'

'Sort of,' Greg echoed. He knew that Striker would hear the whole story soon enough – how he was shacked up with his dead son's widow – but it was easier if someone else told him. 'Without benefit of clergy. Kids?'

'Pretty much grown up. Now, here's something ironic: my eldest has just dropped out of college to go and work on a kibbutz and suddenly I understand exactly how my dad felt twenty-five years ago. I hear myself telling him the same stuff: "You're ruining your life. The kibbutz will still be there when you've got your degree".'

'I'm sure he'll be fine.'

'So long as he doesn't do anything stupid like joining the Israeli army!'

'Do you have regrets?'

'No, you're right. I regret nothing. Then there's the twins, Hannah and Elizabeth. They've just turned eighteen and took their A levels this summer. Now it's the ubiquitous gap year before college, which seems to consist of them hanging around at home doing not very much so far.'

'Do they live locally?'

'London. Hampstead. Sarah's father was a rich man and he left the lot to her, which means I don't have to contribute, which makes life simpler. I'm renting an apartment while I get my bearings: a loft conversion at West Mills, used to be a bakery.'

'Handy for the station,' Greg said. He'd seen these new flats and they were pricey.

'Two bedrooms, so there's room for the girls if they want to come and visit. In fact, they're threatening to come this weekend; I think they're worried I shall be lonely in a strange town. I suppose to them it must seem easier for Sarah, still in the marital home and the same job – she has a small art gallery in Fitzrovia. They can't know with what exhilaration I contemplate a completely new life.'

'And are they really into "House" music?'

'Not so much. More classical. Elizabeth's got a place at the Royal College of Music. She plays the cello rather well and wants to be a professional musician. Hannah's a little more vague about her future and will be studying French and Italian at Cambridge. Not that they aren't both up for clubbing when they're in the mood.'

There was a few minutes of silence while both men made a start on the food.

'So what sort of name is Striker?' Greg asked eventually.

He grinned. 'It says Isaac on my birth certificate so I was called Ike. I was pretty good at cricket at school and one day, after a particularly flash innings, my mates started calling me Striker and I liked it so it stuck.'

Interesting man, Greg thought; maybe a bit too interesting.

'We need to talk to the parents of the first victim,' he said, 'now that we know she *was* the first victim. They live at the other end of Newbury, geographically and socially.'

'Would you like me to do that?' Striker pushed away his empty plate and looked a challenge at Greg, good-humoured but determined.

Fair enough, Greg thought. When he'd been a DCI, he hadn't appreciated his senior officers poking their noses into his investigation.

'Sure,' he said. 'Show me this plan of yours.'

Striker produced Barnett's street map of Newbury and Greg pointed out Donington where the Brownlows lived, close to the golf course.

'I want to have a word with the inspector who looked into Lindsey's death,' Greg said. 'He's on duty at two o'clock today so I'll run you back to the station to pick up your car.'

He paid the modest bill and the two men left.

41

CHAPTER FOUR

The inspector in charge of the night relief on the Friday when Lindsey had died was Martin Nelson. Greg didn't know him, as he'd been promoted from sergeant and moved to Newbury from Oxford only days before the incident, but he'd heard good things about him. He knew that he'd been in CID until his promotion meant an inevitable stint back in uniform, a rule which Greg found incomprehensible when experienced detectives were hard to come by.

He gave him a few minutes to brief his officers at the start of the relief then went to find him. Pausing in the open doorway of his cubicle, he saw a tall, blond man in his mid-thirties, whose muscular frame, visible through his shirt sleeves, suggested he could handle himself.

'Inspector Nelson?'

'Sir.' Nelson's manner as he glanced up was pleasing, polite but not subservient. He rose and plucked the uniform jacket from the back of his chair, putting it on in deference to Greg's rank. He had blue eyes, Greg saw, and regular but undistinguished features. 'What can I do for you?'

'It's about the death of Lindsey Brownlow at the Kismet Klub back in the summer.'

'I thought it might be,' Nelson said. 'I hear there's been another death connected with the club.'

Greg nodded. 'What you might not have heard is that the second victim didn't die from an Ecstasy mishap. So we've carried out tests on the samples we kept from Lindsey, which suggest that she didn't either.'

Nelson murmured a mild expletive and his pale face flushed. 'So what did they die of?'

'A new drug known as Entry – a very unstable chemical compound which is as likely to kill as to make them high.'

'I cocked up,' Nelson said glumly. He covered his mouth with his left hand as if he might be sick and Greg noticed a slim wedding band. 'I should have had the full battery of tests done on Lindsey.'

'It's an easy mistake to make,' Greg said with sympathy, though he'd been thinking the same thing himself while talking to Dr Chubb earlier.

Nelson shook his head. 'No, I can just imagine what I'd have said as a DS if some woodentop had bodged a suspicious death like that.'

'Well,' Greg said briskly, 'spilt milk etc. I need to talk to you about the night Lindsey died, see the statements you took from staff and clubbers.'

'And you'll be wanting the CCTV tapes we recovered from the Kismet.'

Greg felt like kissing him. 'You kept them?'

'I never chuck out anything like that – well, not for years. They're tucked away in the evidence cupboard but they may not be that easy to find, as they're not listed as part of a current investigation. Let me go and dig them out for you.'

As Greg followed Nelson out into the hall, the custody sergeant, Dick Maybey, hailed him with relief.

'Mr Summers, there you are. I've been looking all over for you. They said you'd gone out but what with your car being in the car park...'

'What is it?' Greg snapped. 'Only I'm pretty busy.'

'Young man came in half an hour ago, asking to speak to someone about the suspicious Friday night, only the CID office is like a morgue. Says his name's Craig Warnock and he was with the deceased earlier–'

'Craig!' Greg said. 'Where is he?'

'I didn't know what to do with him so I've stuck him in interview room two, him and his dad.'

'Can you set those tapes up for me?' Greg called to Inspector Nelson as he made for the door into the custody suite and was buzzed in. 'I'll be along later.'

So Craig had come forward of his own accord. Interesting. He was either innocent or a very cool customer indeed. A third possibility was that he had given Erin the drug in good faith, not knowing how dangerous it was, and had the guts to bite the bullet and own up.

He entered interview room two and found both men sitting at the bolted-down table. They were very alike in appearance, the main distinction being the father's mane of white hair where his son was dark. Mr Warnock rose as he came in, while the youngster stayed sitting, staring at the blank walls, hardly aware that they were no longer alone. His face was pale and he exuded an aura of desperate unhappiness that you could almost smell.

'At last!' the older man said.

'I'm very sorry you were kept waiting, sir. I was only just told of your arrival.'

'Tom Warnock.' He offered a firm handshake. 'This is my son, Craig. We heard on the local news about a sudden death in Newbury and believe we can help.'

'Detective Superintendent Gregory Summers. I'm told Craig wishes to make a statement about the death of Erin Moss. Do you want a solicitor?'

'I *am* a solicitor,' Mr Warnock explained courteously, 'so I'll stay with Craig during his interview. My son is here solely, you understand, Superintendent, as a witness, that you may eliminate him from your inquiries.'

'And I'm grateful to you for coming forward,' Greg said, with matching courtesy.

'I know from my work that innocent bystanders are often afraid to get involved. Then, when you track them down, it looks much worse than it is. When Craig told me that he'd made a date with the unfortunate young lady in a chat room, I explained to him that you would certainly identify him through his Internet connection.'

'We certainly would have,' Greg said. Both he and Warnock knew that the young man had earned brownie points by not making extra work for them.

Greg sat down opposite Craig and the lad's father resumed his own seat. Greg judged Warnock junior to be in his early twenties, but he looked like a frightened schoolboy now, his pale T-shirt damp with sweat under the arms.

He said gently, 'Tell me what happened on Friday night, Craig.'

'Is Erin really dead?' The boy found his voice. 'I mean, I only met her the once, for a few hours, but we'd chatted on the Net a lot and I liked her. She was fun. Funny. Know what I mean? Not many women are funny.'

'Erin Moss died some time in the early

hours of Saturday morning,' Greg confirmed. 'When did you see her last, Craig?'

'It must have been one-thirty, two o'clock. I dropped her off at her place on my way home.'

'He got home not much after two,' Mr Warnock added, 'so it was more like one-thirty.'

'Now, I want you to think carefully, Craig. Did you, at any time during the evening, give Erin a tablet, a pill–'

'No!'

'Something you'd bought at the club, maybe, not knowing what it was.'

'He said no,' Mr Warnock interjected.

'There were people at the club doing Ecstasy,' Craig volunteered, 'but Erin didn't like that. She said they were fools who didn't know what they were doing.'

So perhaps Julie Moss hadn't been over-optimistic in her insistence that Erin was anti-drug, Greg thought. He said, 'Were you and she together all evening?'

Craig considered this. 'Not all evening. We stuck together for the first hour or two, but then we realised that it wasn't going to be love at first sight...'

His father caught Greg's eye and the two middle-aged men exchanged slight smiles at the innocence of youth.

'So we split up, danced with other people, but then we ran into each other again at the bar around one o'clock and we were both still on our own and I offered her a lift home.'

'So somebody might have given her the drug during that period of – what? – an hour? Two?'

'Hour and a half,' Craig said, 'but, like I said, she was dead against drugs of any sort.'

'Someone could have slipped it in her drink without her knowing, couldn't they?' Mr Warnock offered. 'You read about such cases – date rape drugs.'

Greg wished he knew more about Entry: whether it dissolved in alcohol; whether you'd be able to taste it. He said, 'Did she seem odd to you while you were driving her home?' Craig shook his head. 'Did she mention feeling unwell?' Greg persevered. 'Did she talk or act in any way abnormally?'

'I didn't know her well enough to know what was normal,' Craig said slowly, 'but she just seemed mellow, like she'd had a few glasses of wine or a couple of vodkas.' He paused for a few seconds. 'She was happy, though, laughing. Said she'd had a bloody great evening. That's a good thing, isn't it?' He looked hopefully at the two older men. 'That she was happy just before she died.'

'Yes,' Greg said after a pause. 'I think it is a good thing.' He stood up. 'I'll get someone to take a formal statement for you to sign, Craig, and I hope we shan't have to bother you again.'

Striker Freeman had telephoned ahead to make an appointment with Lindsey's parents. Mr Brownlow had answered the phone and said, tersely, that his wife had been unable to work since their daughter's death and that he was working from home as much as possible to keep an eye on her.

The unspoken fear was that she would kill herself.

He had followed his map and the superintendent's directions and now found himself outside a detached, red-brick house which must have been built between the wars. It stood in a row of others along a tree-lined avenue, each with some distinguishing feature to prove that they were not identical boxes. The Brownlows' house still had its original stained glass – pale pink tulips with perky heads – in the small riser windows above the casements.

He had to break the news that the investigation into Lindsey's death was to be reopened, following fresh information. He wondered how he would feel in their place. There would surely be a sense almost of relief that their daughter had not died from the sheer stupidity of an Ecstasy overdose, but had lost her life to a new drug, one she could not have been warned against.

He parked in the road, opened the well-oiled gate and walked up the drive. The plots were generous, far larger than a developer would allow today with building land in the south-east of England fast running out. A two-car garage stood to his right with a hatchback on the hard standing in front of it. Crazy paving forked, leading to the front door in one direction and a gate into the back garden in the other.

He turned left.

The front door opened before he could ring and a balding man of about his own age looked at him uncertainly, perhaps doubting that he was a police officer. He wore casual trousers and a tweed jacket but with a collar and tie, as if that made it feel more like a normal working day.

Striker produced his warrant card. 'Chief Inspector Isaac Freeman, Mr Brownlow. We spoke on the phone.'

The man merely nodded and stood aside for him to enter, not offering to shake hands. He gestured to a door on his left which led into the sitting room at the front of the house and Striker noticed that his fingernails were bitten, with dried blood lodged along the edges; he wondered if this was a recent vice, a response to the stresses of the last few months.

He passed through the door as indicated, into a large, square space, which curved into a bay window, giving a good view of the front lawn and the quiet street. The fireplace had been bricked up and an electric fire installed in its place. Double doors stood open to the adjacent room, through which the DCI could see an unnaturally tidy dining table, set for five.

Mrs Brownlow sat in an armchair looking out of the bay, but Striker got the impression that she was not seeing much. She must normally be a good-looking woman, he saw, like her daughter, but she was uncared for, with no make-up and a flat hairstyle which suggested that her husband had brushed it for her when she could not be bothered, with no real clue as to how her style worked, since he was not that sort of man.

'I'm Donald Brownlow,' his host said, 'and my wife is Mary. Won't you sit down, please.'

Striker sat at one end of the sofa, where he had a good view of Mary, while Donald took a second armchair in front of the former fireplace. He was of medium height and nursed the beginnings of middle-aged spread, but looked fit and healthy despite the hollows under his grey eyes.

'You said you had some news for us,' he said. His fingers twitched up towards his mouth to make further inroads into his nails, but he caught the gesture in time and balled the hand into a fist to remove temptation.

On the sideboard next to him stood a full-length photograph of a teenage girl.

'Is that Lindsey?' Striker asked with a nod at the picture.

'Yes. Last year in Cornwall.' Donald reached the picture down in its silver frame and handed it across. Striker saw now that the girl was on a coastline, with large, white-tipped waves behind her. He recognised the North Cornish coast, popular with surfers. Lindsey wore a one-piece swimsuit in scarlet and white, a matching sarong wrapped round her waist to make a skirt. She was laughing into the lens.

'And she was just seventeen,' he said softly.

'Yes, she was seventeen.' Donald's voice grew belligerent. 'And, no, she wasn't old enough to drink legally in nightclubs, but they all do it and what were we supposed to do – keep her locked up in her room?'

Striker let him finish, not attempting to interrupt his indignation. When he subsided, he said, 'I meant only that she was so tragically young. I have two daughters barely a year older and I know how hard it is to get them to do *anything* they don't want to, or stop them from doing anything they do.'

'...Sorry,' Donald muttered.

'No, *I'm* sorry,' Striker said.

Mrs Brownlow spoke for the first time, her

voice a little staccato, as if she was out of practice. 'What are their names, please?'

'Hannah and Elizabeth. They're twins.'

'How lovely. May God preserve them for you.'

'Amen,' Striker said. 'And thank you.'

She turned to face him. 'You said you had some news.'

'There's been a second death connected to the Kismet Klub,' he explained, 'last Friday. I don't know if you heard about it on the local news.'

They shook their heads. 'It was a Friday when Lindsey died,' Mary said. 'Can't they close that place down?'

'Is there a connection?' Donald asked.

'I fear so. The second girl had not taken Ecstasy but–'

'Our Lindsey had more sense than to do drugs,' her father snapped, getting clumsily to his feet as if he wanted to hit someone but had no obvious target.

Striker sighed inwardly but couldn't bring himself to contradict the bereaved man. He was the same – every parent was – convincing himself daily that the twins had too much sense to mess with drugs.

It was Mary who spoke up. 'Oh, Donald, we know for a fact that she took the drug! Her friends admitted as much, to us and to the police. Why won't you accept that?'

'Then she was led astray by her so-called

friends.' Donald walked stiffly to the window and stood for a moment looking out, clenching and unclenching his fists as he calmed himself.

'Please go on, Chief Inspector,' Mary said.

'The autopsy showed that she had taken a different drug, a much more dangerous one. When we learnt that, we did some more tests on Lindsey's ... samples–'

'Samples?' Mary echoed hollowly.

'From her organs,' he said apologetically, 'which were removed at autopsy.'

'You kept her organs?' Donald Brownlow's face was a mask of baffled fury. 'So we buried what – half of our daughter?'

'Only a few tissue samples were kept,' Striker explained, 'against just such an eventuality, since the Coroner released the body for burial before the final inquest verdict.'

'Oh, well that's a great comfort! Have you got more or less than a butcher's window display?'

'That's enough, Donald. Don't you want whoever was responsible for Lindsey's death brought to justice?' Mrs Brownlow turned politely to Striker. 'Please go on.'

'Lindsey had taken the same drug, perhaps in mistake for Ecstasy, perhaps slipped to her without her knowledge. We don't know enough about the new drug yet. We're getting in contact with the American police to find out more about it.'

'So Lindsey's death was not an accident,' Donald Brownlow said. 'Not her own foolhardiness. She was killed.'

'It could be a case of manslaughter,' Striker agreed carefully, 'if we can find the pusher and prove that he knew the dangers of the drug, or that he was reckless.'

'Good!' Donald glanced at his daughter's photo. 'I could never accept that she was responsible for her own death – that she was so stupid.'

'Or she,' Mary said.

'Pardon?' Striker turned to her.

'Why do you assume your drug pusher is a man?'

'We keep an open mind, I said *he* for the sake of convenience. Can you tell me if Lindsey had a boyfriend?'

'She was far too busy with her school work,' Donald said quickly. 'Plenty of time for that later.'

Striker looked enquiringly at Mrs Brownlow, who seemed to have looked at her daughter with less rose-tinted spectacles, but she agreed. 'She'd been on a couple of dates but never anything serious.'

'Was she in contact with anyone over the Internet? Did she go into chat rooms?'

Her mother hesitated. 'The computer was in her bedroom. I never went in without knocking. I thought she was old enough to deserve that respect for her privacy.'

'What a mistake that was,' Donald growled.

'Not necessarily. I don't know what she did on line, but you can find out, can't you? I've read about it.'

'We can find out what websites she visited,' Striker agreed, 'read her emails, with your permission.'

'Of course.'

Mr Brownlow took him upstairs, into a large room at the back, overlooking lush lawns and a water feature. It was not especially girly – Lindsey favoured greys and blacks over pink – with a few posters on the wall, bands he recognised from his own daughters' CD collections. He disconnected the hard drive and carried it downstairs. Mrs Brownlow was waiting in the hall and opened the door for him.

'What was her name?' she asked. 'The second girl.'

'Erin Moss. She was nineteen.'

'Erin Moss,' Mary echoed thoughtfully. 'What a pretty name. Was she Irish?'

'I don't think so. I suppose her mother just liked the name.'

'Erin. And Lindsey.' She threw her head back, letting her limp hair fall about her shoulders. 'Who next?'

CHAPTER FIVE

Greg found Inspector Nelson on his haunches in the video room, sliding a tape into the machine. Nine more stood on top of the television.

'From eight p.m. till two a.m.,' the younger man commented. 'But Lindsey didn't get there till almost ten.'

'Did you watch them at the time?'

'I watched them, hoping to identify a pusher, but I saw nothing. Maybe you'll have better luck. One covers the door and one the central area – bar and dance floor. What they don't cover, of course, is the toilets, which is where most of the trans-actions we're looking for take place.'

He made to leave but Greg called him back. 'I need you to show me which one is Lindsey. I've never seen her.'

'Good point.' Nelson sighed and drew up a couple of hard plastic chairs in an unpleasant shade of burnt orange. 'If only we had popcorn.'

'If you can just point her out to me when she first appears,' Greg said, taking his seat. 'I can go on from there.'

Nelson fast-forwarded for a few minutes,

stopping occasionally to look at the time check in the bottom right-hand corner of the picture. When it said nine-fifty, he slowed to twice normal pace, saying, 'Not long now'.

Greg watched intently as celluloid people scurried about, their legs a blur. The Kismet Klub was still quiet at that time; many clients would not arrive till the pubs shut since the drinks were pricier here. Only the hard-core dancers liked to turn up before eleven when there was room to move on the floor.

The trickle of arrivals began to pick up as ten o'clock approached. Greg thought that there were more girls than boys, mostly in their early twenties, a few older and looking, to his jaundiced eyes, a bit out of place. Why did so many thirty-five-year-olds try to pretend they were still kids?

'Not long now, not long.' Nelson's hand hovered over the pause button on the remote. 'There! There she is with her mates.' The picture froze and Greg found himself looking at a group of girls, no different, superficially, from the many others. Nelson's finger indicated a tall, blonde girl and he saw Lindsey Brownlow for the first time.

Or was it?

He realised that he had seen her before. Newbury wasn't a big town and he'd been policing there a long time so it was not so odd. He searched his memory. It had been quite recent, certainly within the last year.

'She was still at school, right?' he said.

'North Park Comprehensive.'

'Did she have a part-time job?'

'She worked Saturdays at Goodrich's – that little bookstore on Northbrook Street – maybe the odd evening if they had a special event.'

'I know it,' Greg said quietly. That was where he'd seen her, the night Liam Sullivan had given a reading last May. She'd been on the till, selling copies of the former terrorist's autobiography for people to get signed and had given Angie a big, friendly grin as she'd paid for her copy. She'd had her hair back in a ponytail that night, and no make-up, but he was trained to recognise faces.

'And she died in the middle of June?' he asked.

'Friday, the seventeenth,' Nelson confirmed. 'Rough end to my first week as an inspector.'

Less than a month later, Greg thought. What a tragedy. He didn't know why it was worse when it was somebody he'd met, however casually, but it was. 'Play the tape,' he said, his voice a little harsh. 'Slow as you can.'

He watched as Lindsey exchanged smiles and banter with the bouncers. Then she linked arms with another girl as they moved on towards the bar. He was vaguely aware that their Bohemian clothes were the current fashion, but they reminded him too much of the cheesecloth craze of the early Seventies. Still, he preferred them to the other prevailing teen style: Streetwalker Barbie.

While the clothes looked good on Lindsey, the others merely looked messy and unkempt.

'Who's the best pal?' he asked.

'Her name's Gina Trethowan. School friend.'

'I'll take a look at her statement.' Gina was a lot shorter than Lindsey and a little dumpy, although that didn't stop her from sporting a bare midriff between a tiered white skirt that did her backside few favours and a flimsy mauve top, overly busy with beading and tassels. Her red hair was cropped too short for her round face.

The plain friend, he thought, the one who makes a pretty girl look beautiful. Some things never changed. In his own courting days there had always been a pretty one and a plain one and he and his mate would tacitly take it in turns to chat up the looker. He had met his ex-wife Diane that way, in a dance hall in Swindon – so different from the clubs of today; it had been his turn for the pretty one and he'd often wished that it hadn't been, since it would have saved him a lot of grief.

The two girls walked, with the jerky gestures of slow-motion, out of shot of the camera. Nelson pointed to the pair following and said, 'The rest of Lindsey's gang – Maria-Teresa Antonelli and Celia Wing.'

The second girl would be Hong Kong Chinese, Greg thought, judging by her English forename; the first from fairly recent immigrants from the Italian peninsula, since they clung to the familiar forenames. Both were short, like Gina, but much slighter and both had black hair. But for Celia's Oriental features, they could be sisters.

He said, 'Lindsey's gang? Like she was the boss?'

'That was the impression I got, certainly.'

The prerogative of height, he thought.

A fifth girl, close behind the main group, began to dance prematurely to the music, throwing her head back theatrically and turning her face directly to the camera, her eyes closed, a fringe flopping forward. Greg grabbed the remote and froze the frame. 'Who's the fifth girl?'

'No, she's not one of the group,' Nelson said, 'just arriving at the same time. Do you know her?'

After examining her features, Greg slowly shook his head. 'I thought for a moment that I did, but I guess not. Does Lindsey appear on the tape again?'

'On the other tape, dancing, having a couple of vodkas.' Nelson clicked the video off, bringing up a blue screen. 'She used the back door to go out onto the towpath where she was found and there's no coverage there.'

'There's a back door?'

'Exit only. Push bar to open. You know.'

'But anyone could open the door from inside, then hold it to let people in.'

'They keep a bouncer stationed on it to make sure no known troublemakers try to get in unnoticed. The girls get in free anyway, so it doesn't matter that much. They make their money at the bar more than on the door. Plenty of people go out there for a breath of air, private snog, romantic stroll by the water, even to be sick.'

'Did the bouncer see anything?'

'He made a statement. Bloke called Usher.'

'Not Ted Usher?'

'Do you know him?'

'Used to.'

Usher had belonged to the same rugby club as his son Frederick, probably still did. He'd always struck Greg as a bit of a wastrel, never sticking at any job for more than a few months, but he certainly had the build for a bouncer.

He'd come to Fred's funeral, which was a mark in his favour, but had shuffled away after the internment, his head down, to avoid being invited back. Greg couldn't blame him for that; who knew what to say on such occasions?

'Usher said she was looking peaky, rushed past him with her hand over her mouth, so he assumed she was going to throw up. Her mates came after her and they were all laughing and joking about how she couldn't hold her booze. Then, suddenly, she was convulsing and the others were screaming. It was Gina who called for an ambulance.'

It was all fun and games, Greg thought, till somebody lost an eye. 'Was Usher trained in first aid?' he asked. 'Bouncers are supposed to be.'

'He knew the basics, but he was a bit panicky. Hadn't been on the job long. He just ran up to the bridge to direct the ambulance. It arrived within ten minutes but it was too late for Lindsey. DOA.'

This is a statement made by Gina Trethowan concerning the death of Lindsey Brownlow at the Kismet Klub, Newbury, on the night of Friday, June 17th.

Nelson had given Greg everything he had concerning the night of June 17th: a boxful of witness statements, the CCTV tapes and the 999 tape.

We usually went to the Kismet Friday and Saturday nights. They let girls in free. Fridays we didn't stay late because most of us have Saturday jobs, including Lindsey. We mostly left about midnight.

Lindsey liked to do a tab of E occasionally, usually Saturdays when she could have a lie-in the next morning. I don't know why she did one that

Friday – just in the mood, I suppose. We'd had mock exams all week and we were a bit stressed out. I don't know who she got it from. She didn't have a regular supplier, as far as I know. There was always someone with a few tabs for sale.

Gina was making it sound as if she didn't do Ecstasy herself, Greg noticed, afraid she might be in trouble. He found her claim that she couldn't identify Lindsey's supplier suspect. They would have to lean on her a bit harder.

It was gone midnight and we were thinking about calling a taxi. Mr Brownlow always gave Lindsey twenty for a taxi home, didn't want her walking or taking a late bus. She used to drop us off on the way.

Lindsey was dancing with some bloke I'd never seen before, just come up and asked her to dance, but she suddenly started swaying and she had her hand over her mouth. Then she ran off the dance floor. He didn't come after her but I thought she was going to be sick so I followed her out onto the towpath and she was throwing up by the wharf. I went to hold her hair out of her face–

A true mark of friendship, Greg thought.

–But she couldn't seem to stop, just went on retching after everything had come out. I noticed that Terry and Celia had come out too and I sort of shrugged and said we should maybe get her home but then she collapsed on the ground and started convulsing and Terry was screaming.

The bouncer on the back door came over but he

was more scared than we were. I rang the ambulance, but she was dead long before it got there, maybe two minutes after the convulsions began.

Greg glanced through the statements made by the other two girls – Celia and Maria-Teresa, who clearly preferred Terry – but their stories didn't vary. None of them knew – or admitted to knowing – who supplied Lindsey with her drugs.

He idly clicked on the 999 tape and let it play through. The cool operator spoke, with her 'Emergency. Which service please?' Then Gina, a thin, girlish voice, unformed. She was lucid, though, as she spoke to the ambulance service, keeping the panic well tamped down, giving clear directions. He could hear a girl screaming in the background and a man's voice saying dully, 'Oh my God, oh my God!'

Ted Usher, he thought. He'd not been much use, but it was unlikely that anyone or anything could have saved Lindsey Brownlow's life that night.

'Have you been here before?' Nick asked.

Barbara shook her head. 'It only opened about a year ago and I'm getting a bit old for clubbing.'

Nick grinned. 'Thirty next birthday, right?'

'I'm not afraid of growing up,' she said loftily.

'Meaning that I am? Let me remind you that I'm the one who's getting married.'

'Oh, yes! Just as soon as your fiancée's first husband kicks the bucket.'

'...Er, yeah.'

'Sorry to keep you waiting.' The door to the office of the Kismet Klub opened and a man in his thirties bounced in. He obviously spent a lot of time at the gym as his muscles bulged in a sleeveless white vest above black cargo pants. He was heavily tanned in the manner of a sunbed enthusiast and was already showing the wrinkles that went with it. 'Douglas Heap. Call me Dougie.'

'DS Carey. DC Nicolaides.' Barbara showed him her warrant card and he shook hands with both of them before hurling himself into the swivel chair on the far side of the desk, making it skid alarmingly along the grey nylon carpet.

'I'm here until the small hours most nights,' he explained, 'in my penguin suit, so I try to get a lie-in in the mornings, especially Monday.'

Nick had not been surprised to find the Kismet Klub locked and apparently deserted at ten o'clock in the morning. Luckily, a cleaner had eventually responded to his knocking and, when he'd managed to make himself understood (the woman was Bulgarian and seemed to think he was from Immigration, desperately trying to explain her legal status in broken English) she'd dug up a mobile phone number for the manager who had quickly agreed to come in.

Barbara had arrived shortly after and the two officers had taken a quick walk round the club before making themselves at home in Heap's office.

'So. Friday night.' Heap seemed willing to lead the conversation and Barbara was happy to let him. You learnt a lot more from the garrulous, which was why 'No comment' was such a deadly weapon. Heap shook his head. 'Sad business.'

'And not the first,' Barbara said.

'What?'

'Lindsey Brownlow, back in June.'

'Oh, but that was... I mean, the kid'd been popping Es like there was no tomorrow.'

'There wasn't,' Nick said, 'not for her.'

'No, I didn't mean... It's a figure of speech.'

'Did you actually see her taking Ecstasy?' Barbara asked.

Heap wasn't falling into that trap. 'If I see anyone dealing drugs in here, or even taking them, they're straight out and the bouncers have orders not to let them in again.'

'Of course,' Barbara said.

'Got my licence to think about.'

'Yes. Well. To get back to Friday night and Erin Moss. We need the CCTV tapes–'

'You got 'em.'

'–And I'd like to talk to all the staff who were here.'

'Can you give us a full list of staff who

were here on the nights of both deaths,' Nick added. 'I take it it was largely the same group of people.'

'Yeah, I run a happy ship and turnover is–' He broke off abruptly as the purport of the question hit home. 'You don't think one of my staff... Only we vet people very carefully.'

'We're keeping an open mind,' Barbara said. If anyone had the opportunity to peddle drugs in a nightclub, it was the staff. Neither barmen nor bouncers were especially well paid and the temptation to supplement your wages, free of tax, could be hard to resist.

She didn't want to give Heap a hard time, though, or not yet. His protestations about not tolerating drugs at his club were automatic and inevitable, but it had to be hard to run a nightclub these days if people didn't think they could get a few pills to pep up their vodka.

'I'd like to take a look out of the back door,' she said.

Heap led the way through the bar and past the toilets, where the cleaner was busy with mop and bucket, to a metallic push-bar door labelled Emergency Exit. He pushed the bar down with one quick thrust and the door opened outwards into the unexpected autumn sunlight of the canal towpath. A pair of hikers with massive backpacks and solid boots shied away from them in surprise.

'If it was up to me, I'd close the thing off,'

Heap explained, 'but health and safety are adamant that we must have a back door in case of fire.'

'Why not alarm it?' Nick asked. 'Emergency only.'

Heap smiled patiently. 'We tried that. There's a limit to the number of times I can stand the alarm going off of an evening. Drunken revellers don't stop to read the signs, or they do and they don't care when they're desperate for a bit of fresh air.'

Barbara walked a few yards towards the canal. To her left the towpath ran east to Reading; to the right lay Kintbury and Hungerford. The ground was strewn with cigarette ends and bits of litter; she didn't care to look too closely, although no doubt SOCO had been along here after Lindsey's death and left the place like a fresh pin.

'Occasionally people fall into the canal,' Heap said, as if this was not a matter of any great concern.

'Where did Lindsey Brownlow die?'

'That way.' He pointed east. 'She was no more than a few yards along. Or so I'm told – I wasn't here that night.'

'Wouldn't hurt to put a few lights on the outside wall.' Nick looked up at the mass of tan brick which rose above him.

'They'd get smashed in no time.' Heap turned back into the club. 'I'll get you that list of names.'

CHAPTER SIX

Early that Monday afternoon, Greg gathered his team in his office and made sure that everyone had been introduced to DCI Freeman.

'So,' he said, when the formalities were over. 'The deaths at the Kismet Klub are our priority at the moment. Andy, you first. What have you found out about this drug, Entry?'

'I found quite a few Internet sites about it,' Andy said, 'including one with a recipe for making it.' Greg groaned. Apparently you could find out how to make an atom bomb on line. The world was full of people with no sense of responsibility. 'It seemed pretty complicated,' Andy went on. 'I couldn't make head nor tail of it, but then I'm no scientist.'

'So, any high-street pharmacist could probably manufacture it?' Greg said.

'Any chemistry student, more like,' Striker offered.

'Babs, did you and Nick get anything at the club?'

'Only that the manager doesn't allow drugs there under any circumstances,' she said with a grin. 'Yeah, right.'

'Is he complicit, do you think?'

'Doubt it, but he turns a blind eye.'

'They don't search the clubbers?' Striker asked. 'For drugs, knives, guns?'

'Not on any systematic basis,' Barbara said, while Greg added, 'This isn't London. Guns are not an issue.'

'We got a list of names of staff,' Nick said, 'but none of them have any previous.'

'Did you get the CCTV?'

Barbara nodded. 'It's all set up in the CID office.'

'I've had a quick look at the footage from the night Lindsey died–' He held up his hand as Barbara exclaimed in surprise. 'Uniform had hung on to it, God bless them. I didn't see anything useful but a comparison may help – perhaps pinpoint people who were there both evenings.'

Barbara didn't look hopeful. 'Newbury's not exactly teeming with nightclubs. You'll get the same people there week after week.'

'Do we know of any connection between the two girls,' Freeman asked, 'other than their unfortunate deaths? Did Erin previously go to the same school as Lindsey, for instance?'

'We'll look into it but I doubt it,' Greg said. 'North Park has a pretty good reputation – its catchment area is middle-class families in expensive houses. Erin lived in social housing to the south of Newbury and

71

'almost certainly went to The Greenham.'

'There was an age gap too,' Barbara reminded them. 'Two years can seem a lot in your teens.'

'The Greenham doesn't have a sixth form, though,' Andy put in. 'Erin probably left school at sixteen, after GCSEs, but, if not, she would have transferred to another school – maybe even North Park.'

'Barbara, you're on schoolgirl duty,' Greg said. 'I'd like you to talk to the head of North Park, anyway, see what she thought of Lindsey and her gang.'

'Right on it, boss.'

'I'll come with you,' Striker said simply.

'Now, we've had another lucky break,' Greg said. He explained about Craig Warnock.

Striker asked, 'Did you believe him?'

'I did rather. Let's say that he's not top of my list of suspects at the moment, especially as he has no known connection with Lindsey.'

'But if you can point him out to us on last Friday's tape, we might be able to spot him on the earlier tape with Lindsey,' Striker said.

'Indeed, in which case we'll have him in again and lean on him a lot harder. Anyway, Andy, I don't want you to give up on Erin's computer. If she was having one Internet romance, she may have been having others.' He turned to Striker. 'I take it that Lindsey had a PC too, Mr Freeman?'

'She did, and her parents were willing to let us have it for as long as it takes.'

'Good. More screen time for you, Andy.'

'Thank you, sir.'

'Have we been liaising with the American police about Entry?' Striker asked.

'I haven't had time yet,' Andy said, with a note of defensiveness. 'I've been on Erin's computer all morning.'

'I'll see to it,' Striker said. 'I know a couple of people.' He consulted his watch. 'Mid-morning on the east coast. Perfect.'

'OK, thanks,' Greg said. 'Now I want to mount a big operation at the Kismet Klub this Friday night. I'll borrow as many uni-form as I can and we'll question all the regulars.'

'I was going to be there anyway,' Barbara remarked, 'for Nadia's hen party. Remember?'

'Perfect!' Striker said. 'You'll be under-cover, keeping an eye out for our pusher while he's avoiding the more obvious police presence.'

'Yeah.' Barbara grinned. 'I've always wanted to work undercover. I'll give it out that I'm in the market for something special, bored with everyday old Ecstasy.'

Greg nodded approval. 'OK, that's a good plan.'

'Picking up on what Barbara said,' Striker

added, 'we must remember that there are kids who really are *that* jaded, who'll hear about a new drug and won't care if it's dangerous. In fact, the risk – the thrill – will be what attracts them.'

The new DCI settled himself comfortably into the passenger seat of Barbara's small hatchback, took out his mobile phone and dialled a number that went on for more than a dozen digits. After about thirty seconds, he said, 'Hi, can I speak to Loo-tenant Silverman, please? Striker Freeman from the Thames Valley police in England. Striker. Yeah. He'll know.'

There was a lengthy pause, then he said, 'Oscar? Hi. Good, thanks. You? No, not with the Met any more. I fancied country living.' He laughed. 'No, it's only about fifty miles out of London, nowhere near York-shy-uh. Look, I wanted to pick your brains about a drug called Entry – Entium Trilenium. You have? OK.' He recited his mobile number. 'Thanks, Oscar, talk to you soon.'

He disconnected. Barbara said, 'Any good?'

'He's getting someone from the drug squad to call me back, but they don't start work till evening – New York time – so I'm not holding my breath.' He put the mobile away. 'Tell me about North Park comp.'

'Best school in Berkshire,' Barbara said promptly. 'Best state school, at the very least. People move house specially to be in the catchment area.'

Striker nodded with the knowledge of a man with three children. 'What's so special about it?'

'General consensus is the head, Caroline Bishop. She's a real motivator and pretty formidable.'

'Yeah?' Striker grinned and produced a ready-knotted tie from his jacket pocket, blue and white stripes, slipping it over his head and tightening the knot about his neck, without doing up the top button of his shirt.

'Don't want to get put in detention for being sloppily dressed,' he explained.

'I'm sorry to keep you waiting, Detectives.'

It seemed to Barbara that this form of address – not one recognised by British police – had sprung up out of nowhere over the past two years.

Too many American cop shows on TV.

Striker said, 'That's quite all right, madam. We're very grateful for your time.' He showed her his warrant card and introduced himself and Barbara.

Caroline Bishop, the head of North Park comprehensive school, was a strikingly handsome woman in her mid-forties. She wore a black and grey striped skirt suit with a vivid silk blouse underneath. Her hair seemed to match the suit: a sweep of black with dramatic streaks of grey. She wore it rather long and flicked it back from her face at intervals in a way that seemed almost flirtatious.

Her voice was mellow, almost hypnotic, and Barbara had a mental picture of unruly teenagers slinking away from her wrath, turned abruptly virtuous. 'What with the school play,' she said, 'and the mixed-gender hockey tournament, it's a bit hectic at the moment. Thank God it's nearly half term. So, Detectives, what can I do for you?'

'We're looking into the sudden death of Lindsey Brownlow last June,' Barbara said.

'Indeed!' Ms Bishop took her own seat, which was an expensive leather swivel chair, and gave it a vigorous workout, reclining it and raising the seat an inch or two. Barbara noticed that her legs were toned, the calves muscular in their sheer nylon, ending in black leather court shoes. 'I thought that had all been sorted out. Ghastly as it was, the uniformed inspector I spoke to at the time – what was his name?' She paused for thought, her tongue protruding slightly between her teeth in concentration. 'Nelson? Yes, Inspector Nelson seemed certain that it was a bad reaction to Ecstasy.'

'There've been developments,' Striker said. 'Another death occurred in relation to the same nightclub on Friday night.'

'Oh Lord! Another young girl?'

'I'm afraid so.'

Caroline Bishop sighed. 'How dangerous the world has become. Why do they have to do it – take drugs, I mean? In my day, being seventeen was exciting enough without artificial stimulants. Well, the odd drink ... occasional joint. We tell them and tell them and tell them about the dangers of drugs, but I sometimes think that's half the attraction. So you're reopening Lindsey's case?'

'There may well be a connection,' Striker said. 'I'd like to know about Lindsey, and her friends.'

The headmistress looked sad for a moment. 'I had hoped her chums would be able to put the tragedy behind them over the summer but, of course, if they can help...'

'Perhaps you could give us your impression of Lindsey, first of all,' Barbara said.

'She was a model pupil,' Ms Bishop said with a helpless gesture. 'The sort of kid every teacher longs to see in their class. Ten GCSEs, all at high grades, and doing very well in the sixth form. No discipline problems. She's been with us right through, from the age of eleven, and I don't think she's been in trouble once. Nice family – parents still together, couple of brothers lower down the school. But the person you really need to speak to is her personal tutor, George Reddy.'

'Personal tutor?' Barbara queried, as she made a note of the name.

'It's a system we use in the sixth form, not unlike at college, so that a boy or girl has one member of staff they can turn to with all their problems – personal as well as academic – for the entire two years of A level. Since Mr Reddy also takes – *took* – Lindsey for chemistry, he knew her better than anyone else in the staff room.'

She glanced at her watch. 'Quarter past three. He should be finishing his last class about now.' She pressed a button on her telephone and spoke to the secretary in the adjacent office. 'Karen, can you ask George Reddy to come to my office as soon as he's done for the day.'

A disembodied voice said, 'Yes, Ms Bishop.'

'And perhaps we might have some tea while we're waiting? Detectives? Can I tempt you?'

Striker answered for them both. 'Yes, thank you.'

'Three teas and some Hobnobs, Karen.'

'We were also wondering,' Striker said, 'if the other girl had been a pupil here at any time. Her name was Erin Moss.'

Caroline Bishop repeated the name thoughtfully. 'It doesn't ring any bells. How old was she?'

'Nineteen.'

'So she'd have left not long ago. I'd surely remember her in that case, but let's check.' She tapped at her computer keyboard as Barbara wondered if she knew all her pupils

78

by name in a school of over a thousand.

'Is that Mosse with an e?' she asked.

'Without.'

'No. No Mosses, not with either spelling, not recently.' The door opened and the secretary came in with a tray. Striker jumped up to take it from her and she gave him a big smile.

'Karen,' Ms Bishop said, 'did we have an Erin Moss here within the last three years, do you remember?'

The woman slowly shook her head. 'Never heard of her.'

'Thanks,' Striker said. 'It was a long shot.'

Barbara took a dislike to George Reddy on sight.

On the surface he was genial enough, but she found his full – rather feminine – mouth hard, almost cruel, and the smile with which he greeted the head's introduction stopped short of his hazel eyes. For some reason, perhaps because she assumed sixth-form tutor to be a senior job, she'd been expecting someone middle-aged, but Reddy was about her own age, barely thirty.

He was of medium height and somewhat overweight, with limp, mousy hair that itched for the scissors of a competent hairdresser. He was wearing a pair of light grey suit trousers but without the jacket, leaving visible a blue, short-sleeved shirt, a tie in a darker blue tight around his thick neck.

She noticed that his fingers were rather discoloured and that there was what looked like a burn on the right index, as if he'd been trying to remove his fingerprints with acid. *He's a chemist*, was the thought that flashed instantly through her mind, along with the recall of the new DCI's comment that any chemistry student could manufacture Entry.

She pulled herself together. Lindsey hadn't got the drug at school, or how had Erin Moss, who had never been here, come to die in the same way? She trusted her own judgements of people, in the main, but maybe the fact that she found Reddy so unattractive as a man was clouding her today.

She drained the last of her cooling tea as she waited for the head to finish the introductions and nibbled the edge of a chocolate biscuit.

'Lindsey.' Reddy nodded sadly as Caroline Bishop concluded her account of the police visit. 'What a loss to the class. I was expecting great things of her and she was applying to Cambridge.'

'Is there somewhere we can go?' Barbara asked, wiping the last crumbs from her mouth. 'This may take some time.'

'No, you three stay here.' Ms Bishop rose. 'I promised to look in on the rehearsal for the school play. It's the first night next Wednesday and I'll be back later to sell you both tickets.' Striker jumped up to intercept her. 'I'd also like to speak to Lindsey's closest friends – the three girls who were with her at the club that night.'

'Then after you've spoken to Mr Reddy, I suggest you make your way to the school hall since all of them are involved in the play in one capacity or another.' She sighed. 'Lindsey was in it too. She wasn't a bad little actress.'

She left. Barbara watched her with admiration. Caroline Bishop was renowned throughout Newbury, both as an exemplary head teacher and for the fact that she and her partner, the beautiful soap actress Luisa Diski, were tireless campaigners for gay rights.

They had recently announced their forthcoming wedding, following a change in the law that would permit same-sex unions from December, in the social columns of *The Times*.

Parents who had qualms about her second claim to fame –and they were few in these enlightened days – were invariably won over by the first.

She turned her concentration back to Reddy, this teacher who had known Lindsey so well, and to the question the DCI had just put to him.

'A boyfriend? Not that I heard of.' Reddy's mouth twisted into a sneer. 'Our esteemed headmistress has made girl power fashionable, if you know what I mean.'

Barbara looked at him steadily, without replying and, after a moment or two he dropped his gaze. 'Tell me about Lindsey's friends,' she said. 'I take it the girls she went to the club with that night were her special friends.'

'You could say that. You know what teenage girls are like – well, you're young enough to remember.' He clearly intended this personal remark as a compliment and Barbara made no reply. 'They did everything together,' he went on, 'even used to see them going into the loos in a big giggling gang. I mean, what's that about?' He looked to Striker for masculine solidarity but looked in vain.

'If Lindsey was doing A level Chemistry,' Striker said, 'would she have the know-how to make illegal drugs?'

'Like Ecstasy, you mean?'

'It wasn't Ecstasy that killed her, but, yes, something along those lines. One of the Methamphetamine family.'

'I ... I never thought about it. Yes. I suppose she would. So long as you know the formula...'

'Which you can find easily on the Net. And your lab would give her access to the ingredients she needed?'

'Well...'

'Did Lindsey have access to chemicals?'

82

Striker persisted. 'Would she have been able to take things unsupervised?'

'We place a lot of trust in sixth-formers,' Reddy said hollowly. He was less full of himself now, Barbara thought. 'We have to – preparing them for college and the outside world. I can't believe that Lindsey would be so foolish. It's not as if she needed the money. Her father was generous and she had that part-time job at the bookshop.'

'For the excitement, perhaps?' Barbara suggested.

'She wasn't that sort of girl. She was sensible – as sensible as a girl of seventeen ever is.'

They were silent for a moment, then Reddy rose saying, 'Is there anything else I can help you with, because I have a dentist's appointment at four?'

'Yes,' Striker said, getting to his feet. 'Point us in the direction of the school hall.'

Reddy led them out into the school yard, pointed to a newish redbrick building to the west of the campus and walked off without another word towards the staff car park.

'Wanker,' Striker muttered.

Barbara grinned. 'Yes, sir!'

'What was all that about girl power?'

Barbara explained.

'Ah!' he said. 'I thought the flirtatious hair tossing was for my benefit. How foolish do I feel? Come on.'

CHAPTER SEVEN

Although it was twelve years since Barbara had left school, the hall brought back a torrent of memories. It was mostly the smell, she thought, and the rows of upright chairs all facing the front. It was the tall windows with the wooden poles to open the top ones, the dust motes whirling in the sunshine.

It was, above all, the sense of communal activity. Barbara had neither liked nor disliked school, been neither happy nor unhappy. She'd done what was required to get the qualifications for a decent career and volunteered for nothing. For seven years, she'd sat in such a hall three days a week and listened to the head teacher delivering a little homily, mixed with practical notices about the seniors' football match and the importance of not running in the corridors. She'd passed notes to boys and signalled boredom to her mates.

She doubted if things were much changed.

Schooldays might not be the happiest days of your life, but they lodged in the memory in a way that few later experiences could compete with. It was the lack of autonomy in childhood, she thought, the absence of choice.

'They're all the same, aren't they?' Striker Freeman said. 'School halls.'

Barbara spotted Caroline Bishop sitting three rows back in the middle, watching the stage, which was set up as a garden, complete with fake lawn. A girl was sitting on a bench and a second one was inspecting her through a pair of glasses that she held to her eyes on a gilded stick. Barbara knew there was a special name for them but couldn't remember what it was.

They were wearing what the sergeant thought was 1920s costumes, while a tired-looking man in green corduroys and a check shirt harangued one of them in a loud voice.

'At least try to sound as if you mean it, Terry!'

The girl on the bench rolled her eyes. 'I don't know how to respond because I don't get whether Gwendolen's being sarcastic, or what.'

'No, of course you don't – we've only been rehearsing for six weeks!'

Barbara looked closely at the girl. She'd read the statements taken by Inspector Nelson on the eighteenth of June and deduced that this was Maria-Teresa Antonelli. She certainly looked as if she was of Italian descent: slight and dark, her skin a little sallow.

Caroline Bishop glanced round and beckoned them to sit beside her.

'*The Importance of Being Earnest*,' she explained in a low voice. 'I'd have chosen something more modern but it's the sort of thing the parents like. At least it's been updated to the 1920s, gives the girls and boys studying textiles – actually, it's only girls – something to get their teeth into. Do you know it?'

'I think I saw a film of it a couple of years back,' Barbara hazarded, not being much of a theatre-goer. 'Reese Witherspoon?'

Striker merely nodded.

'It's all a bit camp for my taste,' Caroline said, 'but, to be honest, it doesn't require the students to be budding Oliviers, which is just as well.'

The drama teacher said, 'Let's take it again from "Pray let me introduce myself to you," but Ms Bishop intervened.

'Tim, a moment, if you please.'

She didn't raise her voice; it was one of natural authority and the young man came immediately to heel.

'What is it, Caro, only we're going to struggle to be ready by next week as it is.'

'This is Timothy Dixon,' Ms Bishop said, 'head of music and drama. He's also by way of being my brother-in-law. Tim, this is Chief Inspector Freeman and Sergeant Carey from Newbury CID. They're reopening the investigation into Lindsey's death.'

'You're Luisa Diski's brother?' Barbara said. She was no more immune to the glow of reflected fame than the next person. After a hard day, she would often slump in front of the TV and *Home Counties* – in which Luisa played the upmarket landlady of the Bell Inn – was on three nights a week. She could see the resemblance now: each sibling tall and skinny with blue-black hair and intense dark eyes that seemed to see beneath your surface.

'Equity already had a Louise Dixon,' Timothy explained, 'and Lou fancied something more exotic, anyway. People used to say she looked a bit Slavic, with her cheek bones. I'm really glad – about the investigation. How can I help?'

'Actually, it's Lindsey's mates we were wanting to talk to,' Striker said.

'We shall need to borrow two of your leading ladies, I'm afraid, Tim,' Caroline added.

'That's Terry Antonelli on the bench,' Timothy said, 'and Gina is playing Miss Prism, so she's around backstage, waiting for her cue. Celia's in charge of scenery and props and she was repainting a backdrop a few minutes ago after someone spilt soup on it. Soup! I tell them not to eat backstage...'

He glanced at the stage where a younger girl in school uniform was now tugging frantically at Gwendolen's blouse, which didn't seem to hang right over her meagre bosom.

He raised his voice. 'Terry!'

'What?'

'I need you down here a minute.'

'We're doing costume!' The girl sighed theatrically and descended to the hall with a rustle of flapper skirt.

'I'll go and find the others,' Tim said. He vaulted lightly onto the stage and addressed the costume girl. 'Do you know where Celia is, Ruth?' The girl's reply was not audible to Barbara but Tim seemed satisfied and disappeared into the wings.

'Terry,' Ms Bishop said gently. 'These are police officers. They'd like to talk to you about the night Lindsey died.'

Terry's face closed up and her voice was suddenly dull. 'I made a statement.'

'We know how hard this must be for you,' Barbara said, 'but we're not satisfied with the current version of what happened that night, so we're talking to all the witnesses again.'

'Will that bring Lindsey back to us?' Terry's jaw jutted mutinously but Barbara wondered if that was no more than an attempt not to cry.

'No,' she conceded, 'but it might help jail the person who was responsible for her death.'

'*She* was responsible, according to most people.' Terry's eyes, as they fell on Caroline

Bishop, were not friendly.

'I did give a talk to the upper school in the wake of Lindsey's death,' the headmistress explained, 'warning them once more of the dangers of drugs, but I did *not* say that Lindsey had only herself to blame.' She addressed the teenager directly. 'You know that I didn't, Maria-Teresa. I would never have said that.'

'All right,' the girl muttered, 'but plenty of people did say it, including the press.'

Ms Bishop took her pupil's hand and squeezed it – a most natural and maternal gesture.

Tim Dixon returned at that moment, accompanied by a girl whose appearance made Barbara smile. Maybe she could pass for an elderly spinster at a distance and under theatrical lighting, but close up Gina Trethowan looked like a child who'd run amok with her mother's make-up box. Wrinkles had been pencilled onto her smooth brow in black and her auburn hair was powdered grey and wrenched back into a bun.

When she spoke, Barbara recognised the voice she'd heard on the 999 call, calm now.

'You wanted to see me, Miss Bishop.'

The head explained again and Barbara saw the two teenagers exchange glances. She sympathised; they had thought the tragedy done with and, while at seventeen you did not believe that such deep wounds could ever heal, they had already, if only subconsciously, resumed their everyday lives, the space that Lindsey had occupied growing daily smaller.

'So what's changed?' Barbara spun round in surprise; she had not heard Celia Wing join them. She took the newcomer in at a glance: medium height and build with a graceful gait; the shining black hair, caramel-coloured eyes and slightly flat features of the orient. Celia wore jeans and an old T-shirt, both with paint splashes on them and there was a dab of green on her left cheek.

'You'll know me again,' she growled with a wholly English curmudgeonliness. 'I asked what's changed?'

Tim Dixon was back on stage with a pair of boys, both incongruous in dated suits, spats and two-tone shoes.

'Perhaps we might go somewhere more private,' Striker suggested. 'Where's the nearest classroom?'

As Gina led the way to the door, one of the boys began to declaim in a forced way:

'"This ghastly state of things is what you call Banburying, I suppose." I mean, "Bunburying". Oh, bollocks!'

'Just relax!' Tim said. 'You had it yesterday.'

Sometimes it was best to interview witnesses separately; today Striker decided to speak to the girls together, to get a sense of the looks they exchanged, of any secrets that were being kept.

'So,' he said, once the door of the empty classroom was firmly shut and they had all sat down, Celia and Terry in chairs, Gina perching on a desk, her short legs swinging free, 'who usually scored the Ecstasy?'

The girls duly exchanged panicky looks. After a carefully calculated pause, he went on. 'Don't worry. You could have been popping illegal pills every night for the past five years and I couldn't touch you for it. I'd have to catch you in possession. Don't be afraid to tell me the truth if it leads us to the person responsible for Lindsey's death.'

Barbara had moved off to one side, he noticed, so that she could see the three teenagers from a different angle, maybe catch an expression he missed. She gave the appearance of making notes but her eyes were not on her pen and paper.

When none of them answered him still, he decided on divide and conquer. 'Maria-Teresa, was it you?'

'No!' Feeling herself accused, the smallest girl protested. 'It was Lindsey. OK? It was always Lindsey.'

Blame the dead girl. Predictable enough. He heard a faint gasp and saw that Barbara was looking keenly at Gina. Would Lindsey's best friend defend her name?

When she said nothing, he goaded her. 'So

Lindsey was the ringleader. She really did bring it all on herself.'

'We're not sheep,' Gina said angrily. 'We were all in it together, all for one and one for all.'

'So who else took a pill that night? Gina?'

'...Yeah, OK. I took a tab. All right?'

'Maria-Teresa?' She nodded dumbly. 'Celia?'

'I wasn't in the mood that night.'

'And it was Ecstasy you took? You're sure about that?' Gina and Terry exchanged looks and shrugged. 'You didn't feel any different effects to the normal?'

'I guess not,' Gina said.

'About Lindsey. You, Gina, you were her best friend, right?'

'We were all mates but, yeah, I suppose.'

'Would she deliberately have gone after the thrill of a new drug? If her pusher had suggested she try something a bit newer and stronger than boring old E?'

Gina didn't answer. It was Celia who said sullenly, 'Lindsey was up for anything.'

'So,' Barbara said, when they had let the girls go, 'does our drug pusher know what he's selling or did a tab of Entry get into the usual batch by mistake?'

'And is it just this pusher, or does the con-tamination go further up the chain of supply?'

'There've been no deaths other than in Newbury,' Barbara pointed out.

'That we've heard about. Lindsey's death passed more or less unnoticed. Who's to say that other towns haven't had the same thing?'

'Good point. We need to ask around.'

'You know the patch better than I do, Barbara. Where should we be looking for club deaths?'

'Reading, of course, Swindon, Slough, probably Oxford. You know, the best person to ask around would be Mr Summers. He's been in the Thames Valley force for thirty years. He knows everyone.'

'Won't he mind being asked to do such a lowly job?'

Barbara laughed. 'Mind? He'll love it.'

CHAPTER EIGHT

When Greg got home that evening, Angie was on the phone in the front hall. As he came through the door, she said, 'Great! See you there,' and hung up.

'Hello, darling.' He beamed at her.

She beamed back. 'Did Nick Nicolaides tell you to invite me to Nadia's hen night?'

Greg switched off his beam abruptly. 'Oh! Yes. Now you come to mention it...'

She surveyed him with her hands on her hips. 'Do you not want me to go or are you just going senile?'

'Senile,' he said. 'I wasn't sure if you'd want to anyway.'

'I love a good hen night, me. I take it Barbara's going.'

'Yes and no,' he said.

'Come again?'

'She'll be at the party, but she's sort of working undercover. It's about these drug deaths at the Kismet.'

'Right.' She picked up the receiver again. 'I'll give her a ring and see what we're going to do about a stripper.' Greg rolled his eyes. 'Unless you want to volunteer,' she concluded.

He decided not to respond to this. Instead he said, 'I'm meeting Piers for a quick drink later so– Agh! What's that?'

Something resembling a large white rat had just wandered out of the kitchen. It was only when it came to sniff his ankles and wagged its tail to welcome him home, that he recognised his West Highland terrier bitch, Bellini, who had apparently been scalped. 'My poor baby!' he said, gathering her up in his arms. 'Who did this to you?'

'We had a day of health and beauty at the dog groomers,' Angie explained. 'We had our claws trimmed too.' She gave him an up-and-down glance and added, 'A haircut wouldn't kill you either.'

'All right, but I draw the line at a manicure.' He gave Bellini a look of sympathy and solidarity and a quick kiss on her bald head. When he'd been a young constable, his sergeant had never hesitated to bark at him to get his hair cut. Life had been simple then.

Now it was again.

It was Greg's turn to cook so he stuck a couple of pizzas in the oven and set the timer for ten minutes. They always told you on the packet to preheat the oven, but years of bachelor experimentation had taught him that it seldom made any difference. He would have liked to pour himself a generous glass of red wine but he'd be driving to Hungerford and back. He went into the sitting room to watch the early evening news.

Five minutes later he was wondering why he put himself through this daily ordeal. Wasn't his life difficult enough without coming home to the aftermath of that summer's suicide bombings in the capital, the huge eyes of the emaciated children of Niger, the dispossessed of the Pakistan earthquake and today's atrocity in Iraq?

He could switch off, but these things would still be happening even if he wasn't watching.

With one ear he could hear Angie still on the phone trying to arrange a stripper for Friday, proving that life went on. She had not been kidding then, except about the last bit, about his – Greg's – volunteering. He hoped.

The programme went over to *Newbury Newsround* and he reached for the mute button as the bland face of local reporter Adam Chaucer – in the top five of his least favourite people – filled the screen. His finger froze, however, at the reporter's first smiling words.

'You thought Newbury didn't keep up with the latest fashions – with New York, Paris and Milan – well, guess again, because the latest designer drug – Entry – has hit town at our very own Kismet Klub.'

Greg watched in horror as Chaucer ran through the events surrounding the deaths of Lindsey Brownlow and Erin Moss, flashing up photos of the two girls taken in better times. Finally, with an exclamation of fury, he clicked the TV off. Chaucer had just been promoted to number one on the most-hated list.

'Makes it sound very glamorous, doesn't he?'

He realised that Angie had come into the room and was standing with her hands on the back of his armchair.

'Yes,' he said. 'What could be more glamorous than convulsing to death on a cold, dirty towpath at the age of seventeen?'

She slid two fingers of her right hand against his jugular. 'Hmm. The rat Chaucer does nothing for your blood pressure. Take a deep breath. Think how happy it would make him to hear you'd had a stroke while watching his programme.'

She made a good point. He inhaled, let the air fill his lungs, and breathed out slowly. The timer began to beep.

'Supper,' he said, adding, 'Thank you, darling.' He wondered briefly if he could ring Piers and dump him, decided that he couldn't since Piers was his best mate and he hadn't seen him for a fortnight.

It wasn't wholly altruistic: somehow Piers always managed to cheer him up.

'Won't be late,' he said, as he let himself out of the front door forty-five minutes later.

Greg arrived a few minutes early at the Railway Tavern in Hungerford and there was no sign of Piers. The saloon was not crowded – a young couple engrossed in each other; another, older, couple who appeared to be quietly squabbling, with angry glances and curled lips; three lads, barely old enough to drink, intent on a booze-up.

He ordered a small glass of Chardonnay and stayed at the bar to sip in contentment. It was nice to have a few quiet minutes after a long day. Had the barman been inclined to chat, he might have moved away, but he was the silent type making him, in Greg's book, a thoroughly good bloke.

After ten minutes a woman came in, scanned the room quickly, and came to sit on a bar stool only two away from his own. Greg gave her the merest glance. She was in her mid-thirties, he calculated, nice-looking and done up to pull with full evening make-up and a little black dress, subtle but effective. She saw him looking and returned his smile, sliding over to the stool next to his.

'Buy a lady a drink, kind sir?'

'Sorry,' Greg said pleasantly. 'I'm spoken for.'

He felt a little guilty since she looked crushed. Guilty and smug. He still had it, the old Summers charm. She ordered a glass of red wine from the barman, moved to a more remote bar stool and sat sipping in what he assumed was a sulk.

Then the door opened and another man came in; Greg wondered if the wall was, in fact, mirrored since the newcomer could have been his reflection: pushing fifty, average height, slim build, greying but full head of hair, office suit but with the jacket discarded, the tie removed and the top shirt button undone.

The woman stared from him to Greg and back again in confusion as he sat down and ordered a large whisky. She crossed her legs, displaying a taut thigh in tan nylon and Greg's *doppelgänger* rose to the bait, asking in a nasal voice, 'Can I refresh that for you at all?'

'That's very kind. Red wine, please.' She moved smoothly across to sit next to him.

The woman had clearly targeted him. Greg had an inkling of what was going on but he wanted to be sure. He asked for a mineral water and kept his ears open. After a few minutes, he heard the new arrival ask the woman if she fancied a bite to eat. She accepted, said she'd just freshen up and disappeared into the ladies. Greg and the barman exchanged looks.

'Will you tell him or shall I?' the barman muttered.

Greg raised his hands to push the idea

away. 'It's none of my business. He deserves what he gets.'

The barman tutted. 'Where's your masculine solidarity?' He went over to the other man and leant urgently across the bar, whispering to him at length. The man looked alarmed, drained his whisky in one go and made himself scarce.

The woman came out of the ladies, realised that he'd run out on her and said, 'Bollocks!'

'Tough luck.' Greg grinned. 'Here, let me buy you that drink after all.'

'Oh, what the hell!' She sat next to him as he signalled the barman. 'There goes my bonus.'

'What are you?' he asked. 'Private detective, or do you just specialise in honey traps?'

She looked dismayed. 'Is it that obvious?'

'It is to me, but I'm a policeman – don't worry, you're not doing anything illegal.'

'I know. I was in the Job myself for a couple of years. Julia Roberts. Not that one. I wish.' She handed him a business card, an address in Marlborough. 'I do general detective work but I've done a lot of this stuff lately – paid by the wife to see how readily hubby takes the bait. Seems a bit sneaky to me, to be frank, but I can't afford to be fussy.'

'And you thought I was him?' Greg laughed.

'I stupidly forgot to bring the photo and you were the right age and physical type. You don't have a wife who'd like to pay me, do you?'

'No wife,' he said truthfully, 'and I'm just buying you a consolatory drink.'

The door opened and Piers finally arrived, waving and calling out that he was sorry to be so late. The young photographer looked effortlessly elegant, as usual, his handsome blond looks enough to turn any woman's head – pointlessly, since Piers was resolutely homosexual. Julia grinned. 'I see now. And I always thought my gaydar was pretty well tuned.'

'No,' Greg spluttered into his water. 'Not gay. No.'

'It's fine.' She laid a friendly hand on his arm. 'Makes me feel better about you turning me down.'

'Oh ... OK then.'

She drained her wine. 'Better be off. People to follow. Summonses to serve. Lost dogs to find.'

She wiggled off her stool and sashayed out with a cheeky smile at Piers.

'Who's your friend?' he asked as he signalled to the barman. 'And can I blackmail you not to tell Angie?'

'Let's sit down,' Greg said, wanting the optimum setting for his humorous anecdote.

CHAPTER NINE

Greg was waylaid coming into the station the next morning by Veronica Doyle, a uniformed sergeant with several years' service under her belt.

'That new DCI of yours,' she said without preamble.

'Mr Freeman. What about him?'

'He's a bit of all right.'

'Er... Thanks?'

'Striker, yeah? I like that. You know Dick Maybey's really pee-ed off because he can't invent a nickname for him, what with him already having one, like.'

'Good,' Greg said.

'Is he married?'

'Separated.'

'Excellent!'

Greg watched as she marched off in her heavy serge trousers and lace-up boots. She was quite good looking, he supposed, if you liked fleshy redheads. Was Freeman 'a bit of all right'? Women's taste in men was, and would doubtless always remain, a mystery to him.

'So,' he said half an hour later when the

CID team were gathered once more in his office, 'what do we know about Entry that we didn't know yesterday. Mr Freeman? Did you get hold of your contacts?'

'Someone in the NYPD drug squad called me back in the middle of the night,' Striker said with a grin. 'They don't even start work till ten p.m. their time. The drug surfaced in San Francisco, as Andy said, about eighteen months ago. Best guess is that some chemistry anorak at Berkeley with too much time on his hands concocted it. It reached New York a month later. Now, you have to understand that NYPD have dozens of drug-related club deaths to deal with every week.'

'I can imagine,' Greg said.

'But they gave priority to this one. Only, after three months, the deaths stopped, as suddenly as they'd begun. About the same time they had three unexplained murders – one in uptown Manhattan, two in Queens. They had all the hallmarks of a gangland execution, except that the victims weren't gangsters. Two of them were high school teachers.'

'Let me guess,' Greg said. 'They taught chemistry.'

'Right!'

'And the organised crime gangs didn't like amateurs muscling in on their territory.'

'There was more to it than that,' Striker said. 'They were killing off the customers.

That doesn't look good on anyone's balance sheet.'

'And dare I ask if these murders were ever solved?'

'Not so far, but those sorts of cases are notoriously hard to close. Mostly, you end up pinning them on some gangland gorilla you've got for something else.'

'I trust the NYPD aren't dismissing them as not worth the effort,' Greg said seriously.

'I hope so too.' Striker was also serious. 'I want to see whoever's making and distributing this drug go to prison for a long time, but I don't want them dead. Anyway, the drug can be dissolved easily enough in liquid, but they say it's got a slightly bitter taste, so you'd need something strong. Vodka and tonic would be no good but vodka and coke, say, might do it.'

'Or these sugary alcopops the kids seem to like.'

'Yeah.'

'Right. Andy, anything to add.'

'Only that the website with the recipe originates in the Ukraine,' Andy said.

'Doesn't mean a thing,' Striker said. 'The Internet is truly the global village. Whoever created that site could be in LA, New York, Paris. Even sitting in his little semi in Newbury.'

Greg glanced at Andy who nodded agreement. 'What it does mean,' he said, 'is we 'haven't a hope in hell of getting it shut down.'

'OK, that's not our priority since our pusher clearly has the recipe. What are you working on now, Andy?'

'I'm still tracking down any Internet contacts Erin might have made in addition to the one who came forward. Then there's all Lindsey's Net activity to go through.'

'Nick?'

'I've been scanning the CCTV from June to see if there was any sight of Craig Warnock. I'm certain as I can be that he wasn't there that night.' He rubbed his eyes. 'And I shall soon be needing glasses at this rate. I'm doing the dead girls' mobile phone accounts today.'

'Good,' Greg said. 'I didn't like Craig for this. Now, I made some calls yesterday afternoon, to Reading, Oxford and our old colleague Tim Monroe in Slough. Remember him, Babs?'

'Of course.' Monroe had briefly been acting DCI in Newbury until he'd punched the lights out of a member of the National Crime Squad and been sent home in disgrace.

'They've had no unexplained drug deaths in the past year. Nor have Swindon.'

'So our supply of Entry is local,' Striker said. 'Interesting.' Seeing that the rest of the team were looking at him expectantly, he

105

added, 'I didn't see Newbury as the centre of the local drug trade somehow.'

'It isn't really the centre of anything,' Greg admitted. 'So what's happening today?'

'I'd like to concentrate on Erin,' Striker said, 'and I'll keep Barbara with me, if that's OK.'

'Then let's get going!' They all rose but Greg called Striker back. 'Mr Freeman, a word, if I may.'

'I'll catch you up,' Striker said to Barbara. He sat down again and Greg waited till they were alone with the door closed.

'I realise you're busy with these deaths but I do have another little task I'd like you to undertake.'

Striker leant back in his chair and put his right ankle on his left knee. Greg noticed that his sock had 'Tuesday' written on the side, which struck a charmingly uncool note in this coolest of men.

'Fire away,' he said.

'Did you happen to catch *Newbury Newsround* on TV last night?'

'Yes. I must say, I was surprised they had so much detail.'

'That's the problem. This isn't the first time that reporter – Adam Chaucer – has had information he shouldn't have. OK, last night it was minor enough but there was an occasion, about eighteen months ago, when we had a toddler kidnapped, little girl.

Chaucer was about to put her life in jeopardy by going public with some confidential information and he didn't give a damn.'

'I'm guessing he's not on your Christmas card list.'

'Luckily we found her just in time.'

'And you think someone at the station is leaking.'

'I can't think of another explanation.'

Striker looked thoughtful. 'Can I ask why you're giving this job to me?'

'Because you're new here, which means you can't possibly be the culprit.'

'That's what I thought. Does that mean you suspect someone in CID?'

Greg thought about it. 'I'd trust Barbara with my life. Andy is as solid as a rock, slow but methodical...'

'Which leaves Mr Nicolaides,' Striker said. 'Do you think he's the type?'

'...I don't know. Come to think of it, the kidnapped toddler case happened shortly after he joined us. On the other hand, he's been in the Job a long time and he had an unblemished record so I can't really believe it's him. He doesn't need the money either, or he soon won't.'

'Planning on winning the lottery, is he?'

Greg explained about Nick, Nadia and the ailing multi-millionaire, Mr Fitzsimmons.

Striker whistled. 'Nice work if you can get it. But this is recent. He might have started leaking for the money and can't get out of the habit.'

'Chaucer is a nasty piece of work,' Greg agreed. 'If someone sold him information once, he could then hold the threat of exposure over them to keep them onside.'

'What happened to not betraying your sources?' Striker asked. 'What about this Nadia? Pillow talk?'

'Nick only met her last autumn,' Greg explained, 'so she couldn't have been responsible for the toddler thing.'

'What other information have we mislaid?'

'I don't know if you heard about our murder in Inkpen over the summer...'

'The IRA woman?'

'Exactly! I tried to keep her true identity secret for the sake of her children, but it was all over the papers two days after we made the arrest. To get back to your original question, I don't think it's anyone in CID.'

'I shall nose around,' Striker said. 'Do the team have any special friends in uniform – people they might chat to in unguarded moments?'

'There's Chris Clements,' Greg said. 'When Andy was in uniform he was mostly partnered up with Chris.'

'Chris Clements,' Striker repeated, apparently committing the name to memory.

'But I'd categorise him as an amiable idiot,' Greg said. 'I sometimes wonder about one of the custody sergeants – Dick Maybey.'

'Ah, yes, I've met him. Every station has one like him.'

'He's been here since Adam was a lad and knows everything that's going on.'

Striker got up. 'I don't promise fast results, but I'll see what I can nose out.'

'Superintendent. Mr Summers, sir?'

Greg turned, not recognising the voice. It was Martin Nelson, the new uniformed inspector.

'Inspector?'

'I hear you're mounting an operation at the Kismet Klub on Friday night,' the younger man said.

'That's right,' Greg said cautiously. 'Not a big uniformed binge, though, a few men in plain clothes, keeping an eye on the place.'

'I was wondering if you were open to volunteers. I'm on afternoon shift this week so I could be there by ten-thirty.'

'You're volunteering?' Greg queried hopefully. Inspectors weren't eligible for overtime.

'I feel a certain responsibility. If I'd ordered the full range of tests on Lindsey then maybe the second girl needn't have died.'

The man had spent some years in CID before his promotion, Greg remembered. You didn't turn down expertise like that, especially not when it came free.

'Glad to have you aboard,' he said briskly. 'Friday night it is, then. See you there.'

Greg went home early on Friday, planning to get a light supper and a few hours' rest before he set off to the Kismet Klub. He'd be fifty next birthday and it might turn into a late night.

Angie had recently started the third year of her psychology degree at Reading university, which meant that she'd just completed three months' of holiday. Although not naturally a lazy girl, she had mastered the art of spending a day doing almost nothing in a way that he slightly envied and suspected would never now achieve, a fact that made retirement a less-than-welcome prospect.

She was lying on the sofa when he came in, wearing sweat pants and an old sweater of his, a paperback book resting against her bent knees. The TV was on but with the sound off and Anne Robinson was curling her lip as she dismissed some poor soul on *The Weakest Link*. Four empty coffee mugs lay on the floor at her side.

He realised that if she had a boyfriend her own age, like most of her mates, then she'd probably have spent the summer backpacking round Europe, or even Asia. Instead, she'd been stuck with her geriatric partner and the demanding job that kept him out of the house all hours and brought him home sad or grumpy.

'You're home early,' she remarked, as if reading his mind.

He thought of something. 'Did you track down a stripper in the end?'

''Course.' She grinned at him, mischievous. 'So I don't need to draft you in. Sorry.'

'Please tell me he's not coming dressed as a policeman,' he said wearily.

'You'll just have to wait and see.' She swung her legs down and gracefully resumed a vertical position, stretching and yawning as if she'd just got out of bed.

'Anything for supper?' Greg asked.

'There's that leftover chicken in the fridge. I was going to have a salad – probably pick up a kebab in town later. I'll go and change.'

She left the room and Greg gathered up the dirty mugs and ferried them to the dishwasher. He took the chicken and the salad things out of the fridge. It didn't look much so he got a packet of pre-cooked rice out of the freezer and zapped it in the microwave for three minutes. For some reason it was yellow, but it tasted all right. He decided not to wait for Angie since he could hear the bath running upstairs and she might be some time if she was preparing for a night out.

Indeed, it was over an hour before she

came down and the transformation was worthy of Cinderella after she'd met her fairy godmother's magic wand. She'd put her hair up at the back with wispy tendrils snaking round her neck and her eye shadow glittered as she moved and caught the light. He was delighted to see that her black tiered cotton skirt fell demurely halfway down her calves, while her burnt-orange sleeveless top highlighted her fair complexion and blonde hair.

'You look lovely, darling,' he said.

'Thanks.' She gave him an appreciative twirl. She'd grown up in Yorkshire where 'You don't sweat much for a fat lass' passed for a compliment.

CHAPTER TEN

Greg became aware of two teenage girls striding silently towards him, as though they were doing synchronised walking. They looked very similar, except that one was a honey-blonde while the other had brown hair, although she'd compensated by adding yellow streaks to it. They were wearing what seemed like unnecessarily short skirts, but he couldn't help noticing that at least they had the legs for it.

He was about to ask, in an unhelpful manner, if he could help them when Striker said, 'Hello, my darlings,' and kissed them both on each cheek.

Together, they said, 'Hello, Dad.'

'These are my daughters,' he added, 'and, girls, this is my new boss, Superintendent Summers.'

While Greg was debating whether he should shake hands with them, or if that would seem too old-fogeyish, the twins stood grinning at him, with none of the self-consciousness he had felt at their age.

'Have you got a gun?' the blonde asked.

'Dad's got a gun,' the striped one added.

'Dad draws a gun from the armoury when

he needs one,' Striker corrected them. 'As seldom as possible. When Hannah and Elizabeth heard about the hen party they wanted to come along,' he explained, 'and Nadia said the more the merrier. Now,' he added, 'remember what I told you.'

The girls rolled their blue eyes in unison and chanted, 'Just say no!'

'I'm serious. I told you about this new drug. Think how stupid you'll feel if you wake up dead in the morning.' The twins groaned theatrically. 'Well,' he went on, 'if you have no concern for yourselves, have some consideration for me, because your mother would kill me.'

'We'll be fine.' The blonde one laid a kindly hand on his arm as if he were some incalculably old buffer who had to be humoured. 'And we know you can't get pregnant standing up.'

'Everyone's a comedian!'

'Ah, here's Angie.'

Striker looked at the newcomer with interest as Greg made the introductions. He'd heard the whole story now, of course. Luckily, it was from Barbara, so he'd had the sympathetic version, since there were plenty of people at Newbury police station who thought that Superintendent Summers was a bit of an old perv.

Angie glanced over at Sergeant Dave Trafford who was standing in uniform a few yards away, handing out leaflets. Knowing perfectly well who he was, she called over innocently, 'Are you the stripper, love?'

Trafford grinned. 'Soon as I get off duty, Mrs Summers.'

Angie, laughing, turned away to lead the twins down the alleyway, onto the canal towpath and into the club. One of them paused and looked meaningfully at her father.

'Oh, all right!' He produced his wallet and peeled a twenty-pound note off for them. They both looked steadily at him and the stripy one crossed her arms.

'Are you serious?' the blonde said.

He sighed and added a second note. Satisfied, they followed Angie and were soon disappearing from sight. Striker called after them, 'Hannah, watch out for your sister.'

'OK.'

'Elizabeth, watch out for your sister.'

'OK!'

'Are we crazy letting our womenfolk go in there at all in the circumstances?' Greg asked, when they'd vanished round the corner.

'I don't know what it's like at your house,' Striker said, 'but I can't remember when I last *let* my womenfolk do anything.' Greg laughed agreement as Striker continued, 'You can't always prevent disaster. That's one of the first things I learnt in the army.'

'No,' Greg agreed. 'You do what you can

115

to keep your children safe, but sometimes it isn't enough.'

'I heard about your son,' Striker said in a low voice. 'I'm sorry. I should think before I speak.'

'That's all right.'

'I do tell the twins' putative boyfriends that I own a really big gun,' Striker added.

Greg had had leaflets printed and the uniformed officers he had stationed in the surrounding streets were handing them out to clubbers as they arrived. It wasn't hard to determine which of the young men and women heading through the pedestrianised area of Bartholomew Street, up Northbrook Street or round from the Market Place were on their way to the Kismet Klub.

Most of them had already had a few drinks and looked at the leaflets in a puzzled way before screwing them up and letting them drop to the ground. Some of them laughed, secure in the knowledge that they could handle any substance, legal or illegal, that came their way that night.

It was going through the motions, Greg thought. He hadn't expected anything else. If they were to gain any useful information tonight it would be from plain clothes officers inside the club. Apart from Barbara, he had sent Nick and Andy in, but decided that neither he nor Striker was young enough to pass for a clubber, or only one best described as 'Sad'.

Also, he was fond of his hearing and wanted to hang onto it for a few more years.

'I'm thinking of getting two of those testing kits for the twins,' Striker remarked. 'You know? Lets you test your drink for keta-mine, GHB, roofies. Some forces up north have been handing them out to clubbers. You use a pipette and three little strips of paper, like litmus.'

'That'd put a dampener on a hot date,' Greg said.

'I certainly hope so.'

Nadia was in understandably high spirits as she unloaded a tray of drinks onto the corner table she had bagged earlier that evening. She was dressed to kill, making the most of her impressive breasts with a tight, bright basque, giving more than a hint of flesh every time she bent over, which she did often. Black harem trousers clung to her womanly hips.

She was wearing an enormous diamond on her ring finger and held her left hand out from time to time to gaze at it with satis-faction.

Barbara hoped that she wasn't on the pull tonight, the way the bride so often seemed to be at hen nights these days. Barbara was no prude, as many men in Newbury could testify, but there was something very tacky about a woman who was committing herself to a man she presumably loved having a last drunken knee-trembler with a stranger, up against a wall, in an alley smelling of stale urine.

God! She must be getting old. At this rate, she'd soon be voting Conservative and tutting when anyone swore. She was probably just jealous: her relationship with DCI Trevor Faber of the National Crime Squad had cooled considerably since she'd called off their holiday at the last minute in June, leaving him to head out to Corfu on his own so that she wouldn't miss being part of a murder investigation.

Still, she reminded herself, Nadia was not committing herself to the man she loved, not this time round. It was such a weird situation, one quite outside her experience. Nick was somewhere nearby, she knew, although he was under strict orders from Nadia to steer clear of the hen party.

'Bacardi Breezers.' Nadia handed bottles of orange liquid to the twins, who had made themselves perfectly at home among a group of strangers. 'White wine.' That was for Angie. *'Mineral water* for the party pooper.'

She grimaced at Barbara who didn't bother to remind her that she was on duty.

'Lager and lime for yours truly,' Nadia

concluded, flopping down in her chair. 'Cheap date, that's me. After tomorrow it'll be champagne for breakfast every day. I shall bathe in the stuff.'

'I've never seen the attraction,' Angie said. 'It sounds cold and sticky.'

'Asses' milk then.' Nadia raised her glass. 'Here's to marriage. If it wasn't for marriage, men would be wandering about thinking they had no faults.'

'My maiden aunt says being single is like death by drowning,' Barbara said thoughtfully. 'A delightful sensation once you stop struggling.'

'Are you wearing a wedding dress?' Angie asked. 'A proper white one, I mean.'

'Hardly worth it,' Nadia said. 'It's just registry office, then back to his place for a buffet with a bunch of his mates – old people, mostly. I bought a cream suit at Primark.'

'You and Nick were planning to marry next spring, weren't you?' Barbara asked.

'Yeah, probably still will.'

While Barbara pondered whether this was callous or just pragmatic, Angie said, 'Back in a minute,' and rose, ostensibly to visit the Ladies, actually to see if there was any sign of the stripper.

'Good evening, Superintendent.'

Greg, who had seen Adam Chaucer approaching and tried to ignore him, said

119

evenly, 'Mr Chaucer'.

Striker looked at the newcomer with interest. 'You're a lot older than you look on TV,' he remarked.

Greg grinned as Chaucer flushed with annoyance.

'And you are?' the reporter said.

Striker made him a small bow. 'DCI Isaac Freeman at your service, sir.'

Chaucer laughed. 'The latest through the revolving door, eh? Well, you're both a bit old for clubbing, aren't you—?'

Striker batted the ball straight back. 'Could say the same about you.'

'But I know Mr Summers likes his women young.' Chaucer looked pleased with himself, apparently under the impression that he had won the point, then was disappointed at getting no reaction from Greg.

'Well, I'm here to work,' he added.

'What do you imagine we're doing?' Greg asked.

'Keeping the young women of Newbury safe, I trust, since you haven't done a very good job up till now.'

Satisfied with this final impertinence, he turned on his heel and went into the club, pausing to show a press card to a bouncer who nodded him in free of charge.

'Well played,' Greg said.

'I look forward to finding out who his informant is and stitching them both up like kippers,' Striker replied.

'Here, Babs...' Nadia was topping up her lagers with vodka now and growing confidential. They were alone at the table; the Freeman twins were dancing with two young men who also appeared to be twins – which would presumably give them all something to talk about when the music stopped – and Angie had excused herself once more. 'Is it true that Mr Summers' son died of AIDS.'

'It certainly is not!' Barbara felt a cold anger growing within her and swallowed it with difficulty. Bloody Nick Nicolaides was the worst gossip in Berkshire and, like most gossips, he didn't care how accurate his tattle was. 'Fred had leukaemia and keep it down in front of Angie.'

'That's why I waited till she'd gone to the loo,' Nadia said indignantly. 'I'm not inten ... inseniv ... *insensitive.*' She looked around. 'She keeps going to pee. She got cystitis, or what?'

Probably tired of your company, Barbara thought. She noticed that all the women at this hen party were connected to Newbury police: friends of Nick's, in other words. Didn't Nadia have any friends of her own? She said, 'None of your mates from London made it, then?'

Nadia shrugged. 'They're mostly nurses.

121

Shift work. You know how it is. Plus it's a long way when you're a Londoner.'

This statement might have struck some people as odd but Barbara knew that, while people from Newbury thought nothing of travelling up to London for the evening – only an hour's ride on the train – Londoners considered any excursion outside the capital to require maps, sherpas and, probably, inoculation against smallpox.

'Hope I haven't missed anything.'

Greg turned in surprise to see Martin Nelson, looking younger in civvies. He introduced him to Striker, who said, 'Seen you in the canteen'.

'Glad to meet you, sir.'

'Inspector Nelson volunteered to help out,' Greg explained, 'inside in plain clothes. He has CID experience.'

'Bit old for clubbing,' Nelson laughed. He held up his left hand with the wedding ring on it. 'Also too married. I thought of taking this off but decided it'd help keep me out of temptation.'

He looked bright eyed, happy, and Greg guessed that he'd been missing CID and was eager for a chance at a bit of detective work.

'By the way,' Nelson said as he headed towards the club, 'message from Sergeant Maybey. He says don't go arresting anyone as his cells are full.'

Greg groaned. Britain's prisons were now so overcrowded that remand prisoners were being held in police cells, making life hard for provincial stations.

They'd be billeting them in his spare room next.

'There you are!' Barbara joined Angie who was leaning against the back wall of the club, on the towpath, having a cigarette. 'Didn't know you smoked,' she added.

'Don't really. Special occasions. Want one?'

'Well, maybe I will. Just this once.' Barbara took a cigarette from the packet offered to her. Angie produced a box of matches and managed to give her a light on the second one after a gust of wind extinguished the first.

'You should get a lighter,' Barbara said.

'But that'd mean I was a real smoker.'

Barbara inhaled, remembering the few years at school when she used to smoke, mostly because it was forbidden. It must be – what? – ten, eleven years since she'd last had one. She inhaled again and began to cough. 'Bloody hell,' she wheezed, a little red in the face. 'I'm well out of practice.'

She thought Angie would laugh but she didn't, just puffed on her own cigarette in a purposeful sort of way, letting smoke out of her nose like a miniature dragon. After a moment, Barbara asked, 'Is anything wrong?'

'Will you tell me something, Babs?'

'If I can.'

'I mean, I know you're really Greg's friend and you probably feel your first loyalty is to him.'

'Whatever's the matter?' Barbara said, puzzled. 'Are you two having problems?'

'You know a woman called Martha Childs? I think she's with forensics.'

'Scenes of Crime.' Barbara was beginning to understand. 'Bloody Nadia! What's she been telling you?'

'So there's something to tell.'

'No, there really isn't. Angie–' Barbara took hold of her by the upper arms. 'Whatever stupid rumour you've heard about Gregory and Martha, it isn't true. I swear to you on ... on my mother's grave.'

'Like your mother's dead!' Angie said.

'Seriously. Do you trust me?'

'I suppose.'

'It's stupid station gossip and I know for a fact there's no truth in it because I asked him myself three months ago. He loves you. Oh! I could kill Nick Nicolaides. If only gossips would stop to think how destructive it all is.'

'Greg says you wouldn't solve half as many crimes if it wasn't for gossip.'

'...Fair point.'

Angie looked at her cigarette for a moment, then dropped it half-smoked to the gravel of the towpath and ground it out with her heel. 'I don't smoke in front of Greg.'

'Oh, yes. He gave up, didn't he?'

'When Fred died.'

'I don't think fags give you leukaemia,' Barbara said gently.

Somewhere nearby, a firework sputtered into the sky, although Bonfire Night was a fortnight away. Green, red and yellow sparks cascaded over the town, beautiful in their way.

Angie said, 'But there are so many ways to die... Sorry! I've had a bit too much to drink.'

'No, you're right. There must be a hundred ways to die.'

Striker noticed the arrival of Lindsey Brownlow's three mates, looking very much as they had on the night of her death. He was surprised they still came. He didn't think he could have borne to frequent a club where a close friend had died, and so recently. He pointed them out to Greg with a nod of his head, his voice low.

He shared his thoughts as the girls made their way towards the club and Greg said, 'Maybe it's bravado – like getting back on a bike after you've fallen off.'

'Hello, Mr Summers.' He glanced round, recognising at once the girl who'd been just behind Lindsey and her friends on the CCTV, the one who had given him pause.

She said, 'You don't remember me, do you?'

'No, I'm sorry.' He'd had a flicker of recognition on seeing the tape but now, even in the flesh and at close quarters, he couldn't place her. 'You'll have to help me.'

'It's Ruth Stratton,' she said.

'Ruthie?' He looked at her incredulously. The last time he'd seen her she'd been fourteen, a pudgy adolescent with a plain face. Her father, DCI Harry Stratton, had been distraught at the time because their GP had put her on the pill and Greg had been amazed that she had any need for it.

Now, just a couple of years later, she looked all grown up. Her fat legs were long and slender, and that wasn't guesswork, since he could see most of them, along with her midriff and its pierced belly button. He saw that her formerly mousy hair was high-lighted and that a now attractive young face was marred by too much make-up.

He cleared his throat. 'How's your father?'

Her face clouded as she pushed her fringe back out of her eyes. 'I wouldn't know.'

'Ah!'

'He moved out eight months ago and the last phone number we had for him's been disconnected for at least three.'

'I'm so sorry.'

'He never got over losing his job,' she said. 'Being a policeman – that was important to him, gave him his self respect. After he got sacked, he got a job doing security but he hated it. He got more and more miserable and more and more impossible to live with. He lost his faith and stopped going to church and that had been a big part of his life. When he finally left, we were glad – me and Mum.'

'How is Prue?' Greg asked awkwardly.

'OK. Like I say, she was glad to see the back of him. She's got a new bloke now.' Ruth shrugged. 'He's nice enough, bit wimpy, writes poetry.' She seemed suddenly bored with the conversation. 'See you.'

'Wait!' Greg called after her and she turned back with a small sigh of annoyance. 'Did you know Lindsey Brownlow?'

'Bit.'

'You're at the same school?'

'Yeah, but she was in the sixth form. I'm year eleven. They've got their own sixth-form block and don't have to wear uniform and they look down on the likes of us.'

'But you were here the night she died.'

'Was I? What makes you think that?'

'I saw you on the CCTV tapes. You arrived right after Lindsey and her three best mates.'

'So? Somebody had to. I'd left by the time the drama started – heard about it at school the next Monday.'

'OK,' Greg said. 'Thanks.' He handed her a leaflet and she stuffed it into her bag without reading it. 'It's a long story,' he added to Striker, when she was out of earshot.

'I thought it might be.'

'He was my DCI for years – Harry Stratton – till he did something really stupid. I'll tell you about it sometime.'

'Is she actually old enough to be going to nightclubs?' Striker asked.

'...Come to think of it, no.'

'This is where the first girl died, isn't it?' Angie looked round the canalside as if seeing it for the first time.

'Lindsey. Yes.' Barbara always thought it important to name the victims, not degenerate into calling them 'the first one' or 'the second victim' or 'the third girl' as if they had lost their identities, their humanity.

'I was reading about the victims of the London tube bombings,' Angie continued. 'There was this young couple and, on a normal day, neither of them took the tube. But that morning, for various reasons, they did, and they both died. What sort of dumb luck is that?'

Barbara put an arm round her shoulder and squeezed. She didn't know Angie that well but liked her, if only because she made Gregory Summers happy, but now she felt a great affection for her and wanted to give comfort, if she could, to a young woman who seemed very low in spirits.

'It's just that,' she said, 'dumb luck.'

Angie accepted Barbara's embrace without being noticeably cheered by it. 'But do you ever get the feeling that we're living at the end of days?'

'Is that like the end of the world?'

'Yeah. Sorry. Nuns.'

'I always forget that you were brought up Catholic.'

'Not so much. I went to a nursery run by nuns because they were cheap and it meant Mum could go back to work.'

'Catch them young, eh?'

'In theory. Didn't work with me. Anyway. Tsunamis, hurricanes, suicide bombers. End of days.'

Now Barbara felt depressed too.

'I have a cool idea.' Elizabeth Freeman stood waiting while her sister, who was a bit of a clean freak, washed her hands very thoroughly and pressed the button for the hot-air drier with her elbow. 'Why don't we see if we can score us some of this drug of Dad's?'

'Are you crazy?' Hannah, though twenty-two minutes older than her sister, had always been the more timid of the two. 'You heard what he said.'

'But don't you see!' Elizabeth's face was flushed with excitement. 'We can find out for him who the dealer is. Think what brownie points that'll earn us.'

'It sounds a bit dangerous,' Hannah said doubtfully.

'We don't have to take any! Listen.' Elizabeth grabbed her sister by the shoulders and shook her gently. 'Dad puts himself in danger all the time.'

'Not really. Mostly he just wanders about asking people questions. It's not like on the telly.'

'Well, what about when he was in the army in Israel? I know some of his friends died there. This is our chance to show him what we're made of. We'd be heroes. It'd liven things up, apart from anything else. Hasn't anyone told these people that Boho is *so* last season?'

'I have an idea!'

'...Well?'

'Let's not be heroes. Let's go and find those twins and see if they want to dance again. They were cute.'

'I don't fancy yours.'

'They're identical!'

'Time for that later. Come on!' Elizabeth turned and marched out of the toilet.

'I have a very bad feeling about this.'

Hannah followed more slowly. 'Daddy's girl,' she added, but not loudly enough for her sister to hear.

'I take it he's not one of ours,' Striker said with a grin.

Greg turned in the direction he was looking and saw a nervous young man who appeared, at first glance, to be wearing police uniform. As he got closer, it became obvious that the bits of blue serge were held together by Velcro, for easy removal.

'Stripper?' Striker asked.

'Stripper,' Greg agreed.

'...I think I'll just pop inside, make sure he doesn't waggle his bits too close to my girls.'

'Catch you later,' Greg said.

Inside the club, Striker found a spot on an elevated section where he had a good view of the small hen party without being visible to them. He leant against a pillar and folded his arms. The twins were enjoying themselves, he could see, but then they were happy girls, bless them, not cursed with that been-there-done-that-seen-it-all cynicism that seemed to blight teenagers now, even if they did live in the endless social whirl of Hampstead.

Barbara Carey was on the alert, her eyes darting frequently but unobtrusively round the room. He'd worked with all types of police officer and knew that he and Barbara would get on.

Nadia Polycarpou: an attractive woman if you liked them fleshy, which he mostly did; not a natural blonde, he thought, but convincing enough, the dark eyebrows a bit of a giveaway; she was already drunk and looking pleased with herself but maybe she had cause to. That top was a bit skimpy for a full-breasted woman – serious danger of fallout.

Angie Summers: he'd liked her at once. She had that look about her of people who had known suffering but not been made bitter by it. He'd met a lot of them in the Middle East, Palestinian and Jew alike. They were ready for anything life could throw at them and knew they would survive.

The young 'policeman' approached them and accosted Nadia, his air still diffident. He must really need the money, poor bloke. He produced a cheap notebook and biro, presumably asking if he could take down her particulars.

'Wanna dance, love?' Striker glanced round, startled at being addressed in this way but, since there was no one else there, she had to be talking to him.

The young woman was half his age, if that, a bit shaky on her spike heels, a bottle of lager clutched loosely in one hand, a minuscule silver bag in the other. Her eyes struggled to focus on him but they had the look of a cat who's seen an especially juicy mouse – one it intends to have sex with before eating it.

'That's very kind of you,' he said gravely, 'but my wooden leg prevents me from much gyration.'

'No way!' She glanced at his lower half and giggled. 'Not really?'

'War wound,' he assured her.

'Which one?'

'Falklands.'

Her face creased up in puzzlement while she thought this out. 'Which leg, stupid!'

He indicated his left leg. She fumbled in her bag and drew out a nail file. 'So if I stick this in it...?'

'Be my guest.'

She shoved the nail file wildly in his direction, making faint contact with the close-woven fabric of his thigh.

He didn't flinch.

'Cool!' she said.

He wondered if he'd miscalculated, if she wanted to add 'one-legged gimp' to the notches on her bedpost, but she tottered off, calling, 'See yer,' over her shoulder.

'Hey!' She turned as slowly as an oil tanker, pivoting on her stilettos. 'What's your name?'

'Britney.'

''Course it is. Listen, Britney.' He lowered

133

his voice. 'Do you know who to score off here?'

'Nah. Don't do drugs. 'S dangerous, innit?' She waved the bottle of lager, her thumb acting as a stopper. He took this to mean that alcohol was her drug of choice.

'It's been charming,' he murmured as she resumed her zigzag course away from him, the British Disease incarnate. Returning his attention to the hen party, he saw that the show was well underway, the twins laughing good-humouredly, while the older women attempted not to smirk.

'I should ask for my money back,' Angie grumbled. 'That must have been his first time.'

'Ah, don't worry.' Nadia leant drunkenly across and slapped Angie's knee. 'A stripper's a stripper. It's the thought that counts. You can do better for my next hen party. Whose round is it?'

'Haven't you had enough?' Barbara asked. 'What time's the wedding?'

'Not till lunchtime. Plenty of time to re-re-recover.' She began to sing.

I'm getting married in the morning. Ding dong, the bells are gonna chime.'

Barbara strolled over to the bar on the pretext of buying another round and stood next to Nick Nicolaides who pretended not to know her. She recited her order to the barman, then said in a low voice, 'Anything interesting?'

'Well, I thought your stripper was quite funny.' He guffawed into his low-alcohol lager.

'I'm starting to think that strippers are so last century,' she agreed. She glanced round. Andy Whittaker was dancing with a pair of girls she thought were sisters. He looked happy. 'You and Andy made up?' she asked.

'Hostilities have been suspended,' Nick said.

'He with both those women?'

'Yup. You ever had a threesome, Babs?'

'No...! Shut up. I take it you're not going to the wedding tomorrow?'

'No, that would be taking *weird* to the extreme.'

'Do you really have no problem with it,' Barbara asked, 'with Nadia marrying this old man?'

'Why would I? It's all my dreams come true.'

'Riches beyond the dreams of ... who is it?'

Nick shrugged, uninterested, except in his own riches.

Hannah had reclaimed her twin, who was called Will, and they were slow-dancing, despite the unsuitability of the music, their arms twined round each other's necks, his breath hot in her ear. Elizabeth watched them for a while with disdain, declined a similar offer from twin Rick and made her way to the bar.

The barman looked her up and down, not because he fancied her – he was gay – but because he had doubts about her age.

'Eighteen,' she said.

'Says you.'

'Let me get this for you.' The man on the bar stool was in his late twenties – a bit old for her – but fit, in every sense. As she hesitated, he added, 'No strings'.

'Bacardi Breezer. Watermelon.'

He nodded at the barman who shrugged and went to get her drink.

'You having a good time?' he asked as she perched on the stool next to his.

'It's OK. I live in London so...'

'Bit tame?'

'I guess.'

'What're you doing out here in the sticks then?'

'Visiting the old man.'

'Divorced?'

'Separated.'

'Aren't you a bit old for access visits?' he asked with a cheeky grin, 'if you're eighteen, like.'

'I am!' she protested.

'What year were you born? Quick!'

'Nineteen eighty-seven. Duh!'

'OK.'

'It's for his sake. I thought he might be a bit lonely.'

'Ah! Recently separated?'

'Very.'

'And – let me guess – you're hoping they'll get back together and you can all be one big happy family again.'

'They're grown-ups,' Elizabeth said, 'and so am I. They'll do what they want to do.'

The barman brought her drink and she took a sip.

'David,' he said, holding out a cool hand.

She shook it. 'Rachel.' If she was working undercover, she might as well have a false name.

Should she have worked up a back story?

'Having a good time?' he repeated.

'You asked me that.' She lowered her voice. 'Don't suppose you know where I could get something to spice things up a bit, David.'

'Well, Rachel, I just might be able to help you there.'

Nadia made her way to the toilets and no one observing her steady progress would have guessed the amount of alcohol she had downed that night. She was still singing, although her tune had changed.

Who wants to be a millionaire? I do!

Her business done, she stood for a

moment, scrutinising herself in the mirror, adjusting her basque, which was revealing a little more than even she had intended. Harold liked a good look at her breasts: he might not be up to much physically these days but he still enjoyed a nice fondle and who could deny a dying man such small pleasures?

Not that she need mention any of this to Nick.

She took her lipstick from her bag and applied a fresh layer, rubbing her lips together and feeling the wax smear. She had never liked lipstick – the way it made everything taste funny – but a single girl had to make an effort.

This time tomorrow she would no longer be single. Soon she would be a widow, which many women believed to be the best state, especially if you were of the rich variety.

Girls and women came and went as she fiddled with her hair, not anxious to get back to her party which was, to be honest, a bit of a damp squib. Barbara was working and was less up for fun than her reputation – happily related to her by Nick – had led her to expect.

Angie seemed low in spirits, but then she was shacked up with a man old enough to be her father and, while Gregory Summers was wearing well for an old bloke, he wasn't to Nadia's taste. He looked like his idea of a fun day was a walk in the park and a nice cup of tea.

The Freeman sisters seemed like decent kids but that's what they were: kids. When you had your thirtieth birthday in view, eighteen was another planet.

"Scuse me. You got a light?'

Nadia scarcely glanced at the girl as she handed her the gold plated lighter she'd found in a drawer at her fiancé's house. He wasn't going to miss it and soon everything would be hers anyway.

'Thanks.' The teenage girl lit up inexpertly and leant against the sink, inhaling shallowly. 'Don't suppose you've got anything on you tonight?'

'Hmm?' Nadia was only half listening. 'Oh, no.' She liked a drink or six but she didn't do drugs. As a nurse, she had seen too much of the consequences in her years in ER. 'Sorry,' she added, to be neighbourly.

'Want some?' The girl's thin hand with its bitten nails snaked out, holding several small white pills. 'Fiver apiece. Three for a tenner.'

'No, really. I don't.' Nadia looked at her more closely now. Young, scarcely old enough to drink in a nightclub, let alone be pushing pills.

'Well, you'll know me again,' the girl said sourly. She left, 'accidentally' shouldering Nadia aside as she went.

'Young people today!' Nadia said aloud,

and laughed. They said England was becoming a country of yobs; well, five million quid bought you an awful lot of protection from the great unwashed.

'So what did she look like?' Barbara asked patiently.

'I dunno,' Nadia snapped. 'They all look the same – too bleeding young and firm.'

'Can you point her out to me?'

Nadia gave the room a cursory look. It was nearly midnight and the pubs were closed so the place was packed. People were dancing to a fast beat, jumping up and down on the spot as there was no room to move, punching their fists in the air. 'Don't see her.'

'What did the pills look like?'

'White, little, like aspirin.'

'Or Ecstasy?'

'I suppose. Bit rough round the edges, maybe.'

'As if they were homemade?'

'I guess.'

Barbara's patience was starting to wane. 'You do know why I'm here this evening, Nadia? Why Nick's here and half Newbury police station. You do know that two teenage girls have died since the summer.'

'I know why *I'm* here,' Nadia said. 'To have a bloody good time on my hen night and I'm not. All right? Wish I'd bloody stayed at home now with a Chinese and a DVD.'

She got up and walked away.

Barbara sighed. Angie had gone outside for another smoke. She'd long since lost track of the Freeman twins who were adults and not her responsibility.

Maybe she should take a trip to the loo herself, see if she could get propositioned by a pusher.

Hannah and Will were getting on rather well and when he suggested that they step outside for a little air, she happily agreed. She hadn't had a real boyfriend yet; her mother made sure that she and her sister concentrated on their A levels and they attended an all-girls school.

Elizabeth had managed to date Jacob Bloom for six months last year without Mum finding out and Hannah, knowing that her sister had gained some useful experience, feared she was being left behind.

The night was cool and Will, seeing her shiver, took his jacket off and draped it round her shoulders, which seemed gallant. He didn't take his arm away, his thumb rubbing rhythmically against the pulse of her neck as they walked slowly away from the club.

She had often seen couples walking like this, the man displaying the badge of ownership.

'We can go into the park,' he said.

'There's a park? I'm not from round here.'

'Victoria Park. It's no distance. We'll be private there.'

Angie had managed to bum the tail end of a joint from a young man in exchange for a quick kiss, no tongues. It was weak stuff, she thought, so she'd been robbed. After a few minutes, she felt a little mellower, however, and arched her back against the brick wall of the club, enjoying the cool breeze from the canal after the frenetic heat of the dance floor.

Through narrowed eyes, she watched one of the Freeman twins – although which one she couldn't have said – heading for the park with a young man. Was that something she should be worried about? They passed under the bridge where Park Way crossed the canal and she saw them stop to snog.

What was she – a chaperone? She hadn't promised Greg or their father that she'd look after them.

She inhaled the last drag of the joint, disposed of it carefully, and went back inside. She looked around for her party but couldn't see any of them. Finally, she noticed Nadia at the bar talking to Nick. As she watched, his hand came up and lovingly caressed her cheek. She looked away, not wanting to play the voyeur.

She sat down and examined the glasses on the table. Hers was still half full of white wine but she knew better than to drink it after it had been left unattended.

Anyway, she'd probably had enough.

Hannah and Will were sitting on a bench by the boating pond in Victoria Park. Hannah was trying to concentrate on kissing Will – or being kissed by him – but kept finding stray thoughts grabbing her attention: that the pond was too big for the park, for instance, and more perfectly round than any she had seen; that somewhere nearby a cricket was chattering; that – heretical thought – maybe this kissing wasn't all it was cracked up to be, a bit wet, to be honest.

And surely less than hygienic.

'Relax!' Will stopped kissing her and she wiped her mouth surreptitiously with the back of her hand. 'You're very tense.' He felt in the pocket of his jacket which she was still wearing, leaning across her and letting his arm brush against her breasts. 'Bet I can find something to chill you out.'

He drew out a match box, slid it open and let two white tablets fall into his cupped palm.

Greg was growing bored on the canal bridge where Northbrook and Bartholomew Streets met, wondering when he had forgotten what it was like to be young. Had he ever known? Half the people who passed him were in their late twenties, even early thirties. He'd been a husband and father with a big mortgage by the age of twenty-four, a divorcé by twenty-six.

As many people were leaving now as arriving, most of them badly the worse for drink, one girl stopping to puke in the gutter right next to him as her mates walked on without her, as if this were an everyday occurrence, as no doubt it was, and not worthy of comment, let alone offers of help.

'You all right, love?' he asked, stepping away for fear of his shoes and trouser bottoms.

Through her curtain of hair, she fixed him with a look of unbridled contempt, her thick, pasty arms alive with goose bumps. 'Fuck off, grandpa.'

He decided to go for a walk, taking himself along the canal and back through the park. People always wanted more policemen walking the streets, but the truth was you'd have to patrol for ten years before you chanced on a crime in progress.

Still, tonight might be the night.

The Kennet and Avon canal wound its way east from Northbrook Street, past a row of attractive houses. There were pubs and cafés on the opposite bank, their narrow balconies opening onto the water, now emptied for the night.

In less than a month the new licensing laws would allow pubs and clubs to open much later – round the clock, if they chose. This, by some deranged logic, was supposed to cut down the problem of binge drinking. Greg was just glad that it was uniform's job to clear up the inevitable mess.

Past the back door of the Kismet Klub, the view opened out, towards the old town wharf, the hub of Newbury's trade when canals were the principal method of moving freight. The bulk of the town's sparkling new library loomed to the south, almost the antithesis of the nightclub.

A flotilla of swans cruised past, on patrol, at least thirty of them, as white and silent as ghosts.

The towpath was busy as far as the wharf, mostly with courting couples who probably didn't know each other's names. Greg strode rapidly past them with eyes averted, in case he saw anything that was illegal in a public place.

Bored, Hannah got up and began to walk round the pond. Will did not even notice she had gone, his head thrown back, his eyes dilated, though from the drug and not the darkness.

Hannah was nervous in the dark; she had lived in London all her life and was used to twenty-four-hour illumination. She clutched

Will's black jacket tightly round her, quickening her pace, as she passed by a building, like a large shed.

Her throat felt dry and she closed her eyes as the faint buzzing in her ears grew louder. Those were the only effects the pills were having; surely she should be exultant, away in some private heaven, like Will. She groped for the shed wall, leaning one hand against it to steady herself. She experimented with opening her eyes but they didn't want to focus and she soon abandoned the idea.

A wave of nausea swept over her. She had almost a phobia about vomiting and she inhaled to quell the sensation, sucking oxygen deep into her lungs.

She was toppled over the railings into the stagnant water with one swift shove. She could swim, in theory, but she'd had a lot to drink and the water was freezing. Besides, there was a choking sensation in her lungs, a feeling as if she'd been punched in the chest by a heavyweight boxer.

She flailed, her eyes wide with fear, feeling the heat leave her body; it was as if the canal was sapping the life from her. Something hit the water a few feet from her, sparkling in the starlight, and immediately sank. One last heave and she turned over, her face in the rancid water, as she lost consciousness.

It was a matter of seconds then, less than

a minute.

As the canal curved round to the right before Greg, he could see how much quieter it was beyond the bridge and headed for the peace of that oasis, passing through the tunnel that took him under the road, momentarily blinded.

He thought he heard footsteps running on the far side, but when he emerged, there was no one in sight. Voices echoed from somewhere behind him and he realised that the canal at night took sounds and distorted them, magnified them.

Hannah was aware of footsteps running towards her. Realising that she might not be visible in the shadow of the building in her dark clothes, she opened her eyes again. More than one person – two, three, four? – loomed out of the night at her. One of them jostled her and swore.

And, suddenly, her eyes focused perfectly on a face inches from her own. She flinched and the face was gone.

All the faces were gone.

Taking a deep breath, she made her way quickly back to the bench and Will.

'Did you see that?'

He asked dreamily, 'See what?'

'People running past. They scared me.'

'So, it was some people *running* past.' He

giggled. 'Why run when you can fly? That's what I always say. Isn't this great? You're brilliant, Anna. I love you.'

Greg walked on past Victoria Park, not noticing the couple on the bench by the pond. Here the canal and the river Kennet briefly parted company, with the river tumbling over a weir. An ugly metal bridge carried the towpath across the weir, with a triangular, stagnant pool, just a few feet across, between the bridge and the sluice gates, a pit of dead leaves and insects.

But there was something more here tonight and Greg quickened his pace in urgent disbelief.

A woman's body lay face down in the water. She was of medium height and had a mass of blonde hair. She was dressed in black and orange, her top indecently merry in this moment of crisis.

'Angie!' Greg screamed in horror. 'Angie!'

CHAPTER ELEVEN

Greg tore off his shoes and jacket, vaulted the railing and jumped into the water, gasping in disbelief at the cold. In the cramped space, he landed almost on top of the body; grabbing it by its fleshy upper arms, he turned it over and flapped one-handed back to the bridge.

Above him a voice he knew well answered him.

'Gregory?'

'Angie! Can you give me a hand?'

She reached her arms through the railings to hold the body steady as he hauled himself back onto the bridge. They both heaved on the drowned woman, her clothes sopping to make her weighty and unwieldy, her spike heels catching on top of the parapet before she half fell, was half carried to the ground.

He wanted to take Angie in his arms in relief but he had pressing priorities.

'Get help,' he snapped.

He began to perform first aid: interspersing mouth-to-mouth with heart massage. He heard Angie speaking into her mobile phone, demanding an ambulance, coolly invoking his name and rank to expedite it, giving clear directions.

Between forcing his own breath between the cold lips, he issued further instructions. 'Get my mobile from my jacket. Call the number listed under "Freeman". Tell him to come at once.'

Within five minutes, he was aware of the reassuring bulk of Striker Freeman looming over him, his fingers against the cold white neck, feeling for a pulse.

'She's gone,' Striker said in a low voice, 'It's no good.'

Somewhere nearby, they heard the wail of the ambulance siren. Striker took out his phone and began to summon all that was needed for a suspicious death. Greg heard Angie's voice say, 'It's Nadia'. He sat back on his haunches and looked at the dead woman properly for the first time.

'Nadia,' he said dully, looking into her opaque brown eyes. How could he ever have mistaken her fleshiness for Angie's slender form, even in his panic?

'Fuck.' Striker glanced down to confirm the fact for himself and ran his hand across his cropped hair. 'Did anyone see what happened?' They shook their heads. 'Could she just have fallen in? She was pretty tanked up.'

'Given the time and the place – the Kismet Klub on a Friday night – we're going to have to assume that she didn't.'

'I'm going back inside to make sure

nobody leaves.'

'Don't let Nick out here, whatever you do.'

'Right.'

'Find Inspector Nelson–'

'I'll get him to cordon off the area.'

Striker turned away and was soon running back along the towpath with the long, easy strides of a fit man. Greg looked round for Angie who was suddenly gone. She was standing just below the bridge, staring into the weir as it tumbled down to the lower level, the water foaming white.

He hurried to join her.

'I didn't want to get in the way,' she said, raising her voice to be heard over the splashing. He put his arm round her and kissed her hair. His wet embrace made her flimsy top damp, clinging to show the shape of her small breasts.

'I thought it was you,' he murmured.

'Me? I look nothing like Nadia.' She sounded indignant.

'You were wearing the same colour top tonight... Have you been smoking?'

'Yes.' Her tone said, *Want to make something of it?*

'Can I have one?'

'Sure.'

She shook out a Benson & Hedges and lit it for him. He took two puffs, grimaced and stubbed it out. 'Can't remember why I ever liked that.' He looked around, taking in the topography with care. Nadia had been in the water only a few minutes and if someone had helped her in, then they were not long gone.

There were a number of possible routes away from the weir. No one had passed him on the towpath between it and the club, but they could have gone in the other direction. They might also have made their escape through Victoria Park or across the football ground to the industrial estate. 'Where did you come from?' he asked. 'Were you in the park?'

'No. Everybody in my party seemed to have deserted me, so I came out of the club and, when I saw you walking on the towpath about twenty yards ahead, I decided to follow you. Then you started shrieking my name like a banshee.'

'Damn,' he muttered, pushing wet hair back out of his eyes.

'You're soaking wet,' she said pragmatically. 'I'm going back to the club, see if I can find you some dry clothes before you catch your death.'

He realised that he was shivering. 'Thanks!'

Two figures came running along the towpath at that moment. The second one was DCI Freeman, the first Nick Nicolaides. Nick had ten yards advantage although Striker was gaining on him.

'What's going on?' Nick demanded breathlessly. 'I overheard the DCI telling Barbara there'd been a death but not to say anything to me–'

Greg stepped in front of him to block his view, bracing both arms against the railings of the bridge to stop him from passing. Striker caught up with him and grabbed him, holding him back. Nick was taller and heavier than he was but he had no trouble in restraining him.

'You don't need to see, Nick,' Striker said. 'Not just now.'

Greg grimaced as, over both their shoulders, Nick caught sight of the dead woman.

'Nadge?' His voice was full of an almost childlike wonder. 'No. No.' He tried to escape from Striker's grasp but couldn't. 'It isn't. Mr Summers, tell me it isn't Nadia.'

'Get him out of here,' Greg snapped.

Freeman almost carried Nick away as the young constable's legs gave way beneath him. Andy Whittaker appeared at that moment and lent a hand with his colleague.

'Don't let anyone leave the club,' Greg called after them. 'Where the hell's Barbara?'

'I'm here, sir.'

'Give me a hand to close off the crime scene.' The sergeant, uncharacteristically, looked a little helpless, gesturing at her party clothes, the absence of the usual paraphernalia of her job.

'Jesus,' she muttered, staring down at Nadia.

153

'Why her? Why tonight?' She was remembering the flippant remark she had made earlier about death by drowning. It didn't look as if Nadia had enjoyed a delightful sensation.

'I thought it was Angie for a moment,' he said. 'She's wearing a top in the same sort of colour. In the dim light...' He held up a hand. It was shaking faintly.

'Must have given you a hell of a shock, sir.'

'You could say that.' He stifled a smile. There was something wrong with the fact that his first thought on identifying the dead woman had been one of overwhelming relief. The unbearable pain of loss belonged not to him, but to somebody else, some other family.

Angie reappeared at that moment, carrying a bundle of clothing. 'The manager came up with a tracksuit and some socks,' she said. 'It'll be a bit big for you.'

'Thank you, Angel.' Greg took the blue fleece jogging pants and sweatshirt from her. 'Can I ask one more favour of you?'

'Sure. Anything.'

'I'd like you to go home.'

'...I walked right into that, didn't I?'

'Babs, can you organise a taxi for Angie?'

'I'll get someone to run her home. It'll only take a few minutes at this time of night.' She took out her mobile phone and asked for a squad car to be ready to go to Kintbury.

Greg walked Angie back to the club where

154

he handed her over to Constable Tom Reilly. 'See you later then,' she said sardonically. 'Much later, I expect.'

'Don't wait up.'

As Greg headed for the toilets to change, he heard a smooth voice behind him say, 'Lost another, I hear, Summers. And you seem to have fallen into the canal.'

He turned round. 'Jumped rather than fell. Aren't you going to call me a hero tonight then, Chaucer?'

He snorted. 'You what?'

'You called me a hero three years ago when I talked that Romany boy into handing over his shotgun. Remember?'

'No. I don't remember.'

'Memory problems at your age? You said it on camera.'

'Got it on tape?'

'No.'

'Then it never happened.' Chaucer's mobile rang and he answered it. 'About bloody time,' he snapped after listening for a few seconds. 'My camera crew is here,' he added, and left.

Greg went into a cubicle to change, folding his wet things into a soggy pile. The manager's socks were so thick that he could cram his shoes on only with difficulty and he hoped that they were fresh or, failing that, that the manager didn't have athlete's foot. He put his suit jacket on over the sweatshirt and ignored how stupid it looked.

He got the worst of the canal out of his hair with the hot-air drier and looked at himself in the mirror: a grey man of nearly fifty, incongruous in the sort of clothing he hadn't worn in twenty years. It would have to do. He went out, giving instructions that Chaucer and his camera crew were not to be admitted to the club.

Hobbling back to the weir, he found Striker Freeman in command there. 'Lucky we have so many men in the area tonight,' the DCI commented, 'but I've called for reinforcements, all the same.'

So many men in the area, Greg thought, a strong police presence, yet they hadn't been able to prevent another death.

'There must have been six or seven hundred people here this evening,' Striker went on, 'so we'll be taking statements for the next week. Inspector Nelson, Andy and as many uniforms as we could find are getting names and addresses. Then I thought we'd better let them go.'

'Where's Nick?' Greg asked, his voice sounding dull in his own ears.

'I put him in the manager's office,' Striker said. 'Left a uniform with him.'

There was no time to offer comfort, not now, they had too much to do. The best comfort they could give Nick was to find out who had done this to him.

'You haven't seen my girls, I suppose?' Striker said.

'Not since they got here. Sorry.'

'OK. I'm sure they're fine.'

'I can wait here for the technicians,' Greg said, 'if you want to get back to the club and look for them.'

'Well, perhaps I will. Thank you, sir.'

Greg was fairly sure that was the first time his new DCI had addressed him as 'sir'.

Dr Chubb was the first technician to arrive, striding across from the football ground where he'd left his car. The lack of vehicular access to this part of the canal was going to be a nuisance, Greg thought, but the narrow tunnel under the road and the bridge over the weir precluded anything on four wheels making it along the towpath in either direction.

'Taking up jogging?' the pathologist asked Greg. 'Could prove fatal at your age.'

He confirmed death. He then had to wait until the photographer came and took pictures of the body from every angle before further examination was possible, even though Greg had, necessarily, moved the body. This took some time since the light was so poor that the photographer had to use every spotlight he possessed, carrying them from his van in the nearest street.

Finally, just before two o'clock, the

pictures were taken and the tent in place to protect the crime scene, blue and white tape creating a cordon for twenty yards in every direction.

'Nothing inconsistent with death by drowning,' Dr Chubb said, his gloved hands probing tenderly across her abdomen. 'Let's just see the other side.' Greg helped him to turn the body over. Rigor had not yet begun and the young woman flopped onto her front, her arms dangling as they briefly lifted her. The doctor ran his hands over the small of her back under her top and shook his head.

'No obvious wounds. Can I take her?'

Greg nodded and Dr Chubb went in search of the waiting mortuary van, returning with two attendants and a stretcher. They zipped the remains of Nadia Poly-carpou into a body bag, heaved her onto the canvas and carried her away.

Greg didn't bother to ask for an estimate of time of death; she could only have been in the water a matter of minutes when he found her.

'PM first thing,' Dr Chubb said, as he left.

Striker found Elizabeth as soon as he went into the club and gave her a brief hug of relief. 'You OK?'

'Fine. Dad, what's happened?'

He hesitated, but there was no point in

dressing it up. 'We found Nadia dead a couple of hundred yards along the canal.' She stared at him, no words adequate to convey her shock. He asked, 'Where's your sister?'

'She went out for some air ages ago.'

'Alone?'

'Um. Yes, I think so,' Elizabeth lied. 'I'll go and look for her, shall I?'

'Please, darling. Have you given your details to one of my officers?' She nodded. 'Then, when you've found Hannah, come back here and I'll get someone to walk you home. You've got your key?'

'Sure.'

Like Greg he said, 'Don't wait up.'

The night had grown cool and misty but Greg felt himself sweating. He groped in the pocket of his jacket for a handkerchief and wiped his forehead and neck.

'Can I leave you to oversee SOCO?' he said to Barbara. 'Of course.' Some time during the last two hours, she had retrieved her coat from the cloakroom, covering the unsuitably festive clothes she wore.

'I'll see what's happening inside ... have a word with Nick.'

'Yeah. Good luck.'

The interior of the club seemed quiet, most of the clientele departed, having given their details to one of the police officers. Three uniformed constables and Andy were still seated at tables, a short queue before each one, Martin Nelson supervising.

He noticed DCI Freeman talking in a low voice to a man in a suit he assumed to be the manager of the club. The man glanced his way and Greg gestured at the tracksuit and gave him the thumbs up.

As he limped towards the office, a very drunk young woman tottered up to Striker and shrieked, 'You have so-o-o not got a wooden leg, you faker.' The DCI hardly paused in his conversation as he passed her over to a uniform who handled her gently but firmly out of the building.

Greg heard the constable ask, 'Where d'you live, love?' and get the reply, '...It'll come to me in a minute'. He shook his head in disbelief and opened the door of the office without knocking.

Nick was sitting on an upright chair behind the manager's desk, his eyes fixed on nothing. PC Chris Clements was sitting on a two-seater sofa against the wall, looking bored. He stood up when Greg came in but Nick didn't even raise his head. Constable Clements' eyes flickered in surprise over the superintendent's unconventional attire, but it wasn't his place to comment on his superior's sartorial choices.

'All right, Chris,' Greg said. 'Go and see if Inspector Nelson has a job for you.'

Clements went off gratefully and Greg

perched on the corner of the desk so that he was necessarily in Nick's line of sight. He thought the younger man was in shock and wondered if he should get him a doctor but, as he opened his mouth to speak, Nick pre-empted him.

'Don't keep me out of this, sir.'

'I have to, Nick. You know that.'

'I want to find the bastard who did this.' Nick clenched his fists. 'I want to kill him.'

'Which is another good reason you can't be involved,' Greg said gently. He put his hand on the constable's shoulder. 'You're on compassionate leave until further notice.'

Nick began to cry, silently and without drama. Greg opened a drinks cabinet beside the desk and extracted a bottle of whisky and one glass. Nick wasn't on duty, not any more. He poured him a generous measure and held it out to him. Nick looked at it in surprise, then downed it in one.

'Nadia was the best thing that ever happened to me,' he said dully.

'I know what you mean. The love of a good woman ... there's nothing like it.'

'He's gonna cut her up. Chubb. Slice her up. I've seen it dozens of times, but now...'

'Yeah, it's different when it's someone you know,' Greg said. 'Look, I think the best thing we can do is get you home. I shall have to ask you a few questions but they can wait till morning.'

The door opened again at that moment and DCI Freeman came in. To Greg's surprise, he offered to take Nick home.

'My car's close by,' he said.

'It's no distance,' Greg said, 'just along the canal a bit.'

'Nick can show me the way. Right, mate?' Striker put a hand under Nick's arm and the young man rose obediently and followed him.

Natural authority, Greg thought. You couldn't learn it and you couldn't buy it.

He walked back out into the bar area, casting his eyes over the last lingerers.

'You got wet, Mr Summers?'

'Ruthie. Yes, I jumped into the weir.'

She laughed, with the natural gaiety of the teenager, even in a calamity. 'Any particular reason?'

'It seemed like a good idea at the time. Have you given your name and address to one of my officers?' She nodded. 'Then you'd better be getting home. It's late.' He looked at his wrist before remembering that his sodden watch was with his clothes, presumably ruined for good. It was high time he got a new one, anyway.

'There's no rush,' Ruth said. 'Mum's got her new bloke round tonight so I'd only be a third wheel.'

'Have you got the money for a taxi?'

162

'I'll walk. It's only a mile or so.'

'I don't want you walking about at this time of night. Not tonight, anyway. Here.' He felt in the zip pocket of the jogging bottoms where he had stowed his wallet and peeled off a ten pound note and a five. 'This should cover it.'

She hesitated then took it, saying simply, 'OK. Thanks'.

CHAPTER TWELVE

'You OK, Dad?' Elizabeth Freeman peered out of the door of the spare bedroom as Striker let himself into his rented flat just before dawn. She was wearing pyjama shorts and a vest top and he was startled anew by how womanly her figure had become.

'I'm fine, sweetie.' He kissed the top of her head. 'I've just come home to shower and shave, then I'm going into the office. Go back to sleep.'

'Got something for you.' She yawned and went back into the room she shared with her twin, re-emerging with a sealed plastic bag. She handed it to him and he saw that it contained two little white tablets.

'Ecstasy?' he said flatly.

'If it is. I bought them at the club last night. Thought they might be this weird new drug you're looking for.'

He looked at her steadily for a moment, then smiled. 'You're a good girl, Elizabeth, but, whatever you do, don't tell your mother about this.'

'As if.'

'And, officially, I strongly disapprove.'

'Noted.'

'You even got an evidence bag.'

'It's a freezer bag,' she said proudly.

'I have freezer bags?'

'They were at the back of the cutlery drawer.'

'Ah, I remember! Substituted on an Internet order for frozen peas but I just didn't fancy them with my fish fingers.'

She looked at him sternly, with a great deal of her mother in her eyes. 'Are you sure you're eating properly?'

'Oh, stop it. Who sold you these?'

'A bloke called David, or so he claimed. This tall.' She demonstrated with her hand. 'Medium build, blond hair, blue eyes, pale complexion, late twenties. Good kisser.'

'Too much information!'

'I'd know him again.' She added eagerly, 'I could come into the station and do you a photofit.'

'You do remember that you're going to be a musician,' he said, 'make Mum and Grandma Esther proud?'

'I want to make you proud too, Dad.'

'Always, sweetie.' He raised his voice. 'You too, Hannah.' Her voice emerged from the darkness of the spare bedroom, a little foggy, as from one half asleep.

'Thanks, Dad.'

'Look, I'm not going to be getting today off, like I thought, so I think the best thing is if you both catch the train back to Padding-

ton this morning, OK? We'll do our weekend's sightseeing in Marlborough another
time.'

'Sightseeing?' Elizabeth said in mock
surprise. 'I understood it was shopping.'

Greg glanced up as the door opened and
DCI Freeman came in, not looking in the
least as if he'd been up all night; he'd even
found time to shave.

'You've been a long time,' he said, though
not in the spirit of criticism.

'I know. I should have rung.' Striker sat
down, explaining, not apologising. 'I drove
Nick back to his place but, as soon as I
pulled up outside, he burst into tears and
said he wanted his mum. Turns out she lives
in Finsbury Park, which took us an hour
and a half, even driving like the clappers in
the middle of the night. We woke her up,
then I had to explain it all to her and she's
nearly as upset as Nick is – already looked
on Nadia as a daughter. I ended up making
her a cup of tea and letting her cry on my
shoulder.'

'Couldn't you have got someone from
uniform to drive him?' Greg asked.

'I didn't want anyone else to see him in
that state.'

'Fair enough,' Greg said. CID looked after
their own and uncontrollable weeping was
unmanly, however great the provocation.

'It seems that Mrs Nicolaides didn't know about Nadia's other wedding,' Striker added.

'Ah, no. I believe not.'

'She was rather upset about it and suggested to me on the quiet that the poor girl's death might be a judgement from heaven, but I'm inclined to seek another explanation.'

'We still have to eliminate Nick as a suspect,' Greg said.

Freeman drummed his fingers on the desk. 'Why would he kill Nadia? She was his passport to wealth.'

'But was she? They got engaged before this whole "arranged marriage" project cropped up. Why would she share her new-found riches with anyone?'

'Because she loved him?' Striker suggested.

'*He* loved *her*. I'm sure of that.'

Freeman looked at him, considering. 'You didn't like Nadia? I didn't know her, so I'm in no position to judge.'

'I *hardly* knew her,' Greg admitted, 'but I thought she was hard. Call it a hunch.'

'Well, I never ignore a hunch. You think that if Nick had an inkling she planned to dump him, he might have killed her in the heat of the moment?'

'He was *there*,' Greg reminded him.

'Do you honestly think he's a serious suspect?'

'No,' Greg said after a pause. 'Nick may be

167

a bit rough and ready but he's a decent bloke. Plus, as a detective, he knows how unlikely it is he'd get away with it!'

Striker drew the freezer bag his daughter had given him from his pocket. 'Regarding the two earlier deaths.' He explained about Elizabeth's freelance snooping.

'Proper little Miss Marple,' Greg said. 'Doesn't it worry you?'

'Shit, yes. I'll get these to the lab. They look like plain old Ecstasy to me, but maybe the Entry does too.' He looked at his watch. 'So who's going to break the news to Nadia's official fiancé? I understand the wedding was scheduled for noon today. That's less than four hours.'

'I thought we might both go,' Greg said.

Striker laughed. 'You like to be out in the field, don't you?'

'Never have felt comfortable stuck behind a desk all day,' Greg conceded.

'I can identify with that,' Striker said.

'And we are a man short without Nick. I want to see Mr Fitzsimmons' reaction.'

'Me too. I'd also like to find out who his heir is now that Nadia's dead.'

Greg looked at him for a moment. 'I see our minds are moving along the same lines.'

'We can't assume this is the latest in a string of connected deaths at the Kismet Klub,' Striker agreed. 'Nadia was drowned, not killed with a rogue recreational drug.

It's gone eight, so I don't think it's too early for a house call. Do you?'

'One way to find out,' Greg said, getting up.

Custody Sergeant Dick Maybey called to Greg as he was leaving the station. He turned back with a certain irritation as he found Maybey a trial.

Striker said in a low voice, 'I'll drop these at the lab and meet you in the car park.'

'What is it, Dick?'

'Heard the news, sir,' he said. 'Only me and some of the boys thought we might go round to Nick's place when we get off shift, take a bottle of Scotch. Or two.'

'That's a nice thought,' Greg said sincerely, 'but he's in London, with his family.'

'Oh well, can't be in better hands then,' Maybey conceded. He looked awkward. 'There's no question...?'

'No,' Greg said briskly. 'No question.'

'Thank God for that. Bring back hanging, I say, and the do-gooders and the human rights mob can get stuffed.'

169

CHAPTER THIRTEEN

Greg was accustomed to the grandeur of houses on the Downs, home to Berkshire's many millionaires, but Down View Manor was something exceptional, or had been once.

Striker, who was driving, whistled as he drew to a halt in a courtyard dotted with weeds. He peered up at the building, which surrounded them on three sides, through the windscreen. 'Jacobean, if I'm not mistaken. Looks like it's been left to go to seed, though. Shame.'

'If he's old, and alone in the world, and ill, I guess household maintenance isn't his primary concern.'

There was only one other vehicle parked: a private ambulance, presumably summoned to take the groom to the registry office. The driver was sitting at the wheel, reading the *Sun* and ignoring them.

Greg got out and squinted at the house, shading his eyes with his hand. The roof of one wing was clearly in need of repair and he shuddered to think of the ancient beams rotting beneath. The bricks looked soft, as if they would crumble beneath his touch. The windows in both wings had their blinds drawn; only the central section looked lived-in.

'Looks like most of it's shut up,' Striker commented, standing beside him. He produced a mobile phone from his inside pocket and took a photograph of the building. 'For my records,' he explained. Greg, whose phone didn't have a camera, made no comment.

'Let's see if anyone's home.' Freeman strode across to the front door, looked in vain for a bell and lifted the heavy iron knocker, letting it fall on the scarred oak door. As Greg joined him on the doorstep, he could hear movement inside, followed by the squealing turning of a key and a creaking of unoiled hinges as the door swung inwards.

He felt as if he was in a somewhat clichéd horror film.

The door had not been opened by a hunchbacked retainer, however, but by a pleasant-looking middle-aged woman who was protecting her fuchsia-coloured suit with a voluminous green apron emblazoned with the words 'Mum never retires'.

She smiled enquiringly at them.

'May we see Mr Fitzsimmons please?' Greg said. 'We're police officers.' He held up his warrant card.

'Oh? Well, it'll have to be quick.' She stood

aside to admit them, not bothering to look at the card. 'He's getting married in three hours' time and I have to get him ready.'

Greg lowered his voice. 'Actually, Mrs...?'

'Mrs Alderson. I'm the housekeeper.' Her Berkshire accent was strong and her gaze was shrewd and steady.

'Perhaps we should speak to you first.' Greg's eyes adjusted to the dark interior and he took in the hallway, which was the size of a small house, its stone staircase soaring to the upper floor. 'Is there somewhere we can go?'

'Follow me.' She strode away, passing through a curtained doorway, then turning to face them. Greg saw that they were in a room which had been fitted out as an efficient modern kitchen some time in the past ten years.

'Mr Fitzsimmons lives on the ground floor,' she explained. 'He can't get upstairs any more, so the dining room's now his bedroom and the butler's pantry's an en suite.'

On the table were a few plates, the makings of a modest buffet, each one covered in clingfilm.

'The marriage feast.' Mrs Alderson gestured with a smile.

'I have some bad news, I'm afraid,' Greg said, 'about Miss Polycarpou.'

'Would you like to sit down?' Striker added. She looked from one man to the other and sighed. 'Well, perhaps I will then. Why do people on the telly always refuse to sit down when the police tell them to?' She pulled out a Windsor chair from the table and sat squarely on it, her back straight. Greg noticed that her stockinged legs, threaded with plump, blue veins, ended in trainers. A pair of court shoes that matched her suit sat in a regimented pair near the door, waiting for painful last-minute service.

'I'm afraid there's not going to be a wedding,' he said. Mrs Alderson didn't reply, but waited for him to continue. 'Nadia Polycarpou died last night in Newbury.'

The housekeeper breathed in sharply and, just as sharply, out again. Her right hand flew to her face, depositing a smear of flour on her nose.

'Died?' she asked. 'You mean an accident?'

'We're not wholly certain until we get the results of the post-mortem. She appears to have drowned, in the Kennet & Avon canal, outside a nightclub.'

'The Kismet Klub!' Mrs Alderson was suddenly angry. 'She told me she was having her hen night there and I was worried about the deaths they'd been talking about on the local news, but she just laughed and said not to worry and that she had police protection.'

There was a note of accusation in her grey eyes as she looked at Greg and Striker.

'Poor Harold,' she added, as they did not

answer her unspoken allegation of negligence. 'He was that set on this wedding. Quite excited.'

'Harold is Mr Fitzsimmons, I take it,' Greg said. She nodded. 'I gather he's very frail.'

'He's dying,' she said bluntly. 'No secret about that.'

'Which is why I asked to speak to you first,' Greg went on. 'A shock like this could be dangerous and it might be easier if he hears the news from someone he knows well.'

She nodded and got up. She made for the door, then thought better of it, turning to remove her apron, tossing the garment on top of the buffet as if it had offended her. She wiped her hands on a tea towel and smoothed her skirt, as in preparation for a formal occasion.

'He's tough, mind you,' she said, as they followed her back into the hall. 'Tougher than any of us, I often think.'

'Hattie?' A voice called at that moment.

'Coming!' She jerked her head. 'This way, gentlemen.'

'I thought I heard the door,' the old man was saying as Mrs Alderson led the way into the sitting room.

He might have been a dictionary definition of the word *Old*, an illustration in an encyclopaedia. He was emaciated and

174

faintly yellow – both manifestations of his illness, Greg assumed. He was sitting with his back to the door, in a wheelchair, looking out over the rear garden, a green-and-white checked rug over his knees. By his side was a table on which stood a decanter of brown liquid, possibly whisky, a jug of water and a book in a hard binding.

'Only,' he went on, not turning his head, 'I trust it isn't Nadia. Bad luck for the groom to see the bride before the wedding, don't you know.'

'It isn't Nadia, Harold.' Mrs Alderson went over and gently turned the wheelchair to face into the room. Greg was surprised to see that he was no more than seventy, an age at which a man is often still vigorous, when not attacked by an incurable cancer. He was wearing an old-fashioned but immaculate morning suit with a white carnation in his buttonhole, over a linen shirt of the quality that no one made any more, soft as butter. 'These gentlemen are from the Newbury police.'

'Hah! Friends of young George Nicolaides?' Mr Fitzsimmons examined them over the top of his reading glasses. 'Bit late for a stag do.'

'There's bad news, Harold.' The housekeeper didn't speak to him the way people often spoke to the old and infirm, as if they were not only deaf but slightly stupid.

175

'Nadia...' she faltered. 'There's been an accident.'

He turned his face up to her. 'Accident? Spit it out, woman. Is she hurt bad?'

'She's dead,' Hattie blurted out. 'I'm so sorry.' Harold Fitzsimmons sat staring into space for a moment without speaking. Finally, she said, 'Should I send for the doctor?'

'For whom?' His voice was harsh. 'It's too late for Nadia and, come to think of it, it's too late for me. Go and ring round the guests, Hattie. Tell them the wedding's off. Some of them may have set out already. Can't be helped. We must do our best. Oh, and tell the ambulance driver he need not wait.'

She left to obey him without looking at Greg and Striker. He called after her, 'And get onto the agency for another nurse!' After a moment to collect himself, the old man said, 'What happened, please?'

'We don't think it was an accident, I'm afraid.' Greg walked over to the man in the wheelchair and, not comfortable looming above him, took a seat on the nearby sofa. He leant forward, his hands, suddenly huge, dangling uselessly between his knees. 'We believe that Nadia Polycarpou was murdered in Newbury around midnight.'

'Murdered in what way?' His thin voice lacked inflection. It was hard to tell if he was numb with shock or if this was his normal manner.

176

'She appears to have drowned, in the canal. She can't have felt much pain. I'm so sorry for your loss.'

'She was twenty-nine.' The old man's head bowed. 'I can't even remember being that young.' His head jerked up suddenly, causing two tears to fall on his sleeve. 'George!' he said. 'Poor George. She was going to marry him, you know, after my death. He'll be devastated.'

'Nick – George – is with his mother,' Greg explained. 'She's looking after him.'

'Ah! Every man should have a mother.'

Striker had quietly taken an armchair by the massive oak fireplace. He spoke now for the first time since entering the room. 'May we ask you a few questions, Mr Fitzsimmons? Do you feel up to it?'

The old man shifted slightly to examine him and Greg was surprised by the look that passed into his hazel eyes – dislike, even contempt – but his voice stayed even as he answered. 'If it will help to catch Nadia's killer.'

'Who is your heir at present?'

'My heir?'

'I assume you already have a will – one made prior to this marriage idea.'

'You assume too much, young man! I have never made a will. My solicitor has drawn one up in favour of Nadia, my wife, which I was to sign this afternoon after the cere-

177

mony.' He let slip a thin smile. 'We had decided to forego the honeymoon, in the circumstances.'

'You've never made a will.' Greg wanted to be perfectly clear about this. 'Ever?'

Fitzsimmons drew himself up, as far as he was able in his wheelchair, and looked sternly at Greg. 'You sound like my solicitor. Nag, nag, nag. At least he wanted the fees for doing it; what's your excuse?'

'Then who will inherit under the intestacy laws?'

He shrugged. 'I have no family. I never married – didn't get round to it somehow – and have no children, that I know of. My estate would have passed to the crown. *Will* now so pass, I suppose.'

So that was it, Greg thought, Nadia Polycarpou had been murdered by the Chancellor of the Exchequer. All they had to do was scan the CCTV of the nightclub for a middle-aged Scotsman who seldom smiled.

He forced his mind back from this levity and asked, 'What about your housekeeper?'

The old man raised his eyebrows. 'What about her? Hattie's worked for me for eighteen years and I've made her many generous presents, including her house in the village, but she doesn't expect to inherit anything.'

He sighed. 'I feel very tired now and should like to rest. Thank you for coming. Would you mind ringing the bell – yes, there by the fireplace.'

Striker pressed the bell and they heard a distant tinkle. When Hattie responded, he said, 'Please show these gentlemen out.' His voice failed into a gasp at the end of the sentence and he doubled over, clutching his abdomen, his face a paroxysm of pain.

'Morphine,' he stammered.

'I'll get it.' Hattie took a hypodermic kit from the drawer of the nearby dresser and looked at it doubtfully. 'I don't know how... There was supposed to be a locum nurse for last night but she rang at the last minute to say she couldn't come because one of her children was sick.'

'Give it to me,' the old man rasped, his withered hands reaching out like claws. 'I'll do it myself.'

'I thought of ringing Nadia,' Hattie went on, not relinquishing the hypodermic. 'If only I had.'

'Let me.' Striker took the syringe from the housekeeper, rolled up the old man's sleeve and injected him quickly and with a steady hand. Mr Fitzsimmons grunted what might have been thanks but Greg wouldn't have bet good money on it. His face cleared as the opiate pumped into his system and he let his head fall gently forward.

Hattie signalled to the two police officers that they should leave and they followed her on tiptoe out of the room.

'Did you get hold of the guests?' Greg asked, in the hall.

'Such as they were! He talks as if we'd invited hordes. Apart from me and the solicitor, who were to witness the marriage and the will, there were only a few neighbours, a couple of old friends. Nadia didn't want to invite anyone from her side. Saving that for her real wedding, I suppose.'

Greg examined her tone mentally for criticism but found none. 'You didn't disapprove?' he asked.

'Why should I? I liked Nadia, right from the first – always polite and friendly, not like some of the nurses we've had who seemed to think I was their servant. To be honest, he's been through quite a few girls and none of them lasted more than a fortnight, because he can be a cantankerous old sod.' She spoke the words with affection, as a term of endearment.

'But Nadia was different. She made Harold happy, made him laugh. It wasn't like she was deceiving him or anything. He knew she had a proper boyfriend – *fiancé*. Seemed to me she might as well have the money – it's not like he was disinheriting his children.'

'Has he really no family at all?' Striker asked. 'I mean, for your estate to go to the Crown, there have to be no living descendants of your grandparents, which is quite unusual.'

'It's not for me to gossip,' Mrs Alderson said.

Greg reflected that people only said this when they wanted to tell you and needed a nudge.

'Hardly *gossip*,' Striker said dutifully.

She spoke with a show of reluctance. 'Well, he had a sister, or so I'm told. Long before my time. They fell out in about ... must have been the Fifties.'

'Blimey!' Greg said. 'That's quite a feud. Do you know what it was about?'

The woman looked faintly apologetic. 'She married a Jew. A *Welsh* Jew.'

Greg glanced automatically at Striker who said, 'And?'

'He didn't like it, that's all. He doesn't like Jews. Maybe that's why he liked Nadia, with her being Greek.'

'Huh?' Greg said.

'Well, they're like the opposite, aren't they – Jews and Greeks?' While Greg thought about this, she went on. 'In the Fifties, Harold got very friendly with Oswald Mosley and his wife. He used to say what a shame it was that he'd been too young to join the British Union of Fascists in the Thirties.'

Greg wondered why he was surprised. Fitzsimmons hadn't always been old and stuck in a wheelchair, and anti-Semitism had been rife among the British upper classes all those decades ago. Much as he admired the

181

novels of Dorothy L. Sayers, he could still be brought up short when Lord Peter Wimsey – surely the most urbane and civilised of men – referred to a character as 'An East-End Jew Boy'.

Sir Oswald Mosley, baronet, had formed his own version of the Nazi party in Britain in the Thirties, but no one had taken it very seriously – except the East-End Jews they had beaten up – and Mosley and his wife had been thrown in prison in 1939 when Britain declared war on Germany.

'It wasn't only Jews,' Mrs Alderson said, as if to soften the old man's views. 'He dislikes Asians and, um, coloureds too. Though maybe not as much as Jews. Don't see it myself. Live and let live. Except for these Arabs who keep trying to blow people up.'

Greg said, 'But then the sister is his next of kin.'

'He disowned her,' she said with a shrug.

'Maybe,' Greg said, but there was no legal method of 'divorcing' a sister that he knew of.

'She's dead anyway,' Hattie said. 'Fifteen years back.'

'May I ask how you know that,' Striker said, 'if he'd had nothing to do with her in decades?'

She frowned, considering. 'A letter came one morning, handwritten envelope. I took it in to him with the rest and I was tidying up as he opened it. He swore, which isn't something he normally does. He apologised when he realised I was there, told me his "stupid sister" had died and that it was a damned impertinence to think he cared. Then he chucked the letter in the fire – it was winter.'

'So you don't know who it was from?'

'He didn't say and I didn't ask.'

'Perhaps we should talk to him some more about it,' Striker suggested.

'You'd be wasting your time. He'll be out of it for a good while now. Anyway, he'll tell you he has no sister and you won't get him to say anything else. Only time I've ever heard him admit to her existence was when that letter came.'

They could not harass an elderly and dying man, so had no choice but to retreat from the fray for the present.

Greg asked, 'Do you live in?'

'No, I have a cottage in the village which Harold bought for me years ago. But I stayed last night, what with the relief nurse not turning up. That way, if the worst came to the worst, I could at least call for an ambulance.'

As she showed them to the front door, the housekeeper came to a sudden halt as she remembered something. 'Wait here!' She disappeared into the kitchen and returned after some minutes with a black and white photograph, badly creased, as if someone had screwed it up. 'I found this a few years ago,' she explained, 'stuck at the back of a drawer. I don't know why I kept it, but I did.'

Greg took it from her and examined it, holding it up to the light. As with all old photos the creases had formed white lines across the exposure, but he could see a beach party – dating from the immediate post-war years, by their costumes – half a dozen young men and woman, happy and laughing.

He could just recognise Harold Fitzsimmons on the extreme right, which seemed apt.

'There's some writing on the back,' Striker pointed out.

Greg turned it over and read the crabbed hand aloud. 'Daisy, Rupert, Ursula, Tom, Isobel and HF. Brighton 1951.'

'Ursula,' Mrs Alderson said. 'That's the sister.'

Greg turned back to the image, the third figure from the left. He saw a girl of perhaps nineteen, dark-haired insofar as it was possible to tell from the monochrome print. She was tall – taller than her brother – slender, no doubt from years of food rationing, with one of those wasp waists that women – even the half-starved actresses of Hollywood – seemed no longer to possess.

'May I borrow this?' he asked and she nodded assent. 'And – one more thing –

who is Mr Fitzsimmons' solicitor?'

'That's young Mr Faulkner,' Hattie said. 'Michael. Used to be old Mr Faulkner – Terence – but he keeled over on the golf course eighteen months ago. Good way to go.'

She glanced back towards the sitting room, doubtless comparing it with the long, slow and painful death that her employer was undergoing.

CHAPTER FOURTEEN

'So now we know why he looked at me like I'd crawled out from under a stone,' Striker said, as he unlocked the car.

'I wasn't sure if you'd noticed,' Greg said, embarrassed.

'Oh, don't worry. There's always a few, even today. They seem to have a sixth sense too; it's like they can *smell* us – reeking of the blood of murdered Christian babies, no doubt. I may not like his opinions but I'll defend his right to hold them – though probably not to the death. At least I'm not *Welsh*.'

'And yet you gave him his painkiller.'

'Of course I did! Just because he chooses to be an arsehole, doesn't mean I have to be.'

'What did she mean by Jews and Greeks being opposite, do you suppose?'

'Cavaliers and roundheads,' Striker said cheerfully. 'The circumcised and the un-circumcised. I don't think he had Nadia whacked out of jealousy, do you? He seems wholly comfortable with her having a proper fiancé, worried about him even.'

'I really don't think so either,' Greg said

186

with a sigh, 'but he may not be as short of heirs as he makes out.'

'You think the sister and her *Jew* husband had children?'

'No reason why not, and they'd have motive to kill Nadia – five million of them. If the envelope was handwritten then that suggests a family member, rather than, say, a lawyer.'

'Good point. Harold Fitzsimmons may not acknowledge his sister's existence, but the state will have her documented: hatched, matched and dispatched.'

'Sounds like someone's in for a long session at St Catherine's House,' Greg said. 'What about the housekeeper? Is she in the frame?'

Striker shook his head at once. 'I can't see her motive, since she's not in any existing will, and she struck me as a thoroughly nice woman.'

'Me too.'

His mobile phone rang at that moment and the display told him that the pathologist was calling. He pressed the button.

'Dr Chubb?'

'I'm starting the post-mortem in fifteen minutes,' the doctor said, 'and no one's here from CID.'

'I'm right on it.' Greg disconnected and said, 'How do you fancy a PM? I usually send Nick but obviously...'

'Fine. I'll go.' Striker seemed unconcerned and Greg assumed that he'd seen plenty of blood and guts in the Middle East. 'Er, where is it?'

'I'll show you the way. Drive me to the mortuary and I can walk back to the station from there.'

Greg decided to take a short detour via the crime scene on his way back to the office. Striding across Victoria Park, he encountered a cross-looking middle-aged couple – a pair of hikers, by the look of them – coming in the other direction.

'If you're planning a walk along the canal,' the man called, 'the bloody police have got it shut off. God knows why. One of them was quite rude. I mean, it *is* a public right of way. I've a good mind to write to my MP.'

'I heard a woman died last night,' Greg said mildly.

'Yeah? I'm not surprised. The way young people carry on these days.'

'They might as well just arrest the husband,' the woman said with a smirk. 'Save time.'

'That's right,' the man agreed. 'All this nonsense about forensic evidence. Dixon of Dock Green never bothered with it.'

Greg went on without a word, lest he say something he'd regret. When had people become so self-absorbed?

188

Seeing his approach, Sergeant Dave Trafford, who was in charge of the scene, began to write his name and time of arrival on his pad, but Greg held up his hand.

'I'm not going in.'

Trafford scratched across the entry.

He stood looking for a moment at the bustle, as overalled SOC officers carried out a minute search of the area.

He remembered the day he had met Nadia Polycarpou for the first time, running into her and Nick in Newbury one Sunday afternoon last spring. She had struck him as ordinary and he had marvelled anew at how such a commonplace woman could arouse the love he saw in Nick's eyes.

All over England, ordinary couples like Nick and Nadia were planning their future, but Nadia's future – fifty years or more of might-have-been – had been erased last night, in a matter of seconds.

He found that he was clenching his fists and forced himself to relax as he walked away.

Striker erupted into Greg's office late that morning, hotly pursued by Susan Habib who wanted to 'announce' him. The fact that Susan didn't seem to like him was a mark in his favour.

'It was definitely murder,' he said.

Greg said, 'It's all right, Susan. You can go.'

She glared at them both resentfully and walked out with her head held high, letting the door slam behind her.

Striker sat down. 'Just come from the PM. She died by drowning, all right – lungs full of canal water – but she'd been stabbed first.'

'The water would have washed away any blood, of course.'

'It was an amateurish sort of blow. Looks like it was meant to pierce the heart but missed, nicked one of her lungs.'

Greg picked up the phone. 'SOCO are still on the scene. Looks like we'll have to get the divers out. Did Dr Chubb say what sort of weapon we're looking for?'

'Short blade, less than half an inch wide, three inches long, possibly a kitchen knife, sort you'd use to peel vegetables.'

Greg dialled a mobile number from memory and soon heard a woman's voice answer, 'Martha Childs'.

He explained the situation to the chief SOC officer. 'There's a possibility the weapon was discarded at the scene,' he concluded.

'We haven't found it in the vicinity.'

'If I were the killer, I'd have chucked it in the canal after the victim.' Actually, if he were the killer, he'd have taken it away with him and disposed of it miles away, but murderers often panicked.

'I shall need authorisation to get divers out,' Martha said.

'Consider it done.' Greg hung up.

'I have more bad news,' Striker said.

'Worse than what we have already?'

'I fear so. She was pregnant – seven, maybe eight weeks.'

'Oh, no!' Greg drew in a sharp breath. 'I imagine it's Nick's.'

'Can't see it being Mr Fitzsimmons', can you?'

'As if he hasn't suffered enough. He can't know, can he? He hasn't said anything.'

'Dr Chubb said she might not be sure herself yet, not unless she was regular as clockwork. Even if she was, she might have put off telling Nick in case he wanted her to call off the dummy wedding.'

Greg sighed. At some point, Nick was going to have to know the true extent of his loss.

'Do you think it has a bearing on the murder?' he asked.

Striker stretched his legs out in front of him and let his chin fall on his chest. 'I've been asking myself that all the way back from the mortuary. It seems like a red herring to me, but we'll have to keep it in mind.' He paused. 'She had a tattoo on her thigh – a star of David.'

'Really? Harold Fitzsimmons wouldn't have liked that.'

'Don't suppose he'd ever have seen it.

That reminds me.' Striker reached into his shirt pocket and brought out a small object wrapped in tissue paper. 'Dr Chubb gave me this – afraid it might go walkabout at the mortuary.'

Greg looked at the diamond engagement ring his colleague unwrapped. It was the biggest stone he'd ever seen. 'Technically, it belongs to her next of kin,' he said, 'unless she's made a will, which is unlikely.'

'I suppose the fairest thing would be to give it back to the old man,' Striker said, 'but, as you say, legally it was her property. Can I leave it with you?'

'Yes, OK.' Greg dropped the ring gingerly into his desk drawer and locked it. It was undoubtedly worth more than his house and he didn't want to lose it.

Striker tapped on the door of the forensic laboratory shortly after lunch and was buzzed in. A woman in a wheelchair wheeled herself round to look at him enquiringly. She was in her early forties and strikingly handsome.

'Dr Armstrong?' he said.

She nodded. 'And you are the new DCI.'

'Isaac Freeman. Striker to my friends.'

'Call me Pat.'

He offered her his hand and she shook it firmly. 'How'd you end up in the chair?' he asked.

'Blunt. I like that. Better than people trying to pretend they haven't noticed, anyway. Twelve years ago. Dark night. Rain. Winding country road. Drunk driver came round the corner on the wrong side. Bang. Then nothing. For eight days.'

'What happened to the drunk?'

'He was killed outright.'

'Good. I came to see if you'd had a chance to look at those tablets I sent down.'

'Not so far.' Pat Armstrong frowned. 'I'm pretty backed up since your superintendent deprived me of my assistant.'

'...OK.'

She relented. 'I'll try to get to it today and I'll call you if I do.'

CHAPTER FIFTEEN

Greg was in early on Monday morning and sat brooding at his desk, but not about the case. It was rare for anything to deflect his attention when he was investigating a murder, but this morning's *Times* had brought some wholly unexpected news.

The European Court had ruled that the British law which prevented him and Angie, as father- and daughter-in-law, from marrying was a breach of human rights and it seemed that the government would repeal the legislation.

This could change everything, but would she even want to marry him if they were free to do so? Should he charge out and buy a diamond solitaire ring and not give her time to think better of it? Reminded, he unlocked his desk drawer and examined Nadia's engagement ring anew; it made anything he could afford look pathetic.

If he murdered Striker Freeman and Dr Aidan Chubb, he could probably hang onto it.

His telephone rang. As he answered, almost absentmindedly, absorbed in the best way to dispose of the witnesses, he heard

Barbara's voice, speaking very quietly to avoid being overheard.

'Do you think you could get down here, sir?'

He hung up without reply, locked the ring away again and took the stairs down to the CID office two at a time, pausing only at the door to make it look like a casual visit.

As he entered the room, he was not surprised to see Nick Nicolaides, seated at his usual desk, tapping grimly into his computer terminal.

Barbara mouthed 'Thanks' at him across the room. Andy was pretending to shuffle through some notes, while watching his colleague sympathetically out of the corner of his eye. A glance through the window of the DCI's office-cubicle showed it to be empty.

Odd: he hadn't had Striker Freeman down as a shirker.

'Nick,' he said genially. 'When did you get back?'

'Dad drove me home last night.' Nick didn't raise his eyes from the keyboard – like Greg, he was no touch-typist.

'Can I have a quick word with you in my office?'

'Just let me finish–'

'It's important.'

'OK.' Nick looked warily at him, but got up and followed him silently back upstairs.

Greg held a chair out for him and he sat. He resumed his own chair and leant back in it, looking at his hollow-eyed constable with compassion.

'I can't have you on this case, Nick,' he said gently. 'You have enough experience to know that.' Policemen, above all, always thought the rules didn't apply to them.

Nick clenched his fists. 'I have to find the bastard who did this and...'

'What? End up facing a murder charge yourself? I don't want to have to suspend you, Nick, but maybe it's best if you give me your warrant card for the time being.'

'No!' Nick's hand went instinctively to the pocket where he kept his card. 'That won't be necessary.'

'So we understand each other?'

'Yes, sir.' He met Greg's eye for the first time. 'They told me it was you who dived into the canal to try to save her, sir.'

'I was first on the scene, that's all.'

'Still. I won't forget it.'

'While you're here, we should take a statement from you. Will you give it to me or would you prefer it if Barbara did it?'

Nick looked at him with a steadiness that would have embarrassed Greg if thirty years in the police force hadn't rendered him unembarrassable.

'Do you really think I had anything to do with this?'

'No, Nick. I don't. But it'd be a funny sort of murder inquiry if we didn't take a statement from a man who was in a sexual relationship with the victim.'

Nick flushed. 'You make it sound sordid. We were engaged to be married.'

'I know, and I can only guess what you're going through, but the best way you can help Nadia is to let me do my job and follow normal procedure. OK?'

'OK.'

'So, shall I call Barbara—'

'I'd sooner talk to you.'

'As you wish.' Greg tapped at his computer screen, dispersing the screensaver and bringing the monitor back to life. 'You asked Nadia to marry you in June, as I recall.'

Nick looked confused. 'Yeah... I mean, I don't remember... I didn't actually *ask* her, it just sort of evolved.'

It often did, Greg thought, stifling a smile. He didn't comment but said, 'And that was when she took the job nursing Mr Fitzsimmons.'

'Pretty much. She had to give four weeks' notice at the West Middlesex, but she had a fortnight's leave owing, so she only actually worked two. Then she went straight to Down View Manor.'

'And when did this business about marrying him crop up?'

'Few weeks later. Middle of September?'

'Didn't you think it odd?'

'At first, sure, but Nadge explained it all to me, about the taxes, and it seemed like a no-brainer.'

'Mmm. So you felt no jealousy?'

'Have you met Mr F?'

'Yes.'

'I suppose you would have. I hadn't thought about how he was taking the news. Is he all right?'

'Shocked, of course,' Greg said slowly, 'but I get the feeling that when a man reaches a certain phase of his life – extreme old age or, in his case, knowing that death is close – he moves beyond strong emotion. Nothing can really hurt him any more.'

Nick grimaced. 'Roll on extreme old age.'

'Yeah.' Greg talked Nick through his statement, his relationship with Nadia, his movements at the Kismet Klub on Friday night, tapping two-fingered but with speed.

'Did you actually see her at the club?' he asked.

'I was under strict orders to steer clear of the hen party, but I could see them sort of obliquely.' He gestured with his hand as though pointing round a corner.

'So you didn't speak to her?'

'Not till the end, when she came over to the bar and told me she was leaving.'

'She was actually going at that point? It

was still quite early. I assumed she'd just gone outside for some air.'

'No, she said she'd had enough to drink and needed to get some sleep before the wedding.'

A thought struck Greg. It was deemed bad luck for bride and groom to see each other before the ceremony, as Mr Fitzsimmons himself had reminded him. 'Where was she due to spend the night?'

Nick looked surprised. 'At mine, of course.'

Of course. Where else?

'So,' Greg said slowly. 'At the time of the murder, she had left the hen party and was going to walk back to your house along the canal?'

'I told her I'd see her there later,' Nick said bleakly, 'since I was still working. If I'd only left with her...'

'Yeah.'

If only.

'But the weir is a little beyond where she'd naturally turn off to your place,' Greg pointed out. 'Why would she go up onto the bridge at all?'

Nick shrugged. 'To look at the water in the moonlight?'

'Was that her sort of thing?'

'...Not really.'

Wasn't it more likely that she saw someone she recognised up there, or more than one person, that she went up to speak to them, see what they were up to?

And that what they were up to was illegal, to do with the drug Entry, and so they killed her as a possible witness?

Barbara had mentioned that Nadia had been approached by someone selling drugs at the club but had been unable to give a description. Since it had been in the women's lavatories, that did at least narrow it down to half the population.

'I'm going to sell the house,' Nick said suddenly.

'Oh, Nick! You've only just been through the expense and upheaval of buying it.'

Nick bit his lip. 'Too many memories.'

'I know about that.' Greg paused in his typing. 'My house has memories of my son, Frederick. Some of them are unhappy memories – the months when he was dying and I was so helpless – but there are happy memories too. He lived only twenty-two years but he was a good man and I'm proud to have been his father. One day, you will feel the same about Nadia.'

Nick bowed his head but didn't reply and Greg resumed taking his statement. 'All right,' he said, at length, 'I'll get that ready for you to sign.'

He rubbed his hand across his face and sighed. He had to tell Nick about the baby but he couldn't bring himself to do so. He'd had what seemed like a lifetime of breaking bad news, but this was one of the worst he had faced.

But he couldn't *not* tell him. He had to find out eventually – it would come out at the inquest – and the delay would make the pain only more poignant. In his position, Greg would want to know at once.

'Can I go?' Nick said after a long silence. He half rose.

'No.' Nick sank back down with a moan. 'I have bad news,' Greg said. He wished he were a million miles away; he wished he'd passed his A levels and gone to college, become a schoolmaster, the way his parents had wanted. 'There's no easy way to tell you this, but the post-mortem showed that Nadia was some weeks pregnant.'

Nick didn't react for a moment, stunned. Then he opened his mouth to speak but no words came out.

'I am so very sorry,' Greg said. 'I know there's nothing I can say to ease the burden. Rest assured that we're working as hard as we can to nail the man who did this.'

Nick let slip one quick, heart-wrenching sob, his knuckles rammed into his teeth to stifle it, white with the effort. Greg got up. 'I'll leave you here to sit for a minute. Would you like anything – tea, soft drink?' Nick shook his head. 'Just compose yourself. I'll come back in a few minutes, then we'll arrange for someone to see you home.'

Nick spoke at last. 'Did they say ... was it a boy or a girl?'

'They didn't say. I don't think they can tell at that stage, not without a DNA test.'

'No. Course. Why should it matter, anyway?'

Greg placed a heavy hand on the younger man's shoulder. 'A few days' quiet rest will ... help.' He left the room.

'Yeah,' Nick muttered under his breath, 'like I'm going to rest quietly at home!'

Greg decided that Nick should have a cup of hot, sweet tea whether he wanted one or not. There was no sign of Susan Habib and, anyway, she always made such a production out of being asked to perform what she considered menial tasks, so Greg hastened down to the canteen and ordered a large mug of workman's tea with three sugars.

Turning away from the counter with his dark brown brew, he noticed Striker Freeman in the corner, tucking into a bacon sandwich and deep in conversation with Sergeant Veronica Doyle, who was fiddling flirtatiously with her auburn hair.

Greg grinned: she hadn't wasted any time. That explained why the new man wasn't upstairs, in his office, dealing with a bereaved colleague.

After Nick had obediently downed his tea,

Greg asked Andy to walk him home. It was a good opportunity for the two young constables to make their peace after the ill feeling of the previous week. Andy no longer had any reason to envy George Nicolaides his good fortune.

With one man down, Greg decided to recruit some extra help from the uniformed branch and, to that end, went to see Chief Superintendent Jim Barkiss.

His colleague liked to take life at a leisurely pace, a trait that had probably helped him to survive thirty years in the upper echelons of the force with his sanity intact. He insisted that Greg sit and make himself comfortable and indulge in a few minutes' small talk before getting down to business.

Greg did his usual inventory of the collection of framed photographs on the wall behind the Chief and was unsurprised to see a group photo from the Barkisses' recent silver wedding party, which included himself and Angie, their champagne glasses charged.

'Good do,' Jim remarked, following Greg's eye line.

'Yes, it was.'

'Not every day you've been married twenty-five years.' Barkiss folded his hands over his swelling paunch with satisfaction. He was a short man who could barely have

sneaked in over the minimum height require-
ments of the 1970s and he was definitely
running to fat in middle age. 'Now what can
I do for you? Nasty business,' he said a few
minutes later, when Greg had updated him
on the Kismet murders. 'Almost as bad as
losing an officer.'

'It means Nick Nicolaides is sidelined.'

'Of course.'

'So I was wondering if I might poach a
couple of officers.'

'Did you have anyone in mind?' Barkiss
asked.

'Jill Christie and Emily Foster did some
work for me a while back, during the
Marchant case.'

'Did they?'

'You were away.'

'Ah. Any good?'

'Hard to say,' Greg said. 'It was just
donkey work – watching CCTV footage –
but they were keen.'

'Emily's the pretty brunette?' Barkiss
asked. Greg glanced involuntarily at the
anniversary photo and his boss laughed.
'No, I'm not having my mid-life crisis but
nor am I blind. Have a word with the
inspector on their relief and if it's OK with
him then it's OK with me.'

'Cheers. That reminds me. I thought Inspector Nelson might make a useful addition
to CID when he's done his stint in uniform.

He has good experience.'

Barkiss didn't reply for a moment, then he said, 'Inspector Nelson wants to stay in uniform.'

'Really?'

'Oh, I know you CID people can't imagine anyone not wanting to join your elite ranks,' Jim said mockingly. 'This is just between ourselves, right?'

'Of course.'

'Nelson's wife was diagnosed with multiple sclerosis a few months ago. She'll be incapacitated soon and he needs to be working regular shifts so he can arrange care for her.'

'I had no idea.'

'As I said, between ourselves.'

'Poor bugger.' Greg got up.

'How's the new DCI shaping up?' Barkiss asked. 'Any chance of hanging onto this one?'

'I'd say I'm cautiously optimistic,' Greg said, 'but that would be asking for trouble.'

'How is Nicolaides coping?' Jim asked as he reached the door. 'Is there anything I can do?'

Greg hesitated. 'He's not coping too well at the moment, but there'd be something wrong with him if he was. He'll survive.'

He discovered that Jill Christie was on leave for the next ten days but Emily was on the early relief, under the command of Inspector Nelson, who willingly agreed to let her go on secondment to CID for a week.

With her usual partner away, Emily was catching up on her paperwork in the station and Greg soon tracked her down and sent her to change.

She appeared in the CID room ten minutes later, fit for action in a pair of khaki combat trousers and a thick black sweater, a big grin spread all over her face. Barbara smiled a welcome, disarmed by her obvious enthusiasm.

'I want you to go up to London,' Greg told her, 'to St Catherine's House.'

'Sir!'

'You know where it is?'

'Aldwych?' She was pleased with herself, like a schoolgirl who had given her teacher the right answer. She looked unbearably young, he thought, and Barkiss was right: she was extremely pretty.

'Good. We need to track down a marriage that took place some decades ago and whether there were any children of said marriage. Barbara will fill you in on the details.'

St Catherine's House was where the registers of births, marriages and deaths for England and Wales were kept. If Ursula Fitzsimmons' wedding had taken place abroad, or even in Scotland, then they had a problem; same with the birth of her putative children.

206

At least it was not a common name. There were various websites that offered register searches but Greg didn't trust those to be thorough enough. The central Registry was not yet fully on line and Emily would have to search through the giant ledgers manually.

Mrs Alderson said the marriage had taken place in the 1950s so it shouldn't take more than a couple of hours to find. Children were more of a problem, since they might have come a few months after the wedding or twenty years later.

Nasty thought: what if Ursula had divorced her 'Jew' within a few years, remarried, and had children by husband number two? Then they might never track them down.

Elizabeth went into her twin's room without knocking and found her lying on her bed, staring at the ceiling.

'You've been very quiet since we got back from Newbury,' she remarked, sitting down heavily on the mattress and making it bounce.

'Yeah, well, I never knew anyone who died before.'

'We didn't exactly know her.'

'She invited us to her party. We spent a lot of the evening with her.'

'It's still not like it was a friend.' Elizabeth looked at her sister in concern. 'You didn't have any trouble from that bloke – what was his name?'

'Will. No.'

'Only I saw you go outside with him and you didn't come back for ages.'

'We sat in the park.'

'He didn't, like ... rape you, or anything?'

Hannah snorted. 'I might have mentioned it.'

'Only you've been weird since that night.'

Hannah sighed. 'What are you, my mother?'

'Seriously, Hannah, I thought we told each other everything. Did he make a nuisance of himself?'

Hannah slowly shook her head. 'We made out for a bit but then he seemed to lose interest.'

'Well, more fool him!' Elizabeth slapped her twin's leg. 'Mum's out with Jonathan this evening. Covent Garden. Supper at Pizza Express?'

'You go. I'm not hungry.' Hannah turned on her side, showing her back to her sister, the conversation over.

'We might as well call it a day,' Greg said shortly after eight. 'Until we get the info from St Catherine's house, we can't get much further forward.'

'I'll hang on for a bit,' Striker said. He grinned. 'I've got a date at ten-thirty.'

208

'Bit late,' Greg remarked.

'She doesn't knock off work till ten.'

Ronnie Doyle, Greg thought. He said, 'Have fun.'

'I've been looking at Nicolaides's file,' Striker remarked. 'I see that he's passed his sergeant's exams.'

'Three years ago,' Greg said, 'but he failed twice at the board stage and gave up.'

'We should encourage him to try again. Give him something to aim for, to put his mind to now it seems that his world's fallen apart.'

'Unless he gets knocked back again,' Greg pointed out, 'which would be adding insult to injury.'

'I could give him some pointers,' Striker said, 'bit of coaching even.'

'That's nice of you,' Greg said. 'I'll leave you to suggest it to him when you think he's ready.'

On the way home he found himself brooding on Martin Nelson and his misfortune, as sad for him as it was for his wife. His reasons for not ordering full toxicology on Lindsey were sound enough, even for an experienced CID man.

Was it odd that he had been so keen to turn out at the Kismet Klub on Friday night, given his domestic situation?

Greg's mobile rang just as he pulled up in

his drive half an hour later. He didn't recognise the caller's number and it wasn't in his address book. He pressed the requisite button and said neutrally, 'Summers.'

'Constable Foster here, sir.' The young woman sounded businesslike. 'Reporting in.'

'What have you got for me, Emily?'

'I found the marriage certificate easily enough. June 23rd 1956, Marylebone Registry Office. Trouble is, she married a man with a rather common name.'

'Don't tell me – Jones,' Greg said, remembering that the despised husband was Welsh.

'Not that bad: Dixon. So I've been working my way through the birth registers for Dixon and I haven't found any children yet. I got as far as 1962 but then the office was closing and I got chucked out.'

'OK,' Greg said. 'Carry on tomorrow.'

'Yes, sir.'

'And, Emily.'

'Sir?'

'Good work.'

CHAPTER SIXTEEN

Greg stopped outside a glass door in Hungerford High Street on which the words 'Faulkner & Son, Solicitors' were etched in gold. There was no son any more, only Michael Faulkner, last of the line. Piers insisted that he was gay, but not practising.

'In denial?' Greg had asked.

'No, no one fancies him.'

He pushed the door open and went into the outer office where a woman raised her head from some papers she was reading to look at him.

'Prue!' Greg said in astonishment.

Prudence Stratton, wife (ex-wife?) of Harry Stratton, who had been his DCI for eight years. She did not look pleased to see him. Presumably she blamed him for her husband's losing his job and for all the ills that had come from it.

He'd always found her an attractive woman in an unflashy, wife-and-mother sort of way, but he thought she looked older, more than the passage of some three years since their last meeting could account for. She was dowdy, too, in a brown two-piece skirt suit with pin-striped blouse. The Prue he had known had worn reds and yellows, loud patterns, but those were presumably not deemed suitable for a solicitor's office.

'Gregory.' Her tone was neutral, verging on cool. She removed a pair of reading glasses as if she was ashamed to be caught wearing them.

'I didn't know you worked here,' he said.

'Yeah, well. Somebody has to pay the bills or we'd be out on the street.'

'You used to be a secretary. I remember now.'

'I suppose that's what I am,' she admitted, 'though I'm training to be a paralegal.'

'Good for you!' he said heartily. She grimaced at his patronising tone and he didn't blame her. 'I saw Ruthie on Friday night,' he added.

'Yeah, she said.'

'She told me...'

'Yeah.'

'She's looking well.'

'She seems to cope.'

'All grown up.'

'Yeah.'

'...Well, I spoke to Mr Faulkner on the phone early this morning. He said he could spare me five minutes about now.'

'Oh, yes. Something about Mr Fitzsimmons' will.' A mocking tone came into her voice. 'One of our most important clients.' She pressed a button on the telephone on her desk. 'Mr Faulkner, Superintendent Summers is here to see you.' A muffled reply. 'You can go in.'

She put her glasses back on and returned to her reading, dismissing him.

Michael Faulkner was a little younger than Greg but looked older, his paunch swelling in his smart suit and his hair receding to offer an expanse of forehead. He leant across his desk to shake hands and motioned Greg to the client chair.

'I got a call from Harold Fitzsimmons yesterday,' he said. 'I am instructed to give you whatever cooperation you need.'

'I merely wanted to confirm that he'd never made a will,' Greg said.

'No, well not one drawn up by me, anyway.' Faulkner laid a well-manicured hand on a sheaf of paper on his desk. 'This was the one I drafted recently and which was to have been signed after his wedding. But...'

'Yes.' Greg wondered if the lawyer would still charge for the work. 'I understand the marriage was your idea.'

'My...?' Faulkner looked startled.

'As a way of avoiding death duties.'

'Oh! Yes, if you put it that way. I didn't seriously imagine that he would marry the poor girl.'

'And his relatives? What did they think of it?'

'Oh, he is quite alone in the world,' Faulk-

ner said in a tone that brooked no con-
tradiction.

We'll see about that, Greg thought.

Today, if all went well.

Emily Foster came into the CID room just
before lunchtime, bearing a large buff
envelope and a huge grin.

'Done it!' she announced and flopped
triumphantly into the nearest chair.

'You've found Ursula Fitzsimmons' children?' Greg asked.

She handed him the envelope wordlessly
and he drew out a marriage certificate and
two birth certificates.

'I went up to 1985,' she said. 'I figured she
had to be past child-bearing by then.'

'Here.' Andy placed a mug of coffee on the
desk in front of her and gave her a clap on
the shoulder.

'Cheers, Andy.'

'Two children.' Greg examined the certificates. 'A boy and a girl. Timothy, born in
1966...'

'And Louise,' the young constable supplied.

'Born in 1964.'

'What?' Striker got to his feet in consternation. 'Did you say Timothy and Louise
Dixon?'

'Mmm.' Greg was still reading. 'Both certificates register the parents' address as

214

London – South Kensington, to be precise. We have to find out where they're living now.'

'We can tell you that,' Barbara said, with a glance at the DCI. 'Mr Freeman and I met Tim Dixon a few days ago.'

'At Lindsey Brownlow's school,' Striker added, 'where he teaches drama.'

'Common enough name,' Greg remarked.

'But he has a sister called Louise,' Barbara explained. 'Better known as Luisa Diski, the actress, who also happens to be the head-mistress's significant other.'

'And they're the right age,' Striker concluded, slotting the final piece of evidence into his jigsaw. 'So isn't that a nice little connection between Lindsey Brownlow and Nadia Polycarpou?'

'But ... but...' Greg spluttered. 'That makes no sense! Either the connection between the murders is the Kismet Klub, where they all happened, or Nadia was a copycat crime made to look like the work of the Kismet killer. Now, suddenly, we have someone – two people – with a motive to kill Nadia – Harold Fitzsimmons' lawful next of kin – who just happen to be connected to Lindsey.'

'But not to Erin,' Barbara reminded them.

'This makes things more confused,' Greg complained. 'But you'd better go and talk to the nephew and niece.'

215

'What shall I do now, sir?' Emily asked.

'Your next mission, Emily, should you choose to accept it, is to go through the mobile phone calls Nadia made in the days leading up to her death.' He pointed to the corner where Nick Nicolaides usually worked in chaotic untidiness. 'You can use that desk, if you can find it.'

'Are you thinking what I'm thinking?' Striker muttered to Barbara as they shrugged on their coats and grabbed at their mobile phones, handcuffs and the other necessary hardware that weighed down their passage through life.

'...Apparently not.'

'It's not just the nephews and nieces who have motive, but their spouses.'

'You mean ... you don't mean?' She looked at his face. 'You *do* mean.'

'Caroline Bishop. A woman capable of swift and decisive action if ever I saw one.'

'Got an angry phone call from my wife yesterday evening,' Striker remarked as they drove.

'Mmm?' Barbara wasn't really listening, partly because he was driving and she was used to senior officers asking her to take the wheel; partly because she was still pondering what he'd said about Caroline Bishop. It was disconcerting to have to consider one of your heroes as a murder suspect.

She forced herself to concentrate. 'About you taking the twins to the club?'

'Too much risk, apparently.' Freeman drove fast but very skilfully and they were already turning in at the school gate.

'You can see her point,' Barbara said.

'Life is all about risk, Barbara. Life *is* risk.'

They had come on something of a fool's errand, since the school secretary told them that not only was Mr Dixon, head of drama, away on a school trip to Stratford that day, but that Ms Bishop was at home with 'one of her migraines'.

'She lives in Boxford, doesn't she?' Barbara remembered seeing an 'at home' feature about Luisa Diski in a glossy magazine in the dentist's waiting room, showing off her gorgeous seventeenth-century cottage in Berkshire, and had recognised the place.

'Yes.' The woman gave them the exact address. 'Shall I phone ahead to tell her to expect you?'

'Like we could stop her,' Striker muttered, as they drove away.

Dove Cottage sat at the end of a single-track lane behind Boxford church. It had once been cottages, in the plural, but the terrace of three had been thrown together at some point to form one substantial house. Two of the front doors were now blocked off, with tubs of autumnal flowers emphasising that they were for ornament and not use.

The two police officers left their car in one of the spaces provided, next to a black SUV with tinted windows, and followed a winding gravel path to the leftmost door, their feet noisy on the tiny stones.

'They like to hear people coming,' Striker remarked.

Barbara was silently admiring the grey stone, the neat thatch roof with the mullioned windows that peered out from under it like bashful virgins.

She thought it unlikely that Luisa Diski, or Dixon, would be at home, but the door opened promptly to their knock and she saw the soap star standing before her in a dim hallway. In a rose-pink velours tracksuit, without make-up and with her dark hair back in a pony tail, she was nothing like the glamorous pub landlady from *Home Counties* and looked younger than her forty-one years.

Striker identified himself and Barbara and asked if they could come in. Luisa Diski stepped back to allow them through but raised a finger to her lips. 'Quietly, please. My partner has a migraine and is sleeping upstairs.'

'I hope Ms Bishop is all right,' Barbara said politely.

'She only gets them about twice a year,'

Luisa said, 'but they're crippling when they come. Rest is the only cure.'

'It was you we wanted to speak to anyway, Miss Dixon,' Striker said in a low voice.

Luisa ushered them into a sitting room which ran most of the length of the building, its beamed ceiling showing clearly the history of Dove Cottages, where each had once ended and the next begun, the floor levels rising and falling with each dwelling. She shut the wooden door behind them and Striker resumed his normal tone. 'It's about your uncle.'

She looked baffled. 'Uncle Joshua? What's he done now?'

'Your mother's brother,' he clarified.

'"Harold Fitzsimmons"?' Her voice audibly put the name in inverted commas, rising in incredulity. 'I've never met him and I don't want to. Can't help you. Sorry.'

'But you are his next of kin,' Barbara said. 'You and your brother, Timothy.'

'If you say so.' Luisa's mouth was unsmiling now, her voice cold. When she added, 'Won't you sit down?' there was little welcome in it. Barbara took an armchair on one side of the fireplace, Striker on the other.

Luisa flopped onto a yellow velvet sofa, reclined against a bank of cushions like an odalisque and curled her bare feet up under her, a still beautiful woman aware of her

219

own charms. Barbara realised that she was smaller than she looked on TV, both shorter and thinner.

'So what has "Harold Fitzsimmons" done?' she asked.

'Nothing,' Striker said.

'Then has something happened to him?'

'He's dying,' Striker replied, 'but only from natural causes.'

'Then what interest do Newbury CID have in him?'

'It's complicated,' Barbara said. 'You know he lives not far away, on the Downs?'

'I know. It was my mother's family home, where she grew up, but she wasn't allowed to set foot in it after her marriage to my father. She did point it out to me once, a long time ago, when I was about twelve.'

'But you wrote to Mr Fitzsimmons there when your mother died,' Striker said.

'Not me! That was Tim.' Her voice was full of confident scorn. 'I told him he was wasting his time, but he always thinks the best of people and was convinced mother's only brother would want to come to her funeral. He didn't even reply. Now I really must insist that you tell me what this is about before I answer any more of your questions.'

The two police officers exchanged glances and somehow agreed that Striker should be the one to speak. 'It concerns the recent deaths at the Kismet Klub in Newbury,

Miss Dixon. You may have read about them in the *Newbury Weekly News*.'

'You what?' She laughed. 'And was he a regular there?'

'No, but the latest victim was about to become his wife.'

'I see.' She swung her legs down from the sofa and assumed a sitting position, leaning forward, more tense. 'He was about to marry – what? – some bimbo?'

'His nurse,' Barbara said. 'A woman of thirty. No bimbo.'

'And, as his nearest blood relation, I had a motive to kill her. Is that it?'

'Under the intestacy laws, you and your brother would inherit should he die un-married.'

'He's surely made a will to ensure that none of his money comes to his despised relations.'

'He has made no will,' Striker said.

'Well, more fool him.' Luisa waved a well-manicured hand over her surroundings. 'I'm not exactly hard up. They pay me two hundred thousand a year for appearing in *Home Counties*. I know that for a fact because I read it in *Soap Opera Digest* a few weeks ago.'

Barbara laughed, liking her. 'I'm in the wrong job!'

Striker merely smiled. 'Mr Fitzsimmons is a multi-millionaire,' he said.

'Let me tell you something – is it Chief Inspector?'

'Yes, madam.'

'That man treated my parents shamefully and do you know why?'

'Because your father was Jewish.'

'Exactly. At least you've done your homework. Have you any idea how much I loathe that sort of intolerance?'

'Don't we all?' Striker said mildly.

'As a gay woman, I've had to put up with something similar all my life: producers who wouldn't cast me because they said it would alienate viewers; actually, because it meant I wouldn't sleep with them. If Harold Fitzsimmons knocked on my door now and told me he'd come to give me his millions, I'd tell him exactly where he could stick them.'

'Bit of a coincidence you and your brother both ending up in Newbury,' Striker commented.

'Not really. Dad died when I was eleven and that meant that money was tight. Mum sold the place in London and property was much cheaper here. It was where she grew up, so it was natural for her to gravitate back here. Most people don't actually move far from where they started out, you know, even today.'

She was right, of course, Striker thought; most coincidences were no such thing. 'Where were you on Friday night?' he asked.

'At home, here. Caro and I gave a dinner party – eight people in all, should you require witnesses.'

'And what time did they leave?'

'Two couples left around eleven-thirty, but Johanna and Jane were up from London and staying the weekend. We all four sat up till the small hours, drinking vintage port and putting the world to rights.'

'Perhaps I could have a contact number for them and their full names,' Barbara said.

'I have one of Jo's cards here somewhere.' Luisa rose and rootled inside a desk that looked, to Barbara's uneducated eye, like a genuine antique. 'Here.' She handed her a thick, cream-coloured business card, whose stark charcoal lettering proclaimed that Johanna Eriksson was a film producer, based in Golden Square, near Piccadilly Circus.

'She's also a JP,' Luisa added. She didn't sit down again. 'So, if that's all, Chief Inspector...'

Striker rose. 'Thank you for your time, Miss Dixon. Perhaps you could just tell me where your brother lives.'

'He has a flat by the canal in Newbury.' She recited the address and Barbara wrote it down. 'But he's gone to Stratford today to see *Romeo and Juliet* with the sixth form.'

'I know. We'll catch him later. Was he at your dinner party?'

She shook her head. 'Not this time – women only.' She marched to the front door and opened it. As she stood waiting for them to leave, Striker offered her his hand. After a moment's hesitation, she shook it.

'Lou?' They glanced up to see Caroline Bishop standing at the turn of the staircase, peering down at them. She looked and sounded unwell. 'Did I hear voices?'

Striker stepped forward so she could see him. 'It's us, Miss Bishop. DCI Freeman and Sergeant Carey.'

'The detectives?' She descended another step. She was wearing a simple white cotton nightgown, like a Victorian child, falling to her ankles above bare feet. Her face was pale and her eyes were ringed with red.

'It's all right, Caro,' her partner said. 'It was me they wanted.'

'You? Why?'

'Let's get you back to bed. We'll talk about it later.' She turned to Striker and Barbara and said, 'Please see yourselves out.' She sprang upstairs two at a time, took Caroline gently by the shoulders and steered her back to their bedroom.

'How would she even know her uncle was getting married?' Barbara asked, when they were back in the car.

Striker shrugged. 'It's in the public domain. It'd have to be listed at the registry office for

224

three weeks before the wedding, where any-body could read it and object if they had just cause.'

'But why would you even be at the registry office? It's not exactly on the daily round.'

'Didn't I hear something about Luisa Diski and her partner getting married – or whatever you call it – this autumn?'

'And where did you read that?' Barbara asked tartly. '*Soap Opera Digest?*'

Striker laughed denial. 'Maybe she or Ms Bishop went to the Town Hall to arrange their own ceremony and saw the announce-ment there. Maybe she's made it her business to keep an eye on the old man and his doings all these years, whatever she says.'

'But it would be a reasonable supposition that he'd made a will disinheriting her and her brother. Wouldn't it?'

'True. I assumed it myself. And there's no real way of knowing whether someone's made a will or not.'

Striker didn't start the engine but sat looking at his colleague. 'So you believed her, Barbara?'

'Yes, sir. I think I did.'

He fired up the ignition without com-ment. As they pulled out into the main road through Boxford, he said, 'But she is an act-ress. They pay her – an awful lot of money, apparently – to lie convincingly.'

Five silent minutes later, he added, 'And

Caroline Bishop looks ill, as if she's under an immense strain. As if, say, she'd found out that the woman she loves had committed a terrible crime... Or had done so herself.'

'Or as if she had a migraine,' Barbara said.

CHAPTER SEVENTEEN

Timothy Dixon lived in one of the many new blocks of flats – or, as their developers insisted, apartments – that were springing up in Newbury, each striving for a grander name than its neighbours: Oxford, Paris, Manhattan, Atlantis.

His was the Boston, rising four storeys above the banks of the Kennet and Avon canal with a cramped balcony jutting out on each floor.

'Handy for the nightclub,' Striker commented. 'Five minutes' walk along a quiet towpath. Bit further to the weir.' He glanced along the still waters, their surface faintly gleaming in the autumn light. 'Also a near neighbour of mine.'

Barbara rang the bell, said merely, 'Police' when it was answered and they were buzzed straight in. Dixon's flat was on the second floor and neither detective bothered with the lift, striding up the stairs together, to find the young man standing at his open door, wearing what appeared to be the same corduroy trousers as the last time they'd seen him.

He was saying goodbye to Maria-Teresa

Antonelli, who ducked past them, looking as if she were trying not to cry.

As she almost ran down the stairs, he called after her, 'You'll be fine, Terry. Try not to worry.'

Striker produced his warrant card. 'We met at the school, Mr Dixon. DCI Isaac Freeman, DS Carey.'

'I remember. Come in.' Tim turned away ahead of them and they followed him into his hallway, Barbara closing the door behind them. 'What can I do for you?'

'Weren't you expecting us?' Barbara asked.

'No. Should I have been?'

'We assumed your sister would have phoned you,' Striker said, since there was no way they could have prevented her from doing so.

'I only got home half an hour ago, haven't checked my messages.' He turned to glance at the telephone on the hall stand where a red light was blinking. 'Yeah.' He pressed a button and Luisa Diski's smoky voice filled the corridor.

'Darling, it's Lou. I've just had the police here about "Uncle Harold"—' again the audible inverted commas, Striker noticed. 'They're coming to see you next. Love you.' Then a dialling tone. Not incriminating, almost deliberately so.

'Uncle Har—' The young man looked

228

baffled. 'Oh! You mean Mum's brother.' He looked from Striker to Barbara and back again. 'I don't understand.'

'Perhaps we'd all be more comfortable sitting down?' Barbara suggested.

'Yes, of course.'

He led the way into a room that took up the whole depth of the flat, with a kitchen at one end, its sparkling white units dazzling in their newness. There was a dining area in the middle and seating – two beige sofas – on the canal side where windows opened onto the balcony.

Two wine glasses stood on the circular dining table, a smudge of red in the bottom of each. A bottle of supermarket Shiraz stood open next to them.

Tim looked embarrassed and cleared the items away, dumping the glasses in the sink and stowing the bottle in a cupboard. 'Terry's getting cold feet about the play,' he explained. 'Wanted me to hear her lines when we got back from Stratford. I could hardly say no, although, frankly, after a day's theatre-outing with two dozen adolescents, all I need is a hot bath and an evening in front of the telly. I thought a glass of wine might relax her. I mean, she is seventeen; it's not like she's a child.'

Too much explanation, Barbara thought, answering questions that had not been asked. Neither she nor Striker replied and, after a brief hesitation, Dixon gestured them to be seated. 'I don't understand,' he repeated, ignoring the sofas himself and drawing up a hard chair, as if in penance. 'Has something happened to my uncle?'

'You and your sister are his next of kin,' Striker stated.

'Are we?' He shrugged. 'If I'd given the matter any thought, I'd have assumed that he'd married and had children of his own.'

'No,' Barbara said. 'He never married.'

'And he's dead?'

'What makes you ask that?' Striker said.

'All this talk of next of kin. CID officers knocking at my door. I assumed he'd died in mysterious circumstances and I was in the frame.' He laughed at the absurdity of the notion but stopped abruptly when neither detective joined in.

'He's not dead,' Barbara said.

'Well, good.'

'Let me guess,' Striker said. 'You've never met him and never wanted to.'

'You apparently know that he had a major falling-out with my mother. Still, yes, I have seen him. Once.'

'Your sister didn't mention that,' Striker said.

'She doesn't know.' He grinned. 'Bossy older sister – you know how it is. No, when Mum died, I wrote to him to let him know. When I hadn't heard back by the morning of the funeral I decided to go and see him.'

'At Down View Manor,' Striker said.

'Yeah. I didn't tell Lou I was going as she'd just have told me not to be such a sentimental fool. Anyway, I rang the doorbell and a woman answered, some sort of housekeeper. I asked if I could see Mr Fitzsimmons and gave my name – just Timothy Dixon, which didn't seem to mean anything to her.'

She'd not known the name of the man Ursula had married, Striker remembered.

'She told me to wait in the hall,' Tim continued, 'and went into what I took to be the sitting room. After a couple of minutes she came back, looking very embarrassed and said that she'd made a mistake and that Mr Fitzsimmons wasn't at home after all and that I should telephone to make an appointment.'

'And did you?' Barbara asked.

'No. Call me thick-skinned but I did finally get the message at that point.'

'But you said you'd met him,' Striker said.

'I said I'd *seen* him,' Tim corrected him. 'As I walked away from the house, I glanced back and saw him watching me through the window. He made no attempt to conceal himself, just stood there like a statue, watching me leave.'

'May I ask where you were on Friday evening, Mr Dixon?' Striker said.

'I went to see a friend ... woman friend.'

'Girlfriend?'

'Yes – well, hardly a girl.'

'And for how long were you with her?'

'I went round about seven-thirty. She was cooking dinner for us. I, um, stayed the night.'

'Any witnesses?' Barbara asked. 'To your being at her place, I mean.'

'Her teenage daughter was there early on. She had dinner with us but she went out around ten.'

'I need a name and address, sir.' Barbara took out her note pad and pen.

'Prue Stratton. She lives–'

'Prue Stratton!' Barbara echoed in surprise. 'Wife of former DCI Harry Stratton?'

'I understand her ex-husband was a policeman,' Tim said, 'but he's long gone.'

'Isn't her daughter Ruth at your school?'

'Yes, she's one of my students, but there's no law that says I can't date a parent.'

Embarrassing for the kid, though, Barbara thought.

'So the daughter went out to the Kismet Klub,' Striker said.

'I didn't ask, but I shouldn't be surprised. It seems to be a favourite hangout for the older kids.'

'I saw her there myself. She spoke to Mr Summers.'

He remembered her saying that her

mother had a new boyfriend, one who wrote poetry. She had made it sound like a character defect. He had an open mind about men who wrote poetry, along with a fondness for the Hebrew love poems of Yehuda Amichai, which reminded him of a certain Myriam in Israel more than twenty years ago. Tall and strong, with golden ropes of hair, she could strip a gun faster than anyone he had met before or since, explaining the mechanism to him in her lispingly accented English.

He might have married her, had she lived. *My beloved gave me a few words before she left...*

There was a moment's silence then Striker rose from the deep cushions of the sofa with one cat-like movement. 'Thank you for your time, Mr Dixon. We'll see ourselves out.'

'He seems like a nice bloke,' Barbara ventured.

'Drama teacher,' Striker said. 'That means he's an actor like his sister, just couldn't make it as a professional.'

'He was a bit jumpy about us catching him alone with a sixth-form girl,' Barbara said with a grin.

'The gentleman did protest too much, methinks,' Striker agreed. 'Plying her with drink too.'

'*Plying*'s a bit strong,' Barbara objected.

'Looked like she only had the one glass.'

'True. And she's not below the age of consent.'

'No, but the law forbids relationships between teacher and pupil,' Barbara reminded him.

'A very recent law,' Striker said. 'The Sexual Offences Act of 2003. It's interesting, isn't it, when something is perfectly legal and then suddenly ceases to be so – drink driving, driving without a seat belt, insider dealing, teacher romancing a student – people don't take those laws seriously.'

'Schools do. His career would be over, even if he is the head's brother-in-law. Still, if he's dating Prue Stratton...'

'Some men like to have more than one woman on the go,' Striker said with a grin, '–or so I've been told. Anyway, I'm more interested in the fact that Terry was one of Lindsey Brownlow's best mates, one of her little circle, and with her at the Kismet the night she died.'

Tim Dixon took the open bottle of wine back out of the cupboard and poured himself another glass. It had been a long day and the flat felt stuffy so he threw open the balcony window to the cool October air and stood looking down at the canal without really seeing it.

Terry Antonelli had been in a bad way. It

had to be something more than stage fright, surely, since she was a good little actress and had done school plays before without all this angst. OK, she'd had to take over the part of Gwendolen from Lindsey Brownlow, whom he'd originally cast back in the summer, and maybe that had been hard for her. She'd looked as if she was about to burst into tears half the time and she didn't seem to have taken in anything of the RSC production they'd seen that afternoon.

Which was why he'd agreed to let her come to his flat for a few minutes, to look over the text of the play, which was something he was careful about since kids easily got crushes on teachers and that was dangerous.

He'd offered her a glass of wine in the hope of loosening her tongue, getting her to confide in him, but then the two coppers had arrived. He'd hung up the intercom handset and said, puzzled, 'Police. What on earth do they want with me?' and she hadn't been able to get out fast enough.

CHAPTER EIGHTEEN

Striker hung up the telephone and sighed. 'Well, neither Louise Dixon nor Caroline Bishop was out murdering Nadia on Friday night, and that's according to a lay magistrate.'

'I can't help thinking that Luisa Diski would have been noticed at the Kismet Klub, anyway,' Barbara remarked. 'Probably Caroline Bishop too, since a number of her sixth-formers would have been there.'

Striker glanced at his watch. 'Are we having a team meeting this morning?'

'Yes we are.' Greg said, coming in behind him. Striker told him the bad news about the unshakeable alibi of Newbury's hottest lesbian couple. 'Timothy Dixon has an alibi, too,' he concluded, 'although he seems to have shown more of an interest in his uncle than Luisa does.'

'He's not earning two hundred thousand a year,' Barbara said. 'He maybe can't afford to be so cavalier about losing a possible inheritance.'

'Good point, but his alibi checks out too.'

'Who earns two hundred thousand a year?' Greg asked.

'Soap opera stars, apparently.'

'Huh! Not like it's a proper job. I can't help thinking this question of who inherits the Fitzsimmons millions is a red herring,' Greg went on. 'Nadia died in the same place as Lindsey Brownlow—'

'Though not by the same weapon,' Barbara said.

'True, but it was a Friday night, much the same people were there as for the previous deaths. That can't be a coincidence. Mr Freeman? What do you think?'

'I'm inclined to agree, but there's no harm in keeping our options open.'

It was Greg's turn to provide dinner that night and, tired of takeaways, he decided to make an effort, stopping at the supermarket on the way home for supplies: lamb chops grilled to perfection with boiled mangetout and asparagus. OK, it wasn't exactly Gordon Ramsay, but how many murders had Mr Ramsay solved?

The lamb came from New Zealand, the mangetout from Kenya and the asparagus from Thailand. It seemed strange that his dinner was better travelled than he was.

They ate in the dining room to create a sense of occasion and shared a bottle of Spanish Merlot. Greg would have lit the candles if he'd been able to find the matches.

He confided in Angie about his fears for

Nick Nicolaides – how he would refuse to stay out of the investigation, perhaps do something stupid which would jeopardise a future prosecution, or even land himself in trouble by doing physical harm to the killer.

'Not that I don't understand how he feels,' he concluded, before changing the subject.

After dinner, they settled down to watch the news which moved, after the national and international stories, to *Newbury Newsround* at which point Greg reached for his *Times* as he hadn't had a moment to read it that day.

'And in a sensational development in the search for the Kismet Killer, this programme has learnt that the murderer, responsible now for the deaths of three young women at Newbury's hottest night spot, has taken a souvenir from each victim in the form of a shoe.'

Greg glanced up from his paper in surprise as the bronzed and smug face of Adam Chaucer filled the television screen.

'The taking of such souvenirs is by no means uncommon among serial killers,' Chaucer went on, 'as was confirmed for me by eminent local psychiatrist, Dr Sarah Peach, today, in an exclusive interview for this programme.'

Greg laid aside his newspaper and watched. He'd met Sarah Peach, head of psychiatry at the Kennet hospital, during an investigation about eighteen months earlier, and knew her to be a decent and sensible woman. She looked bemused now, clearly wondering how she had let herself be talked into this nonsense. She was a middle-aged woman and no snappy dresser, drawing her woollen cardigan more firmly round her as she spoke. She repeated what Chaucer had just said, a fact that would have been well known to anyone who'd ever picked up a crime novel.

'And is there a special significance in a shoe?' Chaucer wanted to know. 'Some sort of fetish?'

'I suppose it would depend on the type of shoe,' Dr Peach ventured after a pause, her eyes now fixed firmly on her own sensible footwear, 'and the nature of the victim.'

'So if the victim were a young woman,' Chaucer persevered, 'as in this case, and the shoes, say, high-heeled, the motive might be sexual?'

Dr Peach said, 'Hmm,' and Chaucer thanked her and took the opportunity to ask why Newbury CID were taking so long to make the streets of the town safe for its womenfolk again.

Souvenir shoes, Greg thought. Interesting idea.

'But...' Angie stared at the screen, looking perplexed. 'Nadia was still wearing both her shoes when we dragged her out of the water.'

Greg looked at her seriously. 'Are you sure,

darling?' She screwed up her face the way she always did when concentrating, making him want to kiss her. 'I noticed her shoes especially that evening,' she said, 'because they were orange and you don't often see orange shoes – stilettos, sort of fake Manolos. At least, I assumed they were fake.'

'OK, but that doesn't mean she was wearing both of them when you saw her body,' he said.

Doubt was creeping into her voice now. 'They wouldn't just have fallen off because they had tight ankle straps. And didn't they catch on the railing of the bridge as we pulled her over? I could have sworn...'

Greg moved in for the kill. 'Really? You'd swear in court, under oath, that she hadn't lost one of her orange shoes?'

'I... No. Oh, I don't know! Is that true?'

'That serial killers take souvenirs? Yes, it's quite common. Trophies, we call them.'

'Trophy? Like he's scored some sort of victory?'

'Exactly. Shoes are popular, also jewellery, but often it may be an actual part of the body: eyelashes, say, or nail clippings, if he has time to take them, even a finger.'

She grimaced. 'How sick is that?'

'Well, we weren't starting from the premise that the murderer was exactly normal, were we?'

She laughed, her good humour restored,

240

then stopped and pointed at the TV screen where the weather girl was now strutting her stuff. 'But should Chaucer the Chump be telling people? Aren't those the sort of details CID keep secret so you can weed out false confessions?'

'You would think,' Greg said.

'Cup of cocoa?'

'Yes please.'

He watched her leave the room, wondering if she knew about the ruling by the European Court and how it might affect them. She wasn't much of a newspaper reader and the media had confined its coverage of the story mostly to snide jokes about men marrying their mothers-in-law.

Maybe they could go to Thailand on their honeymoon, show that asparagus who was boss.

Or New Zealand.

'What was that crap Adam Chaucer was talking about a missing shoe?' Barbara demanded indignantly when he got in the next morning. 'I mean, how could he have got a shoe off of Erin? Like she went home not noticing she was missing one?'

Greg merely smiled. 'Giving him a chance to show what a useless journalist he is, I suppose.'

Chaucer the Chump: perfect.

She eyed him narrowly. 'This was your

doing, sir?'

'Not me. No need to correct it, though, Babs.'

She looked puzzled. 'Even Chaucer wouldn't just make something like that up.'

'No, which maybe brings us a step closer to tracking down his mole. Gave me a chance to test out Summers' theory of eye witnesses, anyway.'

'That you can convince them of anything?'

'That's the one!'

A telephone rang.

'Yes?'

'What was all that about a missing shoe on the news?'

'I haven't seen the news.'

'*Newbury Newsround.* They said the Kismet Klub killer took shoes from the victims, like souvenirs.'

'Calm down.'

'We didn't take a shoe off that stupid woman.'

'I guess it just fell off.'

'Don't you watch TV?' The voice rose, near hysteria. 'The police will have searched every inch of the towpath. And they've got divers in the weir. I saw them yesterday. If her shoe fell off, then they found it.'

'Maybe it's like the reporter said, then – one of us wanted a souvenir.'

'Oh, that's just sick! You're sick. I tell you,

I can't take any more of this.'

And the line went dead.

As she breezed through life, Elizabeth Freeman found time to worry about her sister. She didn't know if it was a twin thing or if all sisters were the same. She didn't worry about her big brother Aaron, but then Aaron was so laid back that it would have been pointless.

Nervy though Hannah was inclined to be, Elizabeth didn't remember her being this low in spirits since their labrador Percy had died when they were eleven. She'd jumped when a gust of wind had caused the back door to slam shut behind her the previous evening and she was off her food.

So when their mother had left for her work at the art gallery that morning, she double locked the front door behind her, pocketed both her and Hannah's keys so she couldn't bolt out of the house and went to confront her.

'I'll get it out of you in the end, so you might just as well tell me now.' She grabbed Hannah and pinned her to the bed. 'Don't make me tickle you!'

Hannah wrinkled her nose. She needed to talk to someone and there was surely no one better than the sister with whom she had shared a cosy womb for nine months.

'Did Will pop your cherry at last?' Elizabeth

243

went on. 'And you didn't have any condoms so now you're worried you might be pregnant? Is that it?'

Hannah flushed with indignation. 'I'm not an idiot! If that had happened, I'd know to go to the chemist for the morning-after pill.'

'So did you, with Will?'

'No, I told you. He was keen enough at first but then he seemed to lose interest ... after we'd taken the pills.'

'Aha!'

'He went all mellow and kept on about how beautiful the world was and how beautiful I was, which would have been nice if he'd been able to get my name right.'

Elizabeth released her sister and sat back on her haunches. 'And that's what this is all about – that you took drugs?'

'I feel stupid, after all Dad said. How was I to know it wasn't that really dangerous drug he warned us about? I could have died... You remember when he came in the following morning and told us he was proud of us?'

'Dimly.'

'I felt *this* small.' Hannah demonstrated with her thumb and forefinger.

'Well, there was no harm done,' Elizabeth said briskly. 'You were stupid but you'll know better another time. Right?'

'Right.'

'And Dad need never know.'

Hannah managed a wan smile. 'Thanks, sis.'

'So ... what was it like?'

'Crap, actually.'

'Oh!' Elizabeth was disappointed. 'If it was Ecstasy, then people say it's like this great trip.'

'*He* seemed to be having one,' Hannah said, with a note of resentment. 'I just sat there feeling cold and alone, hearing animals rustling and wondering if it was rats, 'cause you know how I hate rats.'

Her story came out in a rush. 'Then I was getting cold so I took a walk round the pond and felt dizzy and then some people ran past, really like their lives depended on it, and they jostled me and I thought something was wrong, then later you came and told me Nadia was dead.'

'What time was this?' Elizabeth asked.

'Midnight, give or take.'

'How many people?'

'Four, I think. Or five. Or three.'

'Male or female?'

'It was dark and I only saw one of them close up but I thought they were all girls.'

CHAPTER NINETEEN

Angie Summers knocked on the peeling front door of a terraced cottage on the fringes of Newbury town centre. When she got no reply, the knocking became a banging, then a relentless hammering. She was going to make it clear to the occupant that nothing would make her give up, that the only way to restore peace to the world was to answer the door.

Several minutes went by in this manner, while passers-by stared at her as if she were a mad woman before scurrying away. Finally, she heard a grunted, 'All right, all fucking right. I'm coming.'

She didn't stop hammering until the key turned in the lock and the door opened. Nick Nicolaides stood there, his eyes ringed with red, either from lack of sleep or weeping. He wore nothing but dingy tracksuit bottoms, his feet bare on the faded parquet of the hall.

His chest was matted with black hair that had not seen soap and water lately.

Angie swept straight past him and into the sitting room where she clicked the light on.

'Jesus!' she said, looking round. 'Did a

bomb go off?'

'Some of the blokes from the station came by last night,' Nick said, running his fingers awkwardly through the overgrown forest that was his hair. 'They brought whisky.'

'And – let me guess – you rounded the evening off with a farting competition.' She strode to the casement window at the back that looked over the scrap of garden, wrenched back the curtain and flung it open.

'It looks even worse by daylight,' she said.

Nick stood staring at her blearily with his hands on his hips. He had always been a hirsute man, needing to shave twice a day, and now he had a definite beard. 'Angie, what are you doing here? Did Mr Summers send you?'

'He doesn't *send* me anywhere,' she said briskly. 'I'm not one of his staff. I've come to comfort you, and if you think that means holding your hand and saying "there, there" while you feel sorry for yourself, you've got another think coming. I shan't be offering comfort from the bottom of a bottle either. Go and shower and put some clean clothes on while I tidy up a bit and make some coffee.'

It was the voice of authority and it did not occur to him to disobey. He went upstairs and she heard the sound of running water a moment later.

She opened the curtains at the front of the

room too, revealing small, dusty panes looking onto the distant canal. No wonder he
wanted to sell up with the constant reminder
before him of how the woman he loved had
died.

She strode into the small kitchen, loaded
fresh coffee and water into the filter
machine and switched it on. There were
black plastic bin bags in the cupboard under
the sink and she went back into the sitting
room while the coffee was brewing, picking
up the debris from the floor: takeaway
cartons, some still half full of curry, empty
lager cans, full ashtrays. She added the
bottles too: this was no time to worry about
recycling.

She gathered up half a dozen mugs and
went back to the kitchen to wash them. She
opened the fridge and threw away anything
that was past its use-by-date or smelt
suspect, including the only carton of milk.

By now, the bin bag was full and she
twisted the plastic ties into a knot and
dumped it outside the back door. There was
a melamine tray on one of the work surfaces
and she poured two cups of coffee, and
rummaged around for sugar.

Walking back into the sitting room with her
tray, she found Nick flopped in an armchair,
staring at the boarded-up fireplace. He was
wearing jeans and a sweater and had washed
his hair although he hadn't shaved.

'I'm afraid there's no milk,' she said.

'I take it black.'

'Just as well.'

She handed him his mug and sat down on the sofa, which sagged a little beneath her slight weight.

'Nadia had such plans for the place,' he said softly. 'Men are no good at that sort of thing, unless they're poofters.'

Angie did not feel inclined to challenge this lack of political correctness, especially since she largely agreed.

'Only then this business with Mr Fitzsimmons came up, and we figured we wouldn't be here long so there was no point in decorating.' He looked in despair at the wallpaper which was a pattern of rambling mauve roses, too big for the room, and the carpet, which was an acid shade of green. Décor that would drive anyone mad.

'Gregory says this Mr Fitzsimmons is not a very nice man,' Angie remarked.

Nick looked at her in surprise. 'He's always been really good to me and Nadge.'

'I'm not going to pretend I know what you're going through, Nick,' Angie said, 'because we're all different, but I maybe have a better idea than most people.'

'But your husband took a long time to die,' he blurted out. 'You had time to get used to it.'

'Months,' she agreed, although they had

seemed like years. 'And nature took him away from me, not some ... evil person. Which is why I don't claim to know exactly how you feel. I'm not going to say that time heals all wounds either. Ninety-nine per cent of the time I'm fine, but there are days when I remember Fred and everything we had together and I want to lie down on the bed and cry until I'm drained, and he's been dead more than three years.'

'I'm thirty-three,' Nick said, 'and Nadia was the first woman I ever felt I wanted to spend the rest of my life with.'

'Yes,' Angie said. 'We know them when we meet them and we don't hesitate. You will always have the memories – the good ones as well as the bad.'

'Yeah, that's what Mr Summers said,' Nick said awkwardly, since he was thinking that Angie had wasted no time in replacing her dead husband, and with his own father. He put the unworthy thought away, along with the even more unworthy one that he would not be seeking consolation with Nadia's mother.

This faintly humorous thought convinced him, more than anything, that one day life might be tolerable again and his mouth switched in the direction of a smile at the mental image of the short, stout woman who should have been his mother-in-law, fit to bursting in a tight black dress, gabbling non-stop in her inaccurate English.

'However long I live, Fred will always be part of me,' Angie went on, 'although we had such a short time together. He'll be somewhere in my heart, but that won't stop me getting on with living my life and he wouldn't have wanted it to.'

Nick made no reply but drank his coffee.

'I hardly knew Nadia,' Angie said, 'so why don't you tell me about her.'

He did, simply and lucidly, with an articulacy that would have surprised anyone – Greg, for example – who'd had to read one of his reports. How they had met at the West Middlesex Hospital when she happened to live upstairs from a murder victim; a nurse, of Cypriot parentage, Greek Orthodox, his mother's dream girl, and, very soon, his own.

He forgot, now, how he had initially found her garrulous, thought twice, even, about asking her out. How rapidly she had become part of his life, an indispensable part that he was now forced to dispense with. Always. His eyes welled as he remembered that he would never see her again, never hear her call 'Only me' as she let herself in at the front door.

'The old people loved her, Angie. She'd sit with them and hold their hands when they were dying, even if it meant staying hours after her shift ended.'

Clearly there had been a side to Nadia Polycarpou she hadn't seen, Angie thought. 'I remember her telling me how, late one night, she was walking home from the hospital after sitting with an old man till he was gone. She reckoned he was seeing her safely to her door, maybe coming in with her in the hope of catching a glimpse of her in her underwear.'

Angie began to laugh.

'You know she was carrying my baby?' he said abruptly.

Her eyes widened as the laugh died in her throat. 'My God! No, I didn't know.'

'I thought Mr Summers would have told you.'

'He does sometimes discuss some aspect of his cases with me,' she admitted, 'but he would have thought that too private. A baby!' She shook her head in dismay. 'How happy you must have been.'

'That's just it: I didn't know. It was only a few weeks – she may not even have known herself.' He hesitated. 'Part of me wishes they hadn't told me.'

'I suppose it would have come out...'

'Last night, I rolled all her clothes into a sort of bolster and I took it to bed with me and I just lay there holding it and it smelt of her.'

Angie was watching him over the top of her mug as she gently sipped, feeling – perhaps remembering – his pain. 'If anyone can find Nadia's killer, it's Greg and his team,' she said finally. 'Meanwhile, why don't you go back to your Mum's for a few days? Let her cook healthy food for you, cosset you a bit. I bet that's what she wants more than anything in the world.'

'...Maybe you're right.'

'I'll drive you, if you like. I've got no classes today – well, none I can't bunk off.'

'No,' he said slowly. 'I'll drive myself. I can manage.' Angie took his empty mug from him. 'So what say we go upstairs and pack you a case?'

'OK.'

Twenty minutes later, he was ready to go. She said, 'If you had a spare set of keys, I could pop round and pack up Nadia's stuff, save you having to do it.'

'Yeah. It should go back to her parents. Thanks.' He went into the kitchen and returned with a latch key. 'Not very secure, I know. Still.'

On the doorstep, she borrowed his mobile phone and programmed her own number into it. 'Call me any time you need to talk. Doesn't matter if it's the middle of the night.'

'Thanks. For everything. If there's ever anything I can do for you...'

'Well, you can stop spreading bogus rumours about Gregory and Martha Childs for a start.'

He flushed. '...You got it!'

Nick got into his Astra and drove off. Angie sat on a bench by the canal and waited for a while, to make sure he didn't double straight back.

She was no more than a hundred yards from the police tape that marked out the area where Nadia had died. She could see uniformed constables in the distance, keeping out crime tourists. Her keen eyesight made out a diver in his wetsuit.

She began to brood on Nadia and her baby. Accident or design? Probably the first since she would surely have waited until the end of her farce of a marriage to the old man.

When Angie and Fred had married they'd been very young but had agreed that they would not wait too long before starting a family, no more than two years. Except that two years was, incredibly, more than Fred had left. She had put the whole idea of children away after that: why give such hostages to fortune, such opportunities for anguish?

And now? She was twenty-five and would be done with university in another year. She hoped eventually to set herself up as a therapist, perhaps a grief counsellor, which she could do from home. She was in a stable relationship, but with a man who might feel himself too old to go through the whole baby thing again.

She got up and walked slowly back to where she had left her car, with no conclusions reached.

As Greg walked into the station after lunch, he found Striker Freeman deep in conversation with Sergeant Maybey, who was laughing at something the DCI had said.

He was making himself at home, Greg thought, or was he making a pal out of Maybey to see if he was the leak? Was it the custody sergeant who'd been told the lie about the shoes?

'Afternoon, Mr Freeman,' he said.

'Good afternoon.' Striker's mobile instantly rang. He apologised, glanced at the display and switched it off.

'Only Elizabeth. I'll call her back later.'

'He's switched the phone off on me!' Elizabeth stared at her handset in disbelief. 'Come on.'

'What? Where?'

Elizabeth dialled another number. 'Hello? I need a taxi to Paddington Station right away, please.'

CHAPTER TWENTY

Bridget Antonelli, like Angie Summers, was among the ranks of those who are widowed young. When her only child, Maria-Teresa, was five, Gianpaolo had flown home to his native Puglia for the funeral of an elderly aunt and had been killed when his taxi from the airport had ploughed into a container lorry at a complicated junction.

There had been a double funeral in the town of Matera that week.

Gianpaolo's family had not approved of his marrying an Englishwoman and settling so far from home, even if that woman was a good Catholic girl from Hartlepool. She had always been the outsider, sitting on rare visits, uncomfortable as they chatted in their rapid Italian and made no attempt to include her, although they all spoke English to some degree.

Her fault, perhaps, for not learning Italian, but she had never had a flair for languages (her French teacher had begged her to give the subject up at fourteen) and Giampi had been too impatient to teach her, just as his brief attempt at giving her driving lessons had ended in shouting matches.

The widow Antonelli could expect little help from her in-laws and it had been a struggle, albeit one she did not begrudge. It was not easy keeping shameful secrets, like the fact that Maria-Teresa got a council grant to pay for her school uniform and books so that she might attend the prestigious North Park Comprehensive.

The girl had refused point-blank to take the free school lunches she was offered and packed her own sandwiches from the age of eleven.

She, Bridget, worked at one of the supermarkets in Newbury and had clawed her way up by hard work and excessive politeness to customers and management from shelf-stacker, to check-out girl, to manager of the deli counter.

It had been worth it, to see Maria-Teresa flourish, with her ten good GCSEs and the prospect of university before her, though God knew how that would be paid for. They were close, with there being just the two of them, or they had been. Teenagers were difficult; everybody knew that.

Moody adolescents preferred their mates to their mums.

Bridget got off the bus at the nearest stop to the house, a five minute walk home, a bag of groceries in each hand. She dumped them on the doorstep as she fumbled for her keys, opened the door and called a cheery,

'I'm home, love.'

No reply. Maybe her daughter wasn't in yet, but the mortise lock on the front door was not engaged and both women were diligent about using it: they couldn't afford to be burgled and two women living alone had to be careful.

She stowed her food in the kitchen cupboards and fridge and went upstairs to see if Maria-Teresa was engrossed in a book, or, more likely, listening to music with her headphones on or talking to a friend over the Internet via the computer they had picked up secondhand.

The door to the smaller bedroom was closed and she rapped on it, then opened it without waiting for a reply. She respected her daughter's privacy but she was also aware of the warnings about unsuitable Internet sites. The thick curtains were drawn although it was not quite dark, with the clocks not going back till next weekend. Odd.

On the desk in the corner the computer screen glowed. Bridget hadn't got her glasses on but could make out the words I AM SORRY in capitals two inches high.

There was smaller writing underneath, two or three lines.

She switched on the light and walked round the bed for a better look, stubbing her toe against something big and soft. Her daughter lay on the floor, face up, her eyes open and vacant, her mouth agape. From her clenched fist had fallen a small scattering of white pills.

Bridget opened her mouth to scream and fainted.

'So what did the note say?' Greg asked.

'Not so much a note,' Striker said. 'A message left on her computer screen.'

'But anyone could write that,' Greg objected.

'Exactly. It said she was sorry, that she had given the drug to Lindsey and Erin at the club, and killed Nadia and that she got the drug from George Reddy.'

'Who?'

'He's the chemistry teacher at North Park, also her and Lindsey's personal tutor.'

'Is he now? Have we arrested him?'

'I've sent Barbara and Andy to pick him up for questioning. She'll enjoy that.'

'Oh?'

'Not a likeable man, our Mr Reddy.' Striker shrugged. 'But whether that makes him a drug pusher...'

'You have your doubts about this being suicide?'

'Let's see what the pathologist has to say.'

'I think I'll go.' Greg stood up and grabbed his jacket. 'You did Nadia's.'

'I don't mind.'

'No, let's share out the autopsies. I'd like you and Barbara to interview this Reddy, go in hard. Andy's time will be best spent looking at his computer.'

'You got it.' Striker took out his mobile and pressed a few buttons. 'We are spread pretty thin so I've had to leave a junior SOC officer in charge of the divers at the weir while the rest go to the Antonelli house.'

'The divers still haven't found anything?'

'Not yet. They're talking about having to drain it. Andy?' Striker issued clear instructions to the young constable and disconnected. 'It may be that the killer took the knife with him – or her.'

'We'll soon see if there's anything like it at the dead girl's place.'

'By the way,' Striker said, 'I got a call from Pat Armstrong at the lab about those pills Elizabeth bought at the club – common-or-garden Ecstasy, so this "David" is out of the frame.'

'You can let her have them back then,' Greg said.

'Yes. Very funny. By the way, Dr Armstrong said you'd deprived her of her assistant. What's that about?'

'Oh, that is so *unfair*,' Greg said.

'I know what you want but I can't oblige.' Dr Chubb scrubbed his hands vigorously at the sink in his mortuary.

'There's got to be some way to tell,' Greg objected.

'Whether this young woman swallowed the pills voluntarily? Hardly. I found no bruising, nothing to indicate that she was held down and force-fed Entry. I think I can rule out another accident, though, unlike with Lindsey and Erin, since she'd taken several tablets – a dose that would be guaranteed to kill a horse. Some of them were still undigested in her stomach. She died quickly.'

'When?'

'Some time this afternoon is my best guess.'

'We pretty much knew that already,' Greg snapped.

'Well pardon me for not making stuff up.'

'She's a small girl.' Greg looked back at the mortuary table where the slight figure of Maria-Teresa Antonelli lay under a sheet, her autopsy done.

'One metre fifty-five – five-foot one to you. Fifty kilos, which is the skinny end of normal.'

'A man or a strong woman could have subdued her easily.'

Dr Chubb spread his hands wide, pink from their scrubbing. 'What can I tell you? It's not as easy to force pills down people's gullets as you seem to think, and remember that they weren't dissolved into her drink, not judging by her stomach contents.'

'Dammit,' Greg muttered.

'I don't know what you're complaining about,' the pathologist said. 'I'd have thought you had enough murder victims, and rumour has it that this corpse confessed before topping herself, so why argue?'

'It doesn't smell right to me,' Greg said. 'In fact it stinks.'

He got into his car and drove to the Antonelli house. SOCO were still there and he stopped for a polite word with Martha Childs so that she wouldn't think he was avoiding her.

He found her in the dead girl's bedroom, a nice-looking woman in her early thirties with the shadows under her eyes of the permanently sleep-deprived. She favoured him with a wan smile and reported that they'd taken possession of yet another computer hard drive but had so far found no kitchen knives that matched the one they were looking for.

'Do you know where Mrs Antonelli is?' Greg asked.

'That poor woman.' Martha looked glum in sisterly solidarity. She had children of her own, though they were much younger, and was familiar with every mother's nightmare. She too was a single parent, although not as a result of widowhood, her husband having left her for a twenty-two-year-old air stewardess called Mandy, which was how she had ended up weeping in Greg's arms one embarrassing day. 'The people next door have offered her a bed for the night.'

'Thanks.' Greg touched her lightly on the arm and left her to her job. He tapped at the house next door since he had some urgent questions for the bereaved mother.

He found her curled up in front of a real fire, wearing her neighbour's grey fleece dressing gown over pyjamas. She was sipping a mug of hot chocolate. He gave her his condolences and asked what time Maria-Teresa would have got home from school that day.

'It's Tuesday,' Bridget Antonelli said after a pause, 'and she has a free period on Tuesday afternoons, last thing. Sometimes she stays at school; sometimes she comes home. Often, she goes into town, for a look round the shops, or she might have had a play rehearsal ... except I remember she said there wasn't one today.'

'What's the earliest she could have been home?' Greg asked gently.

'Two-thirty? Three?'

'And you found her at...?'

'Quarter past six,' she said hollowly. She looked at him beseechingly. 'She didn't commit suicide, did she? She wouldn't. It's so wrong – she knew that – a sin of despair.'

He didn't know what to answer her, so stuck to facts. 'We've taken her computer in for examination. I assume she had a mobile phone.'

'No, actually.' Bridget grimaced. 'I wanted to buy her one last Christmas but I could only afford secondhand and she said it was no good, that people at school made fun of you if you didn't have the latest gadgets.'

Greg wondered if 'make fun' was a euphemism for bully.

'She was always with her mates,' Mrs Antonelli went on, 'Gina, Celia, Lindsey. They were inseparable. She would use one of theirs if she needed to call me, tell me she'd be late or was sleeping over. Lindsey Brownlow's dad bought her a new mobile every six months, seemed like.' She paused. 'But she's dead too.'

Half the little group of friends dead in the space of four months, Greg thought. He murmured some anodyne words of comfort and thankfully took his leave.

Two-thirty till six-fifteen; it was an annoyingly long period. He rang the station and asked the duty inspector for troops to do house to house.

The Antonelli's lived in a terrace of small houses, two-up-two-down, on both sides of the road. Every house would have to be canvassed to see if anyone had seen Terry come home and, crucially, if she had been alone.

On a stationary train between Slough and Reading, the Freeman twins were arguing in whispers, which wasn't easy.

'I didn't know it was important,' Hannah hissed.

'Nadia was murdered by the weir, around midnight. These people who passed you came running from that direction at that time. It didn't occur to you that it might just be important?'

Hannah sucked sullenly on the cold dregs of the cappuccino she had picked up at Paddington, long gone. She had put on her oldest clothes for this excursion and not bothered with her hair and make-up, unlike her sister who never left the house without looking her best so that, if she happened to run into Jake Bloom, he would realise what he was missing since he'd humped her and dumped her.

Eventually, Hannah said, 'I was ... not myself that evening.'

'Out of your head!'

'I didn't say that!'

'It should have been me. I'd make a brilliant witness. It's so unfair.' Elizabeth raised her voice. 'Why does this bloody train not move?'

'Faulty signals,' the man sitting opposite drawled, without raising his eyes from his *Standard*. 'Happens all the time.'

'You think the girl I saw was one of the people who murdered Nadia?' Hannah whispered.

'We'll soon see what Dad thinks.'

265

CHAPTER TWENTY-ONE

When he got back to the station, Greg noticed that the keep-out light above interview room one was lit up and the custody sergeant confirmed that Striker and Barbara were in there with the chemistry teacher. He made his way up to the CID room where Emily hailed him.

'Sir, please, sir. I haven't found anything strange about Nadia's mobile calls.' He crossed over to her desk and she showed him a list of numbers, efficiently highlighted in different colours. 'Mostly to Nick's house and his mobile,' she reported, 'and to the big house where she was working. One a week to her parents in London.'

'Duty call?'

'I guess... Sir, I went round to Nick's at lunchtime, see if he was OK.' She added hastily, 'I was only gone half an hour.'

'That's all right, Emily. You're entitled to your lunch break. That was nice of you.'

'Only he wasn't in. A neighbour said she saw him driving off late morning, with a suitcase.'

'That sounds like good news. How old are you Emily?'

'Twenty-three.'

So young, he thought. He worried sometimes about how they let youngsters loose on the streets, forgetting that he had been pounding a beat himself from the age of eighteen. 'How long have you had your mobile phone?'

'This one? Four, five months.'

'So you change it often.'

She looked faintly embarrassed. 'Maybe once a year. You know how it is.'

'And what do you do with the old ones.'

'You can recycle them, give them to charity. Some of them even end up in the third world.'

'Suppose you had a mate who couldn't afford a mobile.' Emily's face clouded, as if this was too great an effort of the imagination. 'Would you give her your old one?'

'I suppose,' she said doubtfully. 'It might look a bit...'

'Patronising? Lady Bountiful?'

'Yeah, but if she really needed it – why not?'

'OK. I need you to check calls on a landline.' He gave her the Antonellis' address. 'Get the number from British Telecom.'

'How far should I go back, sir?' Emily was already reaching for the phone.

'Three months should be enough. No, wait. Make it five. Take it back to before Lindsey died.'

His own mobile rang and he stepped away to take the call.

'You have? That's brilliant. Yes, I want to see it now.'

He disconnected. 'The divers have finally recovered the knife from the canal.'

'The one that stabbed Nadia?'

'Sounds like it.'

'Thank God!' Elizabeth gathered up her black leather rucksack. 'I thought we were never going to get here. If only I'd passed my driving test...'

'Yes, if only you hadn't skidded into that skip doing your emergency stop.'

The other passengers who had alighted at Newbury hurried away into the darkness, later than they had expected and eager for their supper. Soon only Elizabeth and Hannah were left on the station platform.

'Which way is the police station?' Hannah asked after a pause.

'...I have no idea.'

A noise behind them caught their attention. They saw two identical young men descending from the train, yawning and stretching as though they had both been asleep. As if it had only been waiting for them, the train promptly beeped, closed its doors and glided off.

'It's Will and Rick,' Hannah said. She raised her voice. 'Will! Over here.'

'Huh?' He looked at her without recognition. 'Yeah. Um. It's... Don't tell me.'

'Hannah.'

'Hannah. Right. Yeah... Are you sure?'

'Never mind that,' Elizabeth said impatiently. 'We want you to take us to the police station.'

Hannah took a certain quiet satisfaction in seeing their startled expressions.

George Reddy had lost the complacent look Barbara had observed on first meeting him. He looked younger and nervous, but that didn't prove anything; people were always nervous when the police came and told them they had to come down to the station for questioning about a suspicious death.

He had accepted the presence of the duty solicitor and Adrian Flint was sitting beside him, listening with keen interest. He was noted for his gaudy ties – his substitute for a personality – and today sported yellow frogs. Barbara also caught a glimpse of scarlet braces every time he moved.

No doubt Reddy found his presence reassuring but she doubted he'd be much practical help. It was a little unfair, when you came to think about it, that there were always two police officers and only one witness. Reddy's small eyes darted back and forth between them as they questioned him, as if watching a miniature tennis match.

'So,' Striker was saying, 'you deny all knowledge of this drug: Entry.'

'I've told you already. I've never even heard of it. You've got it on there.' Reddy pointed at the twin tape deck.

'Never heard of it?' Striker queried. 'Don't you watch the local news bulletins?'

'Well, yeah. Sometimes.'

'But you didn't see the recent item about how Lindsey Brownlow had died from this new drug.'

Reddy shifted uncomfortably on his hard chair. 'That was the first I'd heard of it.'

'Even with Lindsey being your favourite pupil,' Barbara said.

'I never said that!' Reddy looked at Flint for help. 'She was an excellent chemist, guaranteed an A, that was all I said.' He added self-righteously, 'I don't have favourites.'

'So why would Maria-Teresa Antonelli finger you as the maker and distributor of the drug?' Barbara went on.

'Kids!' He almost spat the word out. 'They're monsters. Little bundles of egoism and cruelty.'

'Sounds to me like you're in the wrong job,' Striker said.

'Tell me about it! I've been teaching for eight years and I dream daily of packing it in, doing something else, and I'm at a "good" school, where the kids don't actually knife the teachers or set fire to the staff room.'

'So let me get this straight,' Striker said, 'you're suggesting that Maria-Teresa, even as she prepared to kill herself, thought it would be a laugh to get you into trouble.'

'It wouldn't surprise me,' Reddy said sourly, 'although...'

'Yes?'

'It would surprise me from Maria-Teresa, actually. Some of the others, sure, but she never struck me as a spiteful kid. Not that I knew her that well.'

'She wasn't in your chemistry set?' Barbara asked.

'No, she was in the Arts Sixth: English, drama, history.' He flapped a dismissive hand. 'That sort of thing.'

'Where were you this afternoon?' Barbara asked.

'At school, of course, teaching. I have a full schedule on Tuesday afternoons.'

'But you were done at – what? – three-thirty?'

'Yes, but I supervised a detention until four-thirty, then I had a meeting with the head–'

'About what?'

'She meets the sixth-form tutors every week. Routine. There were four of us there. Then I went straight home.'

'Arriving when?'

'Quarter to six?'

Which gave him precious little time to nip

271

out and murder Maria-Teresa before her mother came home half an hour later and found her, Striker thought. It sounded as if Reddy's alibis were sound, but there was still the small matter of who was manufacturing and distributing the drug.

'You live alone?' he asked.

'Yes.'

There was a tap on the door of the interview room and Andy Whittaker came in without waiting for a reply. 'A moment, sir,' he said to Striker.

He got up. 'DCI Freeman leaves the room at seven-forty-five. Interview suspended.' He switched off the tapes and followed Andy out into the corridor.

'I've been looking at the websites accessed from the computer in Reddy's office,' Andy said. He proffered a printout. 'Take a look at this.'

Freeman's face was wreathed in smiles as he said, 'Good job, Andy.'

Greg sat looking at the knife in its evidence bag, still wet from the murky waters of the canal, a frond of weed wrapped round the blade. It matched the description Dr Chubb had given of the weapon – not the *murder* weapon, he reminded himself, since Nadia had drowned.

You could buy a knife like this in any department store. He had one very similar at home, which he used for chopping carrots. It had become commonplace in the last few years for even quite respectable youngsters to carry knives with them, either for use or bravado.

Minors were no longer able to buy them, but it was the work of a moment to nick something like this from their parents' kitchen drawer. Such things were easily misplaced and the parent would simply buy another.

Going armed was 'cool' and, with handguns illegal in Britain and available only to serious criminals, armed meant knives. Some 'cool' person at the Kismet Klub had thought nothing of jabbing this object between Nadia's ribs before shoving her in the weir.

'Where was it found?' he asked the young SOC officer whose name, he vaguely remembered, was Jenny.

'At the bottom of the weir, sir.'

That left little doubt. He asked, 'Prints?'

'Two partials on the handle but not even possible matches on the database.'

So the assailant had no criminal record. He handed the bag back. 'Take it down to the evidence room, will you, um, Jenny?'

'Janie, sir. Yes, sir.'

'So Reddy has been accessing the website with the recipe for Entry,' Greg said.

'Not necessarily.' Striker folded his arms across his chest and pulled a dissatisfied face. 'The computer sits in his office next door to the chemistry lab and he allows his sixth-form chemistry students free access to it.'

'How convenient. So he denies everything?'

'Everything. He'd never heard of Entry till he saw Chaucer talking about it on TV, certainly never made any, let alone handed it out to teenage girls. He's never been to the Kismet Klub. Oh, and he's going to sue us for wrongful arrest.'

'Was he actually under arrest?'

Striker grinned. 'No, he was helping us voluntarily with our inquiries. When I reminded him of that, he left. I didn't see my way to arresting him and keeping him in overnight, not at this stage. Any joy at Maria-Teresa's house?'

'Nothing so far. Most of the people in the street were out at work. Of those who were home during the afternoon, none admits to seeing the poor girl come home or to seeing anyone else enter or leave the house.'

'Andy lifted some fingerprints off her computer before he started examining its inner workings,' Striker said. 'Two sets, one only partial. One was Maria-Teresa herself, naturally enough. I've sent him round to take the mother's prints, see if they match the second set. If not...'

'So does all this leave us any further forward?' Greg said, half rhetorically. 'We have a print on the knife that we can match to any possible suspect and maybe one on the computer.'

'Both partial.'

'Do we have Reddy's prints?'

'Yes. I'll check them.'

'Is he young enough to pass unnoticed at the club?'

'He's barely thirty, so yes.'

Greg sighed and rubbed his eyes. 'I just had word that both inquests are opening at the town hall tomorrow.'

'Do you want me to go?'

'No, I will. It's just a formality and I'm sure we can make better use of your time.'

'Fine. I trust we haven't had any more unwelcome visits from Nick?'

'No. He seems to have seen sense and gone home to Mum. Clearly the talk I had with him got through to him.'

The phone on Barbara's desk rang and she answered it. 'Yes. He's here... OK, I'll tell him.'

She hung up and turned to Striker. 'Your daughters are downstairs in reception, sir.'

'What in the name of bloody hell–?'

'They say it's important.'

'Can't Elizabeth stay with me?' Hannah

275

looked round Greg's office in dismay and appealed to her father.

'Was Elizabeth with you at the time?'

'No.'

'Then I want to hear what you have to say, sweetie, in your own words.'

Elizabeth had also been reluctant to abandon her sister but Striker had been adamant. He knew the power his younger daughter exercised over her twin.

'I was in the park,' Hannah began slowly, 'near the club.'

'Alone?' Striker could not resist asking.

'No-o. I'd been dancing with this boy, Will, and we went out for some air.' She hurried on before her father could ask more questions. 'Anyway, it must have been about midnight and I was cold, so after a few minutes I got up and walked about a bit. Then I heard some people running towards me. I don't think they saw me, at first, but one of them jostled me and swore at me.'

'They were running from the direction of the canal?' Greg asked.

'Definitely.'

'And you saw this man's face?'

'Like this.' She held up her hand in front of her face. 'Only it was a girl, not a man.'

'How many people altogether?' Striker asked.

'I thought four, but it might have been more.'

'So this Will,' Greg said, 'did he see them too?'

'No.'

'Why not?'

'He was…' This was why she had wanted her sister with her. Elizabeth had promised that their father needn't find out about the drugs but now, in her absence, Hannah knew that it was only a matter of time before she broke down and told him everything.

So she might as well just do it now. 'He was pretty out of it. He'd taken a pill.'

'What sort of pill?' Striker said sharply.

'I think it was Ecstasy, only I don't know because I'd never seen an Ecstasy tablet.' She turned beseeching eyes up to him, willing him to believe her.

'And did you take one too?' he asked gently. 'Hannah – tell me the truth.'

'Yes,' she whimpered, 'but it didn't have any effect, or only to make me a bit woozy.'

The two men were silent for a moment then Striker said, 'All right. Thank you for being honest with me. We'll talk about it another time. Now, this girl, can you describe her?'

Hannah thought long and hard. 'She was about my height, medium build, bit younger than me, maybe. White. I think her hair was light brown…'

'Long, short?'

'Middle. And she had a fringe.'

'Would you be able to work with a police artist to do a sketch?' Striker asked.

'Maybe.'

Greg looked at the new watch he'd bought that morning. 'I doubt if we can get anyone at this time of night. First thing in the morning will have to do. I assume you can keep Hannah overnight, Mr Freeman?'

'Of course. Does your mum know where you are?'

Hannah shook her head. 'She was at work when Elizabeth said we had to come here.'

Striker groaned. 'So I'm going to be Mr Popular again! I'll give her a ring.'

As he walked Hannah back downstairs she burst out, 'I'm sorry it took me so long to come forward. I didn't realise it was important. If only it had been Elizabeth–'

'Sweetie–'

'She's always so much better at everything than I am.'

'Heh!' He stopped and seized her by the shoulders, kissing her on her hair. 'You're the first-born twin. Never forget that. You'll always be twenty-two minutes older. That's why she has to try so much harder. And did we give her a palindromic name?'

'...No.'

'Well, there you are then. And think how impressed Mum and Grandma Esther will be when they hear that you helped solve a murder.' Hannah started to protest. 'The heavily edited version, naturally.'

'Ah!'

'And then you can stop trying to get their attention by threatening to join Jews For Jesus.'

'...I was never really serious about that.'

'I know, sweetie. I know.'

CHAPTER TWENTY-TWO

As he let himself into the town hall by the side door the following morning, Greg noticed two teenage girls sitting on a bench outside the inquest room, holding hands. He recognised them from the video tape of the Kismet Klub: Celia Wing and Gina Trethowan.

They looked woebegone, as well they might.

He strolled over and introduced himself. They looked up at him fearfully and glanced at each other.

'I'm very sorry for the loss of your friend,' he said. 'Could I just ask you a quick question?' He went on without waiting for an answer. 'Mrs Antonelli says that Maria-Teresa didn't own a mobile phone.'

'Oh, yeah, she did,' Gina burst out, then fell abruptly silent.

'Go on,' Greg said. When neither girl spoke, he said, 'Did Lindsey give it to her?'

'Yes.' It was Gina who answered once more. 'Her dad gave her a new one in April and she gave the old one to Terry.'

'That was nice of her.'

'Yeah. Terry was really pleased, 'cause it

was a good one, with a camera and everything.'

'But she didn't tell her mum.'

'Mrs Antonelli's proud,' Gina said. 'Doesn't like anything that smacks of charity.'

'It was pay-as-you-go, I suppose?'

'Yeah,' Gina said. 'Lindsey's was on a contract, which her dad paid every month, but when Terry took it over, she used to buy top-up vouchers.'

'I need her number,' Greg said. As they hesitated, he added, 'I'm sure you both have it in the address books of your own phones, so who's going to give it to me?'

Gina sighed and took out a slimline phone; she pressed a few buttons and read out a number in a dull voice. Greg made a note of it and thanked her.

'Has either of you anything she wants to tell me?' he asked.

'No,' Celia said quickly.

'Like what?' Gina said, her eyes wide.

'You both seem very nervous.'

'We're upset,' Celia snapped. 'Our mate is dead. *Two* of our mates are dead.'

Yes, Greg thought, and either you know more about it than you're letting on, or one of you may be next. 'Was Maria-Teresa friendly with Mr Reddy?' he asked.

They looked surprised. 'She hardly knew him,' Celia said.

'None of the students is *friendly* with him,'

Gina added.

'Not even Lindsey, his star pupil?'

'Not since he put his hand on her bum one day,' Gina said. 'Accidentally on purpose. Creep.'

'What about Mr Dixon?' Greg said, remembering that the dead girl had been at his flat when Striker and Barbara had called on him. 'Was Terry close to him?'

They shrugged. 'She liked him,' Celia said. 'We all like him – his sister's a famous actress, which is pretty cool. But there was no funny business, if that's what you mean.'

He gave each girl one of his cards and said, 'Call me if you change your minds about wanting to talk to me.'

They pocketed the cards wordlessly.

If Maria-Teresa had a mobile phone, why, he wondered, as he turned away to greet Dr Derek Walpole, the West Berkshire Coroner, had SOCO not found it at the Antonelli house?

Both inquests were opened and immediately adjourned. Glancing round, Greg could see nobody from Nadia's family and no Mrs Antonelli. He made his way slowly back to the police station, turning the case over in his mind.

He couldn't help thinking that Lindsey was the key, especially now that one of her best friends had committed suicide, if that's what it was. Nadia had probably just been in the wrong place at the wrong time.

Erin Moss. Where did she fit in?

And why did this case make the hairs on the back of his neck stand up? Why did he think that something peculiarly nasty was going on in the quiet market town of Newbury?

At the station, he gave Maria-Teresa's mobile number to Emily, saying, 'More glamorous CID work'.

'I don't mind, sir.'

He knew from his own days as a DC how time-consuming and tedious it all was, not that they'd had mobile phones in those days, and it had sometimes taken weeks for the GPO, as it had then been, to come up with a list of calls made by a landline. Trouble was, it was so often this sort of spade work that broke a case.

'I'm not sure how much help this is going be.' Striker handed Greg a digital printout from their photofit software. He found himself looking at a girl in her mid- to late teens with pale brown hair falling to her shoulders.

It could have fitted many young woman.

'Hannah didn't see the eye colour, of course,' Striker said, 'as it was dark. She's done her best, poor love, but her visual memory isn't good.'

'OK.'

'But she thinks she'd know the girl if she saw her again.'

It flashed through Greg's mind to wonder if Gina and Celia were still around, but Celia could not really be described as white and Gina was much shorter than Hannah, as, of course, was poor Maria-Teresa. Celia and Gina both wore their hair shorter than this, too, and had done on the CCTV.

'I've sent the girls home,' Striker added. 'If we find ourselves a suspect, Hannah can always come back.'

'Maria-Teresa didn't make many calls,' Emily reported, 'and most of them were quite short.'

'Saving money,' Greg said.

'I've found calls to Celia, Gina and Lindsey, usually to their mobiles, occasionally at home. Calls to her own home, of course. There's one number that crops up a few times, though, a landline.'

Emily's slim finger with its short but neat nail tapped on the sheet of paper.

'Newbury phone number,' Greg commented. It looked familiar but he couldn't think from where.

'It's a house in Stroud Green,' Emily said. 'Westwood Road. It's registered to a—'

'Harry Stratton,' Greg supplied.

'Well, a Mrs Prudence Stratton,' she said in surprise. 'Do you know them?'

'Oh, yes,' Greg said. 'Before your time. I forgot.'

He took out his mobile phone and called Striker's number. 'Mr Freeman, how long ago did your daughters set off? Do you think you can stop them before they board the train?'

If Prue Stratton had not looked pleased to see him at her place of work, she was about to be a lot less pleased.

'This is DC Whittaker,' he said, 'and PC Foster. You remember Sergeant Barbara Carey?'

'What do you want, Gregory?'

'I'd like to speak to Ruth, please.'

'About what?'

'I have a warrant.' Greg handed her a copy.

'A search warrant?' she echoed incredulously, the document hanging limp in her hand. 'For here?'

'Is Ruth at home please, Prue?'

'Yes, she's here.' Prue Stratton stepped away from the front door to let them in.

'If you could call her,' Greg said, 'and I'll need you to stay with her as she's not seventeen yet, is she?'

'Not until next autumn.' Prue raised her voice and called up the stairs. 'Ruth?'

After a few seconds, a surly voice responded. 'What?'

'Could you come down, please? Now.'

A moment passed before the girl appeared at the top of the stairs, emerging from a door to the left. She was still wearing the unisex uniform of North Park School: black trousers with a burgundy sweatshirt. She peered down at them and Greg saw a strange look pass over her face.

'Mr Summers,' she said evenly. 'We must stop meeting like this.'

'Could you come down, please, Ruth.'

She descended the stairs slowly, holding onto the handrail. When she reached the bottom Andy and Emily went up and headed for her bedroom. She turned to look after them, her expression inscrutable.

'Shall we go into the dining room?' Greg gestured to the door to the room which he knew of old – an invitation for Sunday lunch in the distant past when Harry Stratton had still been his DCI.

Ruth walked into the room with Prue behind her. Both women drew up chairs at the mahogany dining table, whose dusty surface spoke of long disuse. Barbara closed the door behind them and Greg sat down opposite.

'I'd like to take your prints, Ruth,' he said. 'Sergeant Carey has the pad. Bit messy, I'm afraid.'

Barbara took an ink pad out of the briefcase she was carrying and placed it on

286

the table in front of the girl.

'Her fingerprints!' Prue said. 'What exactly is my daughter being accused of?'

'Of complicity in the deaths of Lindsey Brownlow, Erin Moss, Nadia Polycarpou and Maria-Teresa Antonelli,' Greg said with deliberate brutality, watching the girl's face as he spoke. He cautioned her.

She did not react.

'This is preposterous,' Prue said. 'I've never heard of Erin Moss or these other women with foreign names. Lindsey Brownlow? Wasn't she that silly girl who took a drug overdose at that nightclub in the summer? Ruth doesn't know her.'

'I asked you to sit in as Ruth's responsible adult,' Greg said coldly, 'that doesn't mean you answer on her behalf. Lindsey Brownlow and Maria-Teresa Antonelli were both pupils at North Park School.'

'If you could let me have your right hand, please, Ruth.' Barbara took the girl's hand and spread-eagled it on the pad.

'But the Brownlow girl was a sixth-former,' Prue said, taking no notice of his warning. 'I remember it from the local news. Ruth didn't know her; she's only in year eleven.'

'But you did know her, didn't you, Ruth?' Greg said, as Barbara pressed each digit in turn onto the white paper, rolling them to take a full print.

'You were doing costume for the school

play,' Barbara commented, 'and Lindsey was in it, until her death.'

The girl ignored Barbara and looked at Greg steadily. 'Never said I didn't. In fact, I told you at the Kismet Klub last Friday that I knew her slightly. Your memory's going, Mr Summers.'

'The game's up, Ruth. We have a thumb print on the handle of the knife and one on Terry's computer.' He nodded at the finger-print kit, which Barbara was stowing carefully away. 'I think we both know that we shall find a match.'

'Knife?' Prue echoed, her voice fading.

'A kitchen knife, Mrs Stratton. The sort you use to prepare vegetables. I don't suppose you've mislaid anything like that from your own kitchen lately, by any chance?'

Her stunned silence was sufficient confirmation.

'Are they good prints, Mr Summers?' There was an almost teasing note in Ruth's voice, as if she was enjoying the game. 'I'm a copper's daughter, you know, or was till you chucked him off the force for a trivial mistake—'

A 'trivial mistake' that had driven a fundamentally decent man to take his own life, Greg thought.

'Do you think I don't know how much police work is bluff?'

'I think we'll continue this conversation

288

down at the station,' Greg said.

'Am I under arrest?' Ruth asked calmly.

'If you want to be.'

'Dad always said that it was better to be arrested – start the clock ticking.'

'So be it.'

Andy put his head round the door at that moment and held up a mobile phone in an evidence bag. 'Maria-Teresa's phone,' he said.

'Where did you find it?'

'Stuffed under her mattress.'

'She lent it to me a couple of weeks ago,' Ruth said.

'That was kind of her,' Greg said, 'given that you apparently hardly knew her or her friends.'

'I forgot to give it back.'

'And hiding it under the mattress would remind you?'

'Ever heard the fairy tale of the princess and the pea?' Greg had a very strong urge to slap her, see if that could put a dent in her façade.

'Mrs Stratton,' he said. 'I'd like to take a look at your kitchen knives, if I may. While I'm doing that, I suggest you get coats for yourself and Ruth. It's cold out.'

Ten minutes later Greg and Barbara escorted Ruth Stratton and her mother out of the house, leaving Andy and Emily to continue their search. As they walked down the front path, Ruth pulled on the black woollen coat her mother had fetched for her and clutched its fur-trimmed hood tight around her neck.

Greg had left a police van parked a few yards along the road and shepherded Ruth towards it.

Directly across from the van, Striker Freeman sat at the wheel of his car, with Hannah in the passenger seat.

'Well, darling?' he said, as Greg stopped under a streetlamp with his charge.

'Yes,' she answered without hesitation. 'That's her. That's the girl I saw running away from the scene of the murder.'

'But will you be able to pick her out from a line-up – half a dozen girls the same age and shape?'

Hannah suddenly had a confidence she had never possessed in her life. 'Yeah. I'll know her.'

He kissed her brow. 'That's my best girl.'

In the van, Greg switched his mobile back on and it promptly rang to tell him he had a message. He recognised the voice of Inspector Nelson before he identified himself.

'Mr Summers, it's Martin Nelson here. Can you ring me as soon as you get this. Only we've finally dug up a witness from our house to house in the dead girl's street.'

Greg let the message finish and, without

taking his eyes off Ruth, spoke as if he was having a conversation.

'You've got a witness, you say, Inspector, who saw someone with Maria-Teresa yesterday evening? A good description? That's excellent news.' He disconnected and put the phone away in his pocket.

Sitting across from him, Ruth pulled her fur tighter and kept her eyes fixed on the floor.

Greg sought Inspector Nelson out as soon as he reached the station, leaving Barbara to process Ruth's arrest and settle both Strattons into an interview room.

He heard Prue say, 'Shouldn't we have a solicitor?'

'We can arrange that, naturally,' Barbara said.

'I can ring Michael Faulkner. I'm sure he would help.'

'I don't need a lawyer,' Ruth growled, 'and especially not that old fart.'

Martin Nelson got to his feet as soon as he saw Greg. 'You got my message, sir?'

'Didn't your shift end some time ago?' Greg asked.

'Yeah. Got the mother-in-law staying at the moment.' He rolled his eyes. 'No rush to get home.'

'Right!' Presumably he'd be seeing a lot more of his mother-in-law as his wife's condition deteriorated. Her visit also explained why he had been free to volunteer his services on Friday night. 'So you've found me a witness? I thought nobody had seen anything.'

'None of the residents had,' Nelson confirmed, 'but the old lady at number eighteen has just come out of hospital after a hip operation and she gets daily visits from the district nurse – make sure she's OK and change her dressing. Anyway, today she was telling the nurse about the excitement of having the police call round and it turns out this woman saw someone leaving Maria-Teresa's house yesterday.'

'Fantastic!'

'The street was quite busy so she'd left her car some way from number eighteen, right outside the Antonellis. She was just putting her case in the boot when a girl came out of the house and rushed past her. Almost running, she reckons.'

'Can she describe her?'

Nelson grimaced. 'Not so much, just general height and build. The girl was wearing a heavy coat with a hood, which she had up so it pretty well hid her face, which Nurse Taylor thought was odd as it wasn't raining and it wasn't windy.'

'Was the hood trimmed with fur, by any chance?'

'Yeah. You know who it was?'

'Oh, I know. What time was this?'

'About half-five.' He handed Greg a sheaf of paper. 'Here's Mrs Taylor's statement.'

'Thanks. Great job … Martin.'

CHAPTER TWENTY-THREE

'Who made the drug, Ruth?' Greg asked. 'Was it you?'

'It was Lindsey and, OK, I knew her, better than I let on.' Her voice was without emotion as the twin interview tapes wound steadily.

'You were one of the group of friends, along with Terry, Celia and Gina.' She nodded. 'Even though you were a year below. You told me at the nightclub last Friday that sixth-formers didn't bother with the likes of you.'

'And since when do you believe everything everybody tells you?' she asked with a sneer. 'Not much of a copper, are you?'

'Oh, I do all right. We're here, aren't we?'

'I became part of their gang when we met doing the school play last year. I was costume and Celia was doing props and the others were all in it.'

'And you were with them the night Lindsey died.'

'Lindsey had nobody but herself to blame for her death,' Ruth said. 'She used to pop Es like they were going out of fashion. Then she heard about this new drug from America and decided they really were out of fashion. She looked up the recipe on old Reddy's computer one lunchtime and made some. Then she had us all take it that night in June.'

'Didn't she know it could be fatal?' Greg asked.

'Of course she did!' Ruth said scornfully. 'That was the whole point.'

'A game of chicken?' Barbara said.

'It could have been any one of us who died that night.'

Prue let out an exclamation of horror and stared at her daughter as if seeing her for the first time. Her eyes bulged with tears and she rummaged in her pockets for a tissue.

'And Erin Moss?' Greg said.

'Never heard of her.'

'OK. If you won't tell me what happened, then shall I tell you? After Lindsey died, the rest of you carried on playing chicken with the drug, only nobody reacted to it the way Lindsey had, so you decided you needed a few more people for your game. You started to dish them out at the club – no, you *sold* them to make a bit of extra cash. Erin Moss didn't do drugs and she told you off for trying to push them so you slipped one into her drink, maybe a double dose.'

'You spin a good tale, Mr Summers,' Ruth said.

'And you were in so deep then, all four of

you. As you'd conspired to kill a young woman, so you conspired to keep silent, because if any of you spoke out you would all be in big trouble. You kept on selling the drug – nice little earner.'

'One of you tried to sell some to Nadia at the club on Friday night,' Barbara put in. 'She told me some kid tried to sell her tablets in the loo, but she hadn't even taken enough notice to give me a decent description. Was that you?'

'No comment.'

'Then she stumbled on the four of you at the weir later that night, when she was on her way home,' Greg added. 'Were you afraid she would tell on you. Is that it?'

'No comment.'

'You stabbed Nadia Polycarpou with a knife you'd taken from your mother's kitchen and pushed her into the weir. Then the four of you ran away across Victoria Park, but you, Ruth, doubled back later and put in an appearance at the club so it would look as if you'd never left. You came over deliberately to speak to me so I'd remember you being there.'

'No comment.'

'But Maria-Teresa was getting cold feet, wasn't she?' Greg went on. 'Celia and Gina too, but Terry worst of all. Nadia's death was the last straw for her, because she'd perhaps been able to convince herself that

Lindsey and Erin dying wasn't her fault, but this was deliberate murder. Was she talking of going to the police? Was that it? Was that why you gave her an overdose of pills and made it look like suicide?'

'Don't be absurd. I wasn't even there.'

Greg turned over the papers he had face down on the table in front of him. 'That's interesting, because I have a statement here from the district nurse who was visiting a patient in Maria-Teresa's street at five-thirty yesterday evening, about three-quarters of an hour before Mrs Antonelli found the body. She saw you leave the house.'

'Saw *me*, did she?' Ruth leant across and tapped her fingers on the statement, her nails bitten so short as to make no sound. 'Gives a good description of me, does she?'

'Actually no, since, as you are well aware, you were wearing your hood to hide your face. The same fur-trimmed hood you put on this evening. The nurse noticed it especially. Silly really, because if you hadn't taken so much care to hide your identity, she might not have taken any notice of you, might not have connected you to the house-to-house inquiries when her patient told her about them today.'

'Oh, Ruthie,' Prue whimpered.

'Shut up! Does she have to stay with me, only she's doing my head in?'

'Unless you'd prefer a social worker.'

Ruth was silent for a moment, then she sighed. 'It *was* suicide. OK? She topped herself because she was weak and feeble and, OK, I was there, and, OK, I wrote the note on the computer, but that's *all*.'

'So you admit you were there?'

'I just said so, didn't I? She had a free period and she persuaded me to bunk off school and come and do some Entry with her. I had no idea what she was planning. We each took one tab, then I went to the bathroom. She must have taken a shitload more while I was in there.'

'Very implausible. And why implicate Mr Reddy?'

'I thought it'd be a laugh. He's an old perv. And I knew you'd find the website Lindsey used on his computer history.'

'If you wrote the note, then you must have known Maria-Teresa was dying. Why didn't you phone for an ambulance?'

'I told you, I'd taken a tab myself. I was well out of it. By the time I sobered up she was dead, so I wrote the note and legged it. That's no offence in this country. You can't pin any of those deaths on me. Now you can charge me or release me.'

'Actually,' Greg said, 'I don't have to do either, or not for several hours. I'm keeping you in the cells – overnight, if necessary – while I make further inquiries. Wait here.'

He went out to talk to the custody officer

who was, once again, Dick Maybey. The old sergeant looked at him in consternation. 'That's never Harry Stratton's little lass?'

'Not so little any more.'

'What's the charge?'

'Probably murder.'

He gasped and raised no objection to her further detention.

Since Andy was still at the Stratton's house, Greg sent Striker with a uniformed constable to pick up Gina Trethowan while Barbara and Emily brought in Celia Wing, then he had Emily accompany him as he interviewed Gina while Barbara and Striker took Celia.

Two sets of anxious parents arrived not far behind their daughters, accompanied, in the case of the Wings, by their solicitor, a man with a designer suit and a loud and arrogant voice.

'Perfect,' Barbara murmured to Striker as the lawyer demanded to confer in private with his client. 'That's Barrington Chitty. He acts for all the rich people in town and what he knows about criminal law would fit on the head of a pin.'

'My favourite type of brief,' Striker said.

Since he didn't have to wait for a solicitor, Greg got started first. Gina Trethowan looked very young, sitting alone and pale across the table from him and Emily, but she was seventeen and he had refused all requests from the Trethowans to be allowed into the interview room with her.

He hardened his heart against her. He would not be deflected by her youth and obvious fear. All the victims had been young and afraid too and if she wasn't the primary killer, she was still in it up to her neck.

'Gina,' he began. 'I have Ruth Stratton in custody in this station, arrested on suspicion of murder.'

She gasped.

'I know pretty much everything,' Greg went on. 'I know that you and your friends made the drug after finding the recipe using the computer in the school chemistry lab—'

'Lindsey,' Gina gabbled. 'Lindsey made the drug.'

'Lindsey made the drug,' Celia told Striker and Barbara about twenty minutes later. 'She said she'd heard about a new high, more fun than Ecstasy. I had no idea it was dangerous.'

'I know that you were playing a game of chicken the night she died,' Greg said. 'You all took the new drug and any one of you might have died that night. It just happened to be Lindsey.'

'She was getting cold feet,' Gina said. 'We

300

all were. But Ruth egged us on. She called us cowards.'

'We know that one of you slipped a tab of Entry into Erin Moss's drink when she refused to buy one from you,' Barbara said. 'Erin hated drugs. Did she give you a lecture about it?'

'I didn't want to do that,' Gina exclaimed. 'It was Ruth's idea.'
   'So she put the drug into Erin's drink?'
   '...No.'

'It was Terry who did that,' Celia said. 'Slipped it into her vodka and coke where she wouldn't taste it.'
   'Maria-Teresa?' Striker asked. Celia nodded. 'You're saying that she was responsible for the death of Erin Moss?'
   'She was always the most timid,' the girl explained, 'and Ruth goaded her into doing it, teach the snooty cow a lesson – lecturing us about the dangers of drugs.'

'We know that one of you tried to sell Entry to Nadia Polycarpou in the Ladies at the Kismet Klub on Friday night,' Greg said. 'Was that you?'
   'That would have been Ruth,' Gina insisted.

'It was Ruth,' Celia said.

'And then you were all gathered together by the weir around midnight,' Barbara said, 'to what – divvy up the spoils? Nadia saw you and came up to speak to you. What did she say that made you think you had to kill her?'

Celia glanced at Chitty who said, 'My client has no comment to make to that ridiculous allegation.'

'Was she threatening to call the police?' Striker asked. 'Was that why you stabbed her and pushed her into the water?'

'That was nothing to do with me!' Celia said in panic.

'It was Ruth,' Gina said. 'I had no idea she was going to do anything like that. The woman recognised Ruth from the toilets and came over to talk to her. She was so pissed, I don't suppose she'd have remembered anything in the morning, but Ruth just rushed at her, like a mad woman, and suddenly she was in the weir. I yelled at her, asked what the hell she thought she was doing, but she ran away, across the park, so we all ran after her.'

'I had no idea she carried a knife,' Celia said. 'I figured that the woman would pull herself out of the weir. It's not like it's that deep and everyone can swim, right? I didn't

302

know till the next day that she'd been stabbed and when I rang Ruth she said that it wasn't true, that it was just the sort of thing the police made up so they could weed out false confessions. She knew stuff like that because her father was a copper. But Terry started to freak.'

'We were all pretty freaked out,' Gina said, 'but Terry was the worst. She was going to pieces and she'd started talking about going to the police.'

'So that's when you decided she must die,' Greg said.

'I don't know anything about that! I swear to God.'

'I don't know what happened to Terry. She was my best friend and now she's de-de-dead.' Celia began to cry, angry, frightened tears pouring down her alabaster cheeks. Barrington Chitty said, 'I think that's quite enough, Chief Inspector.'

'Yes,' Striker said. 'I think it probably is.'

CHAPTER TWENTY-FOUR

'Your "friends" gave you up, Ruth,' Greg said. 'Which was very sensible of them. As it is, they may be charged as accessories after the fact. I'll leave that up to the CPS. But you certainly are going to be charged – with the wilful murder of Nadia Polycarpou for starters, although further charges may follow.'

She stared at him, her lips thin and her eyes cold. 'I dunno why you're making all this fuss. They've been saved a lifetime of disappointment.'

'We're not going to get her for murdering Maria-Teresa,' Greg said grimly. 'I'm morally certain that she did but there's just not enough evidence. We'll have to settle for nailing her for Nadia's death. We have the knife, missing from her mother's kitchen, and her partial print on it. We have Hannah to place her at the scene and we have the evidence of her erstwhile friends. I trust that'll be enough for the CPS.'

'Thank goodness she panicked and threw the knife in the weir,' Striker said. 'If she'd taken it home, washed it and put it back in the kitchen drawer, we might be struggling now.'

'Do you believe Gina and Celia when they say that Lindsey made the drug?' Barbara asked.

'Given that she was North Park's star chemistry student,' Greg said, 'I suppose I do.'

'They told the same story without collusion,' Striker added.

Greg had been right in thinking that these crimes were peculiarly horrible. He had seen a girl, one he had known since she was nine years old, set out on a killing spree with the calm of any psychopath.

As a minor, Ruth would probably be out within ten years. Of what future horrors would she be capable?

'I would have liked to be able to tell Mrs Antonelli that her daughter didn't commit suicide,' he said. 'She's a Catholic and it's important to her.'

'I hope you're not blaming yourself,' Barbara said.

'I'm trying not to, but I'm not having much luck so far.'

'There was no way Harry Stratton could have stayed in the Job after what he did.'

'I know,' Greg said, 'but that was how it all started, surely, with him getting sacked.'

'Who knows – maybe the kid was always a wrong 'un.'

'No!' Mr Brownlow spluttered. 'Not my Lindsey. She didn't make that drug. Those other girls are just trying to blame her because she's dead and can't defend herself.'

When Striker didn't answer, he looked to his wife in appeal but she said, 'Don't you remember what Mr Reddy told us at the last parent-teacher evening, Donald?'

'...Not really.'

'He said that Lindsey was the best chemist he'd ever taught, a natural. He said that he expected to see her win the Nobel prize for chemistry one day.'

'He was joking.'

'Maybe a little.'

'So you believe this of your own daughter?'

'That she was the one who manufactured the drug? Yes, Donald, I'm afraid I do.'

'I don't understand,' Mr Brownlow muttered. 'She had everything – beauty, brains, a loving home and family.' He wiped a hand across his eyes but it was not enough to stem his emotion. He snivelled, 'I'm sorry' and fled the room.

Mrs Brownlow was silent for a moment, then she said, 'Yes, she had everything she wanted. Everything she asked for, he got it. Maybe that was the problem.'

'It isn't easy,' Striker said, 'to find the right balance. When a man adores his daughters, as I do, he finds himself giving in to them again and again, often against his better judgement.'

'Hannah and Elizabeth,' she said.

'You have a good memory.'

'It will be terrible for the other families,' Mary Brownlow said with a sigh, 'the Wings and the Trethowans. I know them both well. John Wing is a surgeon,' she added irrelevantly.

'And Bridget, poor woman. She's had no luck in life and even death won't prevent Maria-Teresa's name being dragged through the mud. The other family you mentioned...?'

'Mrs Stratton.'

'I don't know her or her daughter.' She paused. 'Thank you for coming, Chief Inspector, for telling us the results of your investigations.'

Striker, recognising his dismissal, rose and said, 'I'm only sorry it was such bad news, Mrs Brownlow.' Opening the door of the living room, he found two teenage boys jumping away, trying to pretend that they had not been eavesdropping. He gave them a weak smile. 'All right, lads?' They looked back at him with big, scared eyes, not adolescents any more but disoriented children. They had probably never seen their father crying before.

Striker got back into his car and sat for a moment without starting the engine. Now he had to go and explain the inexplicable to Julie Moss.

Tim Dixon let himself into his flat and headed for the fridge in a gloomy mood. As he'd thought, there was a bottle of sauvignon blanc in there, chilling. He had intended it for his supper with Prue that night but now she had dumped him. There was no other way of putting it, although the verb made him wince when applied to relationships. She had prettied it up and he understood how she needed all her time and energy to support Ruth through her trial and inevitable imprisonment, but he could have helped with that, would have liked to. He wasn't the sort of man to run a mile at the first sign of trouble. He uncorked the wine and poured himself a big glass. There was food in the fridge – a ready meal for two – but he had lost his appetite. Two of his students were dead and one was facing trial for murder, with two more facing possible lesser charges.

He had spoken to his sister that morning and knew that Caroline Bishop was distraught, a loss of poise he would previously have believed alien to her.

Little Ruth Stratton: always so quiet, studious, never in trouble, always first with her hand up in class, keen with the extra-curricular activities like the school play.

There had been some problem with her father, he knew. The man he had never met had left the police force under a cloud a few years ago then slumped into a depression and abandoned his family. Prue had never wanted to go into detail but maybe that was where things had started to go wrong.

Ruth had not seemed to mind him dating her mother, the way teenagers often did. When he had tried to explain to her one day that he was not, of course, attempting to replace her missing father, she had replied, 'My father's a loser' as if she were commenting on the weather, and wandered off to do her homework.

The school play had been cancelled, following the death of his Gwendolen, and his second Gwendolen. At least nobody had said, 'To lose one Gwendolen may be considered an accident...'

The doorbell rang. Tim was not a man who could ignore a ringing bell, much as he would have liked to. He snatched up the receiver on the entry phone and snapped, 'Yes?'

'Superintendent Gregory Summers, sir. May I come up?'

'If you must.' Tim buzzed him in and waited till he heard the tap on his door before opening it.

'What do you want?' he asked inhospitably.

'My sergeant told me you were a friend of Prue Stratton's.'

'Not any more,' Tim growled and turned away.

'Oh, I'm sorry.' Greg followed him in and shut the door. 'Only I was hoping you could be of help to her. I've just come from there and she's concerned about not being able to contact her husband, Ruth's father. She thought he would come forward when he read about the arrest, but I had to explain that Ruth is a minor and won't be named in the papers unless the trial judge decides otherwise, and that wouldn't be for months.'

'Prue doesn't want my help,' Tim said. 'She made that perfectly clear.'

'OK, sorry to have troubled you. I'll be off then.'

'How could this have happened?' Tim blurted out.

Greg paused by the door. He said, slowly, 'It seems to me that there's something very wrong with the way we're bringing up our children.'

'Prue did her best,' Tim protested, 'in difficult circumstances.'

'By *we*, I meant society,' Greg said. 'Look, I'm just going to see Mr Fitzsimmons. Would you like to come?'

Tim thought about it for a second. 'I'll get my coat.'

Harold Fitzsimmons didn't give Tim a second glance when Mrs Alderson showed him in with Greg, doubtless taking him for another policeman. He had his new nurse with him and he told her curtly to leave them.

'Don't like her,' he said, before she was out of earshot. 'Irish. Now there's an inferior race.'

Greg didn't rise to the bait. Instead, he said, 'So you won't be marrying this one?'

'Huh!' The old man almost choked on his saliva at the thought. 'Not got your Jew boy with you today, I see. Oh, you don't like that? Well, tough.'

Greg said patiently, 'We've made an arrest in the matter of Nadia's murder, sir.'

He explained succinctly what had happened.

'So there was no reason for it,' Harold said finally. 'Just plain badness.'

'I fear so.'

'I'd like my ring back, by the way. Do you have it?'

'Sir?'

'The engagement ring I gave Nadia. It was rather valuable.'

'It forms part of her estate,' Greg said.

'I beg to differ.' The old man's voice was dry as ashes.

The housekeeper tapped lightly on the door at that moment and came in. 'I'm sorry to disturb you, Harold, but young Mr

Faulkner's arrived for his appointment.'

'All right, show him in.'

The solicitor bustled in a moment later, all suit and bulging briefcase. He seemed surprised to see Greg and commented, 'We meet again, Mr Summers,' hunching his case under his armpit to shake hands.

'Faulkner,' Fitzsimmons said. 'Your arrival is timely. I'd like you to tell the superintendent why I must have my engagement ring back.'

The solicitor cleared his throat. 'The, um, the *bestowal* of the engagement ring upon Miss Polycarpou was conditional on her marrying my client, which condition she has, um, failed to fulfil. *Ergo*, the ring remains the property of Mr Fitzsimmons.'

'I'll mention it to the Polycarpous,' Greg said coldly. 'I'm sure it's their foremost concern following the senseless murder of their only child.'

'Good, because I don't want to have to see them in court,' Fitzsimmons said. 'Now, Faulkner, about my will.' He turned to Greg and explained. 'I'm leaving my estate to the British National Party – try to make this island a decent place for the Anglo-Saxon race again. Was the girl who killed my little Nadia a darkie? I bet she was.'

Tim stared at his uncle in appalled fascination and even the lawyer looked embarrassed.

'You're a horrible old man,' Greg said in his politest voice, 'and if you weren't dying, I'd tell you so to your face.'

'Very comical.'

'Seen enough, Mr Dixon?' Greg asked.

Harold Fitzsimmons' head jerked up and his eyes narrowed as Tim said, 'More than enough, thank you'.

'We'll see ourselves out,' Greg said, and they left.

EPILOGUE

Greg slept in on Sunday morning, exhausted, not so much from the investigation itself as from the feelings of despair its resolution had awakened in him.

When he surfaced, the bed beside him was empty and a glance out of the front window proved that Angie's car was missing. He took a leisurely shower and walked down to the village to buy his *Sunday Times*. When he returned, Angie's Renault 5 was back in the drive and he found her eating cornflakes in the kitchen.

Unusually, she was wearing a skirt, a plain brown one he didn't remember seeing before, and proper shoes, not trainers.

'You were up early,' he said, beginning to dismantle the paper, throwing all the extraneous bits into the bin.

'I went to early mass in Newbury.'

He stopped, the Business section in his hand on its unread way to recycling. 'Really?'

'Sudden urge for something ... spiritual.'

'OK.' He racked his brains for a suitable comment. 'Did you take communion?'

She shook her head. 'Haven't been to con-

314

fession since – ooh, let's see – *ever*.'

'I thought as you'd missed breakfast...'

'Didn't have time. Then I stopped off at Nick's place to pack up Nadia's stuff, so he doesn't have to look at it. I know how hard that is.'

She cleared her empty cereal bowl into the dishwasher, poured herself another cup of coffee and went off to change.

'Have you got a moment?' Striker Freeman put his head round Greg's door the following Monday morning.

Here it comes, Greg thought. He said, 'Sure. Take a seat.' When the DCI was sitting, he added, 'Let me guess – you and your wife are reconciled and you'll be moving back to London as soon as possible.'

Freeman looked bemused. 'I did have Sabbath dinner with my wife and the twins Friday night, as it happens, but that was so she could tell me that she wants to press ahead with the divorce. She's met somebody else – opera producer called Jonathan, shares her cultural interests.'

'I'm sorry,' Greg said dutifully. 'So why are you leaving?'

Freeman laughed. 'I'm not! I like it here. Are you really so desperate to get rid of me?'

'No! Blimey. I only thought...' Greg decided to start again. 'Shall we pretend you've just come in? So, what can I do for

315

you, Chief Inspector?'

'It may be more a question of what I can do for you,' Striker said. 'I've identified your mole.'

'Ah! The shoe trophy?'

'Exactly. I gave a different piece of duff gen to a number of suspects to see what surfaced.'

'And?' Greg said as the DCI paused, presumably for dramatic effect.

'It was Sergeant Veronica Doyle.'

'Ronnie? Are you sure?'

'She admitted it when I confronted her.'

'My God! But why?'

Freeman shrugged. 'Chaucer paid her, pure and simple.' Greg was silent for a moment, then he said, 'I hope it was enough to compensate her for the loss of her career.'

'I didn't really suspect her, you know, since I was concentrating on the people you suggested, but when I had that late curry with her the other night, I thought she was showing a little too much interest in the details of the investigation so I decided to throw some fake crumbs her way, just in case. Had to think on my feet so I was quite proud of the trophy thing.'

'As she's uniform, I shall have to refer this up to CS Barkiss but...'

Striker produced a somewhat crumpled envelope from his trouser pocket and laid it on Greg's desk. 'Her letter of resignation. I sort of promised her that if she quit of her own accord, we wouldn't take the matter any further. I may have exceeded my authority rather.'

'I suspect Mr Barkiss will agree that it's for the best,' Greg said, weighing the thin envelope in his hands. 'If we make a disciplinary matter of it, there'll only be unwelcome publicity. I don't think I can ever forgive her for what she put Aoife Cusack's children through.' He hesitated, since the DCI had been more or less dating her. 'Did you like her?'

'I don't like people who betray my trust,' Striker said curtly. 'Is that how Harry Stratton left the force?'

'No, that was another type of letter entirely. Bribing a police officer – that's a serious offence.'

'Doyle's made a full statement.'

'Then I shall be paying Mr Chaucer a visit very soon.'

'It's always nice to have something to look forward to.'

Greg smiled at his junior officer across the desk. 'I'm really glad you're staying, Striker. I think we work well together.'

'Good, and when you retire, bags I get first dibs on your job.'

'OK, but you have to take Susan Habib.'

'Ah!' Freeman's chin sank to his chest. 'Back to the drawing board then.' He got up and left without further ado.

After a moment, Greg rose and went to look out of the window, over his fiefdom of Newbury. He had made up his mind. At lunchtime he would go and buy a diamond ring and this evening he would ask Angie to marry him and be the mother of his children.

And pray to the God he didn't believe in that he made a better job of parenthood than the Strattons, the Brownlows, the Wings, the Trethowans and the Antonellis.

The publishers hope that this book has given you enjoyable reading. Large Print Books are especially designed to be as easy to see and hold as possible. If you wish a complete list of our books please ask at your local library or write directly to:

Magna Large Print Books
Magna House, Long Preston,
Skipton, North Yorkshire.
BD23 4ND

This Large Print Book, for people
who cannot read normal print,
is published under the auspices of

THE ULVERSCROFT FOUNDATION